Goldkorn Tales

Goldkorn Tales

Leslie Epstein

E. P. DUTTON, INC. | NEW YORK

6/1985
Am. Lit.

"The Steinway Quintet" was previously published in different
form in *The Steinway Quintet Plus Four* in 1976 by Little, Brown &
Company. Portions of "Music of the Spheres" appeared in the
Winter 1985 issue of *The Georgia Review*. Portions of "The Magic
Flute" appeared in the January 1985 issue of *Moment* magazine.

Published in the United States by
E. P. Dutton, Inc.,
2 Park Avenue, New York, N.Y. 10016

Library of Congress Cataloging in Publication Data

Epstein, Leslie.
Goldkorn tales.
I. Title.
PS3555.P655G6   1985   813'.54   84-26029
ISBN: 0-525-24286-4

Published simultaneously in Canada
by Fitzhenry & Whiteside Limited, Toronto

Designed by Mark O'Connor

COBE
10 9 8 7 6 5 4 3 2 1
First Edition

For Uncle Julie

CONTENTS

Be not afeard; the isle is full of noises,
Sounds and sweet airs that give delight and hurt not.
—*The Tempest*

The Steinway
Quintet

There's many a beast, then, in a populous city.
—*Othello*

1

Good evening, my name is L. Goldkorn and my specialty is woodwind instruments, with emphasis on the flute. However, in 1963, on the Avenue Amsterdam, my instrument was stolen from me by an unknown person and has not in spite of strong efforts been to this day restored. This is the reason I play at the Steinway Restaurant the Bechstein piano and not the Rudall & Rose–model flute with which my career began at the Imperial and Royal Hof–Operntheater Orchester. An example of my work on this instrument may be found on gramophone recordings of the NBC Orchestra, A. Toscanini conducting, in particular the lively overture to *The Secret of Susanna* by E. Wolf-Ferrari, in which exists, for the flute, a definite solo passage.

I wish to say that I am an American citizen since 1943. My wife is living, too. These days she spends most of her day in bed, or on the sofa, watching the television; it is rare that her health allows her to walk the four flights of stairs to the street. In our lives we were blessed with a single child, a daughter, who did not upon birth thrive. Although the flute was in a case, and the case was securely under my arm, a black man took it from me and at once ran away. It was a prize upon graduation from the Akademie für Musik, Philosophie, und darstellende Kunst, when I was fourteen. Only a boy.

1963. That is what Americans call ancient history. Let us speak of more recent events.

It was at the Steinway Restaurant a quiet night, a Tuesday night, raining, only four tables, or five tables, occupied. The opinion of experts was that soon the rain would turn into snow. Mosk, a waiter, came to the back of the room.

"You got a request," he told Salpeter, our first violinist.

"Yes?" Salpeter replied.

"From the lady. Purple dress. Pearls. Onion herring."

This lady was a nice-looking young person, a nice dress lacking straps, her hair a mixture of red and brown. She smiled—what bright, dazzling teeth!—at the Quintet members.

"Yes?"

" 'Some Enchanted Evening.' "

Salpeter picked up his bow. Murmelstein, second violinist, put his instrument under his chin. Also present were Tartakower, a flautist, and the old 'cellist, A. Baer. For an instant there was silence. I mean, not only from the Steinway Quintet, which had not yet started to play, but from the restaurant patrons, who ceased conversation, who stopped chewing food; silence also from Margolies, Mosk, Ellenbogen, still as statues, with napkins over their arms. You could not see in or out of the panes of the window, because the warmth had created a mist. Around each chandelier was a circle of electrical light. Outside, on Rivington Street, on Allen Street, wet tires of cars made a sound: *shhhh!* Salpeter dipped one shoulder forward and drew his bow over the strings. The sweet music of R. Rodgers filled the room.

It was during the performance of this selection that the door opened and two men, a tall Sephardic Jew, and a short Jew, also of Iberian background, came in. Their hats and the cloth of their shoulders were damp. They walked through the tables to the bar, which is located directly opposite the platform where the musicians are seated. It is possible for my colleagues and me to see ourselves in the mirror of this bar while playing. Without removing their hats, the two men ordered some beer to drink.

After a time a party of four, who had dined on roasted duck, on famed Roumanian broilings, stood up, then departed; as they did so, snowflakes came in the door. The night in the crack looked very dark. Murmelstein, by no means unskilled, received a specific request: "September Song." Of course from *Knickerbocker Holiday.* When this selection came to an end, the lady in the purple dress put on a raccoon-type coat and, with a gentleman companion, went out to Rivington Street. The chimes of the First Warsaw Congregation sounded eleven o'clock. The members of the Steinway Quintet had then some tea. The figs and the cakes were removed from the window. At a side table Martinez, the cook, was eating a plate of potatoes. Tartakower smoked. The heat went off; the temperature dropped. It helped to warm clumsy fingers on the outside of a glass. At eleven fifteen Salpeter nodded. We played selections from Mister Sigmund Romberg's *The Student Prince.*

At this moment the mouth of Ellenbogen's wife, who mixed liquors at the bar, dropped completely open and her hands rose into the air. The explanation for this was in the mirror behind her: both Sephardim were holding big guns. Out of the open mouth of Madam Ellenbogen came a scream. The music, except for the violoncello, ceased. The tall man stood up and put his hand over the barmaid's face. Ellenbogen himself allowed a tray of something, strudel perhaps, to tip slowly onto the floor. Tartakower leaned toward the old musician.

"Mister Baer, time to stop."

The short man climbed to the top of the bar. "We don't want no trouble and we don't want nobody hurt. But you gotta cooperate with us. Anybody who don't cooperate completely is gonna be hurt very bad." This man had still his hat low over his eyes. However, it was possible to see that he had a thin moustache on his lip, and at the end of a long chin were a few added hairs, just wisps. A young man, then. In profuse perspiration.

"The first thing is to cut out that music."

This was a reference to A. Baer, who had come to the end of the vigorous "Drinking Song," and was now beginning again.

"Psssst! Psssst! Mister Baer!" said Tartakower, pulling on the 'cellist's shoulder.

"Mister Baer!" Salpeter echoed. "I insist that you stop!"

"No! No! Reprise!" said A. Baer, and hunched farther forward, peering at the music on the music stand.

The tall man—it was now possible to see that he had also a moustache; yet he was older, not so slight in his physique, with eyes that seemed almost sad, that is, they were close-set, drooping, filled with liquid: this man came quickly toward us, seized the bow from the aged musician, and broke it over his knee.

"*Er hat gebrochen de strunes fin mein fiedl!*"

Murmelstein stood up. "That ain't right what you done. He doesn't hear."

"*Er hat gebrochen mein boigenhaar!*"

"I am the Quintet leader," Salpeter said. "What is it you want? Why have you done this? Never has such a thing happened before! Do you know what Goethe said about music?"

"And H. W. Longfellow?" added the Bechstein artist.

"Up with the hands! Up! Up! Onto the wall!" The sad-eyed man held his pistol in front of the face of the first violinist. Salpeter turned; he joined Tartakower, who was already leaning against the famous murals, by Feiner, of classical Greece. And I? I stood up, I also turned about. From the corner of my eye I observed the first man, the young one, still standing on the bar top, motioning with his gun. He was making the others, the waiters and patrons, face the wall, too. "Oh! Oh!" cried Pearl Ellenbogen, again and again: "Oh! Oh!" Before me was Socrates—Feiner was an artist who put real people into his paintings—with a group of young men beneath a tree. Murmelstein turned around, toward where A. Baer was still talking.

"Young man! You have broken my bowstring. *Mein boigenhaar!* Now how can I play? Do you know what it costs such a bowstring? The horsehairs? I paid for this seven dollars. I am Rothschild? I have such a sum in the bank? *Ai! Ai! Er reis mein bord!*"

Without thinking, Ellenbogen, Salpeter, Tartakower, and I, we all turned our heads. Terrible vision! The tall individual had taken our colleague by the hair of his beard. In only a moment he pulled the old man off his chair onto his knees. What happened next is almost too painful to speak of. The gunman released his hold upon A. Baer and leaped into the air and came down with both feet through the back of his violoncello.

"I am an American citizen since nineteen forty-three!" some person cried. The voice was familiar. Without doubt that of Leib Goldkorn.

"This was no accident! No, no, it was a purposeful act!" Tartakower speaking.

Murmelstein, a young man, not even sixty, began to advance on the terrorist, who, still with sad eyes, was nonetheless smiling. "You done that to an old man. You got no idea how old this man happens to be. Aren't you ashamed? A venerable man? To pull his beard!"

Salpeter reached out his hand. "No, stay, Mister Murmelstein. He does not appreciate music."

"There is a hole in it. A hole in it." A. Baer held his instrument in his lap as if it had been an injured child.

"What's so funny? What is the joke here? This is a tragedy. A tragedy!" The second violinist stepped in front of the man, who, under his hat, still smiled; then that villain raised his pistol so that it pointed straight at young Murmelstein's chest.

Suddenly from across the room his partner cried out in Ladino, "*¡Jesús! ¡El cocinero! ¡Está tratando de usar el teléfono!*"

The gunman whirled about to where his colleague was pointing. There, next to the door to the kitchen, Martinez was dropping nickels and dimes into the box of the pay telephone. The next thing we knew the hoodlum was flying in the air, Martinez was shouting, the weapon was raised and—in front of everyone's eyes—brought down upon the cook's head. More than once. Twice. And the victim fell to the floor. Is this not in many ways an act as terrible as the destruction of a violoncello? To attack a man's head, where great thoughts often are born? Everyone was still. No person dared breathe. Then Tartakower spoke:

"Friends, these two are not Jews."

I felt a chill on my neck. Like a cold hand. Then Salpeter said what we dreaded to hear:

"Hispanics!"

From Murmelstein: "Puerto Ricans!"

The tall man's hat had fallen onto the floor. He put it back on his head, which was pomaded. Without difficulty, with a swipe of his hand, he tore the phone box off the wall.

2

Greetings! L. Goldkorn once again. I have paused for some time. It was necessary to prepare an injection of medicament for my wife. Now she is sleeping, my life's companion, with no obstruction of nasal passages. Sweetly. Also, it is sometimes desirable to settle the nerves. I am too old to speak of such terrible things, the destruction of property, attacks to the head area, without becoming myself upset. This is to explain the presence of schnapps, squeezed from plums. Alcohol is good for you; it allows to breathe the hundreds of veins which surround the heart.

Now I will confess that this lengthy delay was not due solely to what I have already described; no, it is rather a hesitation over what remains to be said. Such abominations! There, out the window, over Columbus Avenue, the huge night sky is growing lighter. Like color returning to the cheeks of a patient. Yet at the Steinway Restaurant, where the temperature continued to fall, it was not yet even midnight. A storm of snow. I shall speak briefly of Tartakower, my successor upon woodwinds. He is a cultured man, born in Bialystok, and like all Bialystokers he possesses a songful technique, and accurate, unwavering intonation. But he lacks volume of breath. We do not permit him a single cadenza. The reason for this is Pall Mall brand cigarettes. It is a habit that has stained his fingers permanent yellow.

Tartakower! Tartakower is not the point!

To comprehend what happened next you must know a detail of the Steinway Restaurant, which is that when you come through the door the men's water closet and the ladies' water closet are together down the stairs to the left. Many times Hispanic people, Colored people, Ukrainians, even, would descend this stairway in order to move their bowels upon the johnnies below. Such hospitality is now and has always been the policy of this dining spot, since the day it was founded by M. P. Stutchkoff and S. Stutchkoff, his bride, in 1901. 1901. By coincidence also the year of my birth. Not in Vienna precisely. To that imperial city, filled with Jews, non-Jews, and Turks, I moved at a somewhat later time, to further my studies upon the flute. Little did I suspect I would one day play within the orchestra pit of the k.k. Hof-Operntheater. Finished, Vienna. Kaputt. In America, on Rivington Street, have occurred similar changes. I have been told there was once throughout this quarter a lively Jewish culture: opera houses, concert stages, recital halls, a theater in the language of Yiddish. Now there is nothing but Pipe, a bedding merchant, and the fish store of Sheftelowitz. Even A. Baer, one year ago, moved away. Living here now are the Negro Americans I have already mentioned, poor as poor Jews, downtrodden, silent, without even workable plumbing.

Also downstairs, next to the two WCs, is the office of the son of M. P. Stutchkoff, V. V. Stutchkoff, a room whose door is perpetually closed. From the time that I joined the Quintet of the Steinway Restaurant in 1959 until the snow-filled night I am describing, no more than ten greetings had been exchanged between myself and my employer. What I know of this man I have learned from others.

They say he was a pale child, a pious child, a non-eater, so thin that he would blow on Eldridge Street like a leaf, a feather, and not a person. When he was a mere seven years of age people would come from north of Fourteenth Street in order to sit with him, to listen for words of advice. Stutchkoff's son! Only a boy! I am the near contemporary of S. Zweig, S. Freud, and L. Wittgenstein, the skeptic. I read each red-covered issue of the *Fackel* of Karl Kraus. I once attended a lecture by Krafft-Ebing. Impossible for such a modernist to believe in wonder-working rabbis, *tzaddikim*, whiz-kids, and such. But the others believed whatever he told them, and finally it was decided to send him to Europe to study. The year, I believe, was 1930. Godiadz was the spot they picked. A town in Poland. Young Stutchkoff was then eighteen.

What occurred in the war years is not clear. It is certain that in spite of his American passport the young scholar was put by the German invaders into a Jewish district, they say in the Lubartowsky quarter of Lublin. After that, all is confusion. According to Margolies, the waiter, a miracle happened. One day the Death's-Headers came to shoot him, only when they fired they missed. He fell into a hole and other Jews fell on top. He waited beneath those bodies until the night, and then he got up and walked away. Let us assume this account of events is a true one. Does this mean a miracle? The gift of life to a scholarly child? In my opinion it is a weakness of human nature to think such a thing. Many died. A few escaped. That is all. If you want to know more, ask Margolies. Ask Ellenbogen.

What is known for a fact is that after the war M. P. Stutchkoff died and V. V. Stutchkoff returned, not quite so thin as he had been before. Also, he took at this time a blond-headed wife. We see the sensualist element here. Yes, he was eating, he put on weight. In the quarter century I have been at the Steinway Restaurant, he developed from a man of average size into a corpulent figure. In the recent past I have seen him only rarely. He remained in his room, on occasion sending requests for the music of Meyerbeer and a tray of potted meatballs. By his wish nothing in the dining area has changed. Thus the window is divided in many panes, the chandeliers have each one dozen bulbs, the bar top is zinc, and a chip remains on the leg of my Bechstein, while, in the mural of Feiner, ladies stand in their togas, and the figure of Archimedes rests in his bath. The windmill bar sign, glowing with neon gas, and the register for cash—these alone are new. Every man has heard some story in which a wild and profligate youth reformed himself and led in his manhood an exemplary life. It must be said of V. V. Stutchkoff, the pious boy, the man of flesh, that he has reversed the traditional tale.

I return to the events of Tuesday night. The door opened. Who then came in? The lady in purple! "I left my handbag" is what she said. Therefore, the many events that occurred—selections of Romberg, A. Baer's persecution, the blow to the head of Martinez—which seemed to take hours, had gone by in only five or six minutes, just long enough for this woman to walk away, to discover the loss of her handbag, to return.

"This it, lady?" The speaker was the young hooligan. He

had in his hand a leather purse, whose contents he then emptied onto the bar.

The woman did not reply. She looked quickly around, saw the patrons with their hands on the wall, saw the two Puerto Ricans holding guns, saw, on the floor, with red blood in his hair, Martinez: And she uttered a scream, *Eeee,* and then, *Eeeeee!*

Now others began also to shout. "Help! Help!" "They will kill us!" Such things as that. The young man with the wisps of hair on his chin jumped down from the bar; his older companion put his pistol into his belt. In my opinion they were on the point of taking flight. But at that instant we all heard, upon the stairs, a tremendous reverberation. It was a kind of snorting, snorting through the nose, and crashing against things, and the thud and bang of heavy feet from stair to stair. Everyone became motionless. There was the sound of whistling breath, a boom, a further snort, and then the rounded dome, followed by the fierce red face, of V. V. Stutchkoff appeared on the stairs.

"What the fuck is going on here?"

With one hand on a banister railing and another hand braced against the wall, Stutchkoff pulled himself higher. He was wearing a black bowtie and a white shirt. It was possible to see the pink skin through it. His mouth was open. Into it he sucked the air.

"I said what the *fuck* is going on?"

The tall Puerto Rican, called Jesús by his colleague, fell to his knees with his arms held before him. In my confused condition of mind I believed he was beginning a Spanish prayer. But I soon saw the weapon in his hands. It was pointed at the spot where Stutchkoff was pulling himself out of the stairwell. Higher and higher, the air rushing into and out of his mouth, he rose. It seemed as if there would be no end to him. With his white shirt he wore shiny black pants, in size large enough to cover the top of my Bechstein grand.

The gun went off and a bullet emerged. A piece of the

bar mirror suffered a hole. Stutchkoff brushed his right ear with the back of his plump hand. It was a fly, an annoyance, to him.

The second Hispanic crouched on the floor. He rested his gun arm on the seat of a chair, tilted his head, narrowed his eye. His weapon detonated with a tremendous report. The ceiling above Stutchkoff's head splintered, and pieces of plaster fell on his shoulders. But Stutchkoff himself continued climbing the last of the stairs. To the men on the floor he must have seemed like a figure in one of Feiner's murals, like some ancient deity rising out of the water, or the god of the sun appearing over the hills.

Both robbers shot once again. Unbelievable fulmination. Salpeter with his hands over his ears. Screams. Screaming. Sulfuric smells. Yet the consequences were not of great moment. Additional plaster dropped from the ceiling. A glass of tea on a table broke into two. Stutchkoff, however, who had emerged from the stairwell and was moving rapidly in front of the window, had not been touched. When he reached the aisle between the tables, he paused, he swung himself around; then he descended upon the assassins.

The shooting stopped. Both Puerto Ricans, the young man with the wisps of a beard and his bright-toothed colleague, crawled backward, got to their feet, and with wild eyes ran toward the rear kitchen door. Stutchkoff took two or three steps, and halted. His mouth fell. His hands went to his chest. He stood there a time, like a basso singing an aria; then his red face went white, and he hauled himself about in the other direction and lurched toward the front of the room.

"Hilda! Hilda!" he shouted.

His wife ran from behind the cash register counter. She had a red mouth painted over thin lips, and wore a fox fur because of the cold.

"Vivian!" she cried. "Vivian!"

"*Hilda!*" said her husband and sought to take her in his arms. But he staggered, he missed her, he clutched only the air as he fell slowly and ponderously, the way a great tree falls, to the earth.

Silence. Utter silence. Slowly Salpeter lowered his hands. A. Baer looked up from his violoncello. One hatted figure, a second hatted figure, peered around the edge of the kitchen door. Then, into this stillness, this hush, came two extraordinary sounds. By this I do not mean they were in any way noises removed from the course of everyday life. On the contrary, what could be more common than this *rip-rip-rip*? This *rattle-rattle*? But after the bang and roar of the gunshots—the first I had heard in what we Viennese thought of as the Wild West of Gotham—no one was able to imagine the existence of such simple sounds. People were looking about. "What's that?" they whispered. "What could it be?" Then Margolies started to move.

"Hildegard," he said. "You shouldn't do it." He came up to where Madam Stutchkoff was standing alone, tearing the sleeve of her dress.

"Why not to do it? How come why not?"

"But this is only a fit. A spell. Something to do with the nerves. You see, there is no blood. I will revive him. Mister Stutchkoff! Mister Stutchkoff!"

At my side the flautist started to laugh, a thin, high, hysterical sound. "Look, look," he gasped, pointing toward Margolies. "He still has his napkin over his arm!" It struck him as something amusing.

"Mister Tartakower, control your emotions." This was Salpeter.

"Not moving! I knew not moving! Not blinking his eyes! Is finish! Is the end!" Hildegard Stutchkoff resumed, in the Orthodox manner, the ripping of her clothes.

But what was that noise like a rattle? At first I believed it came from the throat of our stricken employer. Then a movement above him drew my attention. The brass-type doorknob was twisting around. The door itself shook back and forth inside its frame. A person was attempting to enter;

however, the body of Stutchkoff, with the belly upward, was blocking the way. Now somebody actually pounded.

"Beverly! For Christ's sake, Beverly! I'm double-parked!"

"*Eeeee! Eeeeee!*"

In a windowpane of the Steinway Restaurant the face of a man appeared. The lady in purple saw him, screamed once again, and then the short Hispano-American, the one who had promised that no harm would befall us, snatched the napkin cloth from the forearm of Mosk and stuffed it into her mouth. The gentleman companion stared an instant, and then he vanished. Just disappeared.

"*¡Ay, Diós! ¡Nos van a coger! ¡Vámonos de aquí!*"

"*¡Un momento! ¡La registradora!*"

The young man, in truth only a boy, the perspiration flying from him, leaped to the front counter. He opened the cash register and swept the money from the drawer into his own jacket pockets. No person attempted to stop him. Then he and his colleague ran through the restaurant into the kitchen.

"Are you well, Mister Baer? Mister Tartakower, are you calm? They are gone. They will leave through the door in the rear."

"No they won't, Mister Salpeter. You forgot that door is locked."

"Mister Murmelstein, where is the key?"

The second violinist pointed to where Margolies was shaking the shoulder of the great black-and-white form. "In Stutchkoff's pocket."

"*¡Oh, no! ¡Demonios!* Locked! They got bars on it!"

"*¡Empuja! ¡Empujemos a la vez!*"

Mosk, meanwhile, climbed on a Steinway Restaurant chair. He addressed the little crowd of frightened patrons. "We need a medical doctor. Doctor Fuchs! How about you?"

A half-bald man in a tweed suit turned around, although he kept his hands on the wall. "Freudian analyst. Sorry."

Mosk persisted. "You're a big shot. Well known. You could make an examination."

"Doctor Fuchs! I am asking you, too!"

At the appeal of the grief-stricken woman, the alienist dropped his arms and went toward the prostrate restaurateur.

Now the Ellenbogens, the man and wife, ran to each other. Mosk got down from his chair and began to mop up the pool of spilled tea. Salpeter and Tartakower sought to help A. Baer to his feet. He waved them away. *"Azah teire zach!"* The violoncello, a priceless item, was still rocked in his arms. "This was from Genoa. This was made by Italian hands."

Trotting fiercely, yes, like yellow-eyed wolves, the intruders burst out of the kitchen and went to the blockaded front door. The tall one started to take hold of Stutchkoff's feet, stopped, then said to his junior colleague, *"¡Hala!"*

"¿Yo? No. *You* pull."

"¡Ha-ha! ¡Cobarde! El muchachito es cobarde."

"¿Yo? You are the coward. You!"

"¡Espera! Tengo una idea."

The last speaker turned toward the two elderly men. To Mosk, the Lithuanian. To Margolies, a Steinway Restaurant waiter more than sixty years. "Hey, you mothas! Legs! Legs! Pull the legs!"

Just then Doctor Fuchs, who had been snapping his fingers by the ear of his patient, stood up. "A moment, please," he said, and went to where Hildegard Stutchkoff was standing. He plucked a bit of fox fluff from her stole and with care laid it upon V. V. Stutchkoff's lips. The delicate threads, the ruddy hairs, did not stir.

"Dead," the alienist declared.

From the waiters, an echo: "Dead."

"Blessed be the True Judge!"

From outside, from far off, came the sound of many sirens.

"¡Los policías!"

Each of the killers then jumped for the doorknob and pulled energetically at it; but the son of M. P. Stutchkoff still barred the way. The sirens, already louder, were approaching from several directions. The tall hoodlum, the one with the liquid-filled eyes, abandoned his effort to open the door and began striking his own head, through his hat, with his hands. The other pulled with even more vigor, so that his whole body trembled. Then, on Rivington Street, the police forces arrived. Brake sounds, tire sounds, sirens so grudgingly fading. Now it was possible to see through the Steinway Restaurant window the fall of the snowflakes: red snow, blue snow, holiday snow, lit up by the flashing lights of the autos.

"Chino! Tell me! What to do?"

"Wait a minute! I need a minute to think!"

"*Unschätzbar! Unschätzbar! Eine Antike!* What will I play on? I'm supposed to whistle? To hum? Next they will sew on a yellow star. *Zei hoben gebrochen meine boigenhaar! Zei hoben gerissen mein bord! Ich volt bedorfen zein* a Rothschild? A J. P. Morgan?"

At this time of tremendous tension—police forces outside, inside the guns—the Widow Stutchkoff dropped to the floor and began to untie the laces on her late husband's shoes. As soon as she had completed this task, she crawled to his head and with her long fingers loosened the knot of his tie.

"What's going on, man? What's the chick doing?"

Doctor Fuchs answered. "She is unfastening the knots that might hinder the release of her husband's soul. His anima. It's Jungian psychology."

"No, no," said Margolies in a hoarse whisper. "Not his soul. The Angel of Death! Otherwise it would be tempted to linger. You can look it up in Zev Wolf of Zbarazh."

"In that case," Ellenbogen added, "you must open the window as well. This is according to the Maggid of Mezritch himself!"

"Maggid, schmaggid!" Mosk, a skeptical man, declared.

The tall hooligan waved his gun as the former Madam

Stutchkoff got to her feet. "Crazy lady! Black magic! She got the eye! Jewish lady! Jewish! Viva Puerto Rico!"

But the cashieress ignored him. She began to walk—from her eyes tears were dropping—through the restaurant tables toward the rear of the room.

"Stop, lady! Nobody moves! Stop! You gonna make me kill you!" Chino, the wispy-chinned lad, aimed his pistol at her back: The members of the Steinway Quintet dropped to the floor.

There were those who maintained that this Hildegard Stutchkoff was not a Jewess at all. I have already described how a red mouth was painted on top of her own. Yes, and her long fingers. In addition she curled her hair, her blond hair, until it looked like small sausages. Her eyes were Polish blue. It was necessary to look away from her bust, both parts of which were young, strong, and well-developed. I did not think she had a musical nature until one night, some years in the past, it was also a Tuesday, she sat beside me on the bench of the Bechstein and played the bass notes, while I the melody, of the operetta *Madame Pompadour*. Perhaps I did not mention that, a summer sight, the nails of her toes were painted, too? And in winter squeezed into tiny pointed shoes? After the piety with which she mourned her husband, the rumors on the subject of her Polishness, her gymnastic nature, her fox furs, have ceased at last.

The murderer did not, after all, fire his gun. The fresh widow stopped and removed a tablecloth from a table. With this she began to cover the surface of the bar-area mirror.

"The Spola Grandfather!"

"No, Shmelke of Nikolsburg! The dead man must not see his own spirit depart!"

"Mister Ellenbogen, am I not correct in assuming that the purpose of this action is to prevent the Angel of Death from becoming entrapped in the glass?"

"That is a valid interpretation, Mister Margolies."

"Pfui!"

Doctor Fuchs spoke from the viewpoint of science. "I agree with the negative opinion of our friend Mister Mosk. These are Jungian daydreams. A regression to primitive thinking. Even children—"

"Look, gentlemen! She has finished!" It was Salpeter, our first violinist, who was speaking. "Now dear V. V. Stutchkoff, patron of the arts, may depart!"

Every person's eyes swung back to the corpse. The little piece of fox fur remained attached to its lips. It did not move. It did not tremble.

"This is the police department speaking. You are surrounded. Come out with your hands in the air. You must surrender."

That voice came from an amplification horn. One of the gangsters, an adolescent, a boy, shouted back:

"We ain't going nowhere! We got hostages! We're cold killers! You gonna find out, because we gonna kill them one by one!" He threw a blue-colored pill into his mouth. His colleague smiled, and swallowed a red one.

"¡Mamá!" The cry came from the rear. *"¡Mamá!"* Martinez, the cook, raised his bloody head from the floor.

3

Hello? Hello? Leib Goldkorn here. What a poor thing, memory! Have I mentioned my performance in *Il Segreto di Susanna*? Or have I not? Perhaps, through attentiveness, you will succeed in hearing this disk on radio station WQXR. The difficult aspect of playing in the orchestra of A. Toscanini— naturally there were also many joys—was tempi: tempi and also temper! An artist went as fast as he could and—"No, no, no, no! Allegro! Allegro, *cretino!* Allegro *vivace!*" The key to the overture, with its lively briskness, was breath control:

Whether I possess it or whether I lack it you will judge for yourself.

Now the radio is off; this is because of the Admiral-brand television for spouse entertainment. She is watching from the sofa, with her medicaments on the table. A red cotton night-dress and a white lace cap: adorable, the little mouse! You will pardon me? I am sipping hot milk substitute poured into hot coffee. No sugars. I am fond of sugars. However, Clara has diabetes. I think now we are having a spring morning. The tree on the street has birds in it and the buds of leaves. The clouds are not serious in nature. I have suffered since the events of February from a disturbance in sleeping. Brandy from plums is good for this condition. Yes, but the bottle is nearly empty. An amber inch at the bottom is all that remains.

I remember from the night not fear so much as the cold conditions. No heat, and outside a sudden wind: Snowflakes went from the left hand to the right. The tall Puerto Rican took Salpeter's waterproof, his silk muffler, his fur-lined gloves. Chino, the young man, took the tweeds of Doctor Fuchs, who then rolled himself into a tablecloth and fell asleep. This others did too, lying so that they touched, without concern for who was a man or a woman. But Mosk, Margolies, and Ellenbogen walked up the aisle and down the aisle, wearing black coats. Their breath came out in clouds. Tartakower suffered. He is a thin man, with a thin face, on which there are prominent bones. He wore an orange-and-black-colored muffler and a topcoat which had, in the place of buttons, clips for paper and safety pins. Widower. He sat in his Quintet chair with his knees together and a lit cigarette in his mouth. The platform shook when he trembled.

I too sat at my place, with toes burning. That is the sensation of extreme cold—a fire in parts of the body, in knee-caps and earlobes and nose, and the wish to sleep was the same as the wish to put it out. I then had a dream of Hildegard Stutchkoff. I must say that in this dream she was upon a privy seat, and I must say, too, that she was not wearing clothes. The feeling that accompanied this sight was one of familiarity, and friendliness. My life has been such that I have never seen in this way any woman, not even Clara, my wife. I looked down, of course, and felt great pity for her uncovered feet. I saw the painted toes. I removed my plaid-style jacket and laid it upon them. "You are getting warm," she said, and at once things returned to normal: I heard china piled upon china, and the clink of waiters carrying plates. I woke. It was still night. From the four corners of the Steinway Restaurant came the sound of chattering teeth.

The chandeliers were no longer shining. But the light was on at the bar, as were the illuminations for types of beer. Both villains sat there, facing the room, with their hats pulled to the level of their eyes. They were laughing together, and slapping each other's cheeks. I rose from my Bechstein. I left my colleagues, who now were sleeping. Tartakower's face was white as dishes. I walked alone to the counter of the bar. Rows of red pills and blue pills were lined up on the zinc top. There was Scotch whisky in glasses, and both the gray guns.

"A French cognac, please." This was L. Goldkorn speaking, but the voice came out in the tones of a piping child.

The hooligans looked at each other. They blinked their eyes.

"Courvoisier," I continued. "VSOP."

"What you want, little man?"

"*Un brandy,* Chino. *Un cognac,* ha, ha!"

"Oh, sure, you wanna have a drink!" The youth opened the hearty liquor and filled to the brim a tall highball glass. "So, Mister Weinberg, Steinberg, Feinberg! You wanna make a toast to one hundred thousand dollars?"

"Ha-ha-ha! Weinstein, Feinstein, Steinstein! Ha-ha-ha!" The tall man, the man with the successful moustache, slapped in a playful manner the face of his young companion. "Names of Jews!"

"Ha-ha! Listen, Mister Greenberg—"

"Mister Goldberg!"

"Ha-ha! Drink it down!"

Only once before in my life, forty years in the past, in the chambers of Judge S. Gitlitz, had I tasted a liquor of this class. The Hispano-Americans continued to slap one another. They each swallowed a pill. They put more of the pleasant cognac into my glass.

"My name is L. Goldkorn, specialist in—"

"Ha-ha-ha! We gonna get a hundred thousand American dollars!"

"*No. No. ¡Un cuarto de millión! Y después aceptamos cien mil. ¿Verdad?*"

"Ha-ha! Jesús is smart! We gonna demand a quarter million! Or more! Maybe a million! Then they gonna say, We don't got that kinda money, and then we gonna say, Okay, two hundred thousand, and then they gonna say, We don't got that either, and then we say, Okay, okay, one hundred and fifty, and when they say, No, no, that's too much too, we gonna say, One hundred thousand in tens and twenties and fifties or we gonna shoot every dude in the room! Ha-ha! Goldkorn! It's gonna be a negotiation!"

"*¡El avión! ¡El avión!* Goldkorns! In the air! In the sky! Like a bird! Tell him! *¡El avión!*"

"Yeah, we gonna have a plane, a big silver plane. No other passengers. Just me and Jesús. And maybe we gonna go to Cuba, and maybe we gonna go to Iran, to China—"

"*¡La China! ¡Ha-ha!*"

"We gonna look down from the window and see the ocean, you know, Goldkorn, with ships on it, a blue ocean, and I heard that from a jet you can tell the world is round, like a ball, and the millions of people on it are just like a bunch of ants."

"*Pantalones de* silk! In China I am *un héroe. ¡Un revolucionario! ¡Sí!* Is true! *Pantalones de* silk!"

"What's that?" The adolescent hurled his body forward and picked up his pistol. The whisky spilled on the bar. The weapon was aimed at the front of the room, where something black moved before the window glass.

"*¡Espíritus malos!*" shouted Jesús, and he also leaped for his gun.

"No! Please! That is Margolies!"

It was in truth the aged waiter. He walked slowly to where the corpse of V. V. Stutchkoff was lying and sat down beside it. He put his head on his ex-employer's chest.

"Goldkorn, man! What's the mothafucka doing? Is he talking to that fat-ass's ghost?"

"Ha-ha! Is only jokes! The mirror! Untying the tie! Is stunts, no? No is *espíritus malos*. Listen, little Jewish man. *Un hombre es solamente un hombre. No tiene alma. No tiene nada. No es nada. El resto es superstición.* Chino, tell it to him!"

"He said a man don't have no soul."

"Right? Right, Goldkorns? Right?"

I did not at that moment answer. In faint light, which came through the window as well as from the bar, I saw Margolies listening for his master's heart. Among the patrons one person cried out, as if some dream oppressed him. A woman whimpered: the same dream, perhaps. A. Baer lay upon his back on the floor of the platform. There was his beard, his brow, the curled end of his violoncello. It looked like the tucked-in head of a sleeping bird. The Widow Stutchkoff sat with open eyes, wearing her tight, pinching shoes. I wished to ask if she were comfortable, if there was for her some thing I, Leib Goldkorn, might do. Instead, that same Goldkorn, a Viennese of some culture, a nonbeliever, a twentieth-century man, spoke precisely as follows:

"Well, gentlemen, but what if he does have a soul?"

Margolies rose to his feet and passed once again, in his black coat, in front of the window. The snow was now blowing in the opposite direction, from the right hand to the left, although after a time it seemed to drop down in the normal manner, and still later it stopped. Then that night, in some respects no different from any other, came to an end.

4

Rivington Street in the morning was covered with snow. It was white, sparkling, sweet-looking, like *Schlagsahne* in a cup of black coffee. From the window of the Steinway Restaurant it was possible to see a crowd standing behind the barriers that had been erected at either end of the block. But the street before us was smooth, without even a footprint.

"*Pam!*" said the kidnapper with the perpetual smile. "Ha-ha!"

He was simulating a gunshot at a tan-colored spaniel that ran down the street, stopping at one sugary curb, then the other.

"*Pam! Pow! Pam!*"

The dog disappeared. Down the block a window opened. A person shook out a duster. The window closed. The gangsters drank each a Ballantine beer.

The small group of patrons, the musicians, and the wife of Ellenbogen sat at the tables. The waiters put plates of hot smelt, with hot derma rounds, before them. No person ate. Tartakower had something wrong with his neck. A. Baer was flushed with a fever. Hildegard Stutchkoff, her gown in tatters, did not leave her chair. The heat, which worked by automation, by some kind of clock, came on, and the windowpanes filled up with steam. The two Hispanics rubbed constantly a clear place on the glass. Vivian Stutchkoff, looking alive, started to thaw.

"Goldkorns! *¡Atención! ¿Qué pasa?*"

"A gypsy! A Checker cab! Okay, Goldkorn, you stand in front of the window. You wave."

The automobile which came slowly across the snow was a Checker brand, but no longer a taxi. Taxis are yellow. This vehicle was black, with black tires, a black grille, and black curtains over each of the windows. At a speed of perhaps one mile in an hour it approached the front of the restaurant, then stopped. Nothing happened. No person got out. The engine appeared to be off. It was not possible to see movement inside.

"I don't like it," Chino said. "I don't like how it looks. Why's it sitting there, huh? What's it want? How come you can't see inside?"

"*Pam! Pam!*"

Margolies came up with a tray and three bowls of meat-kreplach broth. He peered through the misted glass. "A hearse," he said.

The tall man, Jesús, vigorously rubbed the window. "Where? *¿Una carroza fúnebre? ¡Sí!* Curtains on windows! Same like the covered mirror! Ghosts! Ha-ha-ha!" He took a bowl from the waiter's tray.

The full-figured widow rose from her seat to look. She wore an orange-blossom perfume and the back of her shoulders was rounded. "Mister Margolies, we must to make preparations."

"Nobody moves, got it? Nobody touches him!"

"But he must be buried by sundown," said the old man, and bent over Stutchkoff's unlaced shoes. The woman knelt by his head.

Jesús spit the ground-round filling upon the Steinway Restaurant floor. "In China! Mu-shoo pork!"

"I like the smooth feeling of killing. Old man, to me you're just a fly." Chino pointed his gun at the head of the waiter. That was the moment for the black hearse, with astounding volume, to break into "La Cucaracha," which it followed with a medley of Latin-American tunes.

"*¡Ay, ay, ay, ay!*" Martinez, holding chicken necks and of course with a bump on his head, sang in the door of the kitchen. *"Come to your window!"*

The two killers swayed slightly, snapping a little their fingers. They too sang the words of the songs: The hardly-haired man did so poorly; but the tall man, what a surprise, was a light and elegant tenor. Then the music stopped. The black Checker-brand car, which had been trembling, as though from exertions, was now silent, and perfectly still.

"More! More!" cried the desperadoes, and as a matter of fact the auto, or rather some person in it, a woman with a low, soft, flavorful voice, began to speak:

"*¡Oigan, muchachos!* Is it lonely in there? No one to talk to? No one who understands? *Sí*, I know you have troubles, such big, sad troubles. You can tell them to me. I am listening. Come on, Yankee boys, put your head in my lap and tell me all about it. My big, brave soldier boys!"

"Womans! Real womans! *Quiero llevarla a la cama. Tengo que mamarle las tetas.* Tell him, Chino. About the tits. Tell this to Goldkorns."

But the adolescent's eyes had rolled up in his head. "Ooooo, I feel like she was blowing those words in my ear."

"Cold, boys? And hungry? Nothing but kreplach to eat? Guess what I am going to cook for you? Hot honey plantains! Black beans! *¡Especialidades cubanas!* Ay! My hero boys!

What about a nice hot bath? Would you like that? That's for me, *muchachos*! Lots of hot steam! Then you can sleep. How tired you are, how much you want to sleep. *Sí. Sí.* I know. I understand. You don't want to hurt anybody. You want a lullaby. Who wants to die because of some old men? Come on, Yankee boys! Come over to my side! Put your heads here, on my *tetas*."

The older villain had climbed onto the belly of V. V. Stutchkoff and was in an insane manner pulling the handle of the door.

"Surrender! Okay! Surrender!"

"No, man, listen, man, I think the whole gig's a trap. You cats—start playing! Play loud!"

This was an instruction to the membership of the Steinway Quintet, who, with lively selections from Mendelssohn, tried to obey. But it must be remembered, first, that our orchestra possessed no means of amplification and, second, that A. Baer, although he sat in his place and moved his arms, had no instrument inside them. Thus, even in the "Wedding March" passage, the voice of the Siren was all too clearly heard:

> *Duerma, duerma, mi niñito,*
> *Duerma, duerma, mi amor;*
> *Su mami lo está cuidando*
> *Y lo besa con amor.*

Ladies and gentlemen, we are adults here. There is not a great deal left in this modern world to cause us surprise. Yet even those with the most experience among us might wish, from the present scene, to turn aside their eyes. The tall man—his name was actually Jesús—took by the arm the lady with the pearls, the lady with the reddish-brown hair, and rubbed his body parts against her. Then he put his hand inside her nice purple dress and pushed a part of her bosom. I cannot tell you how strenuously our orchestra played the "Fingal's Cave Overture"; even Tartakower with his twisted neck produced a full-bodied tone. But we, and all our art, did not prevail.

For there then began the process which each one of us had held, perhaps, in fearful suspension at a dark spot in his mind. By this I mean that here after all were men with great power, but lacking the voice of conscience: and such men were in a room with desirable women. Krafft-Ebing once remarked that—no, no, it is not necessary to recall his statement. We know, do we not, what men are? From my position at the Bechstein I saw the crazed man lower his victim—she did not resist; perhaps she had fainted?—to the Steinway Restaurant floor.

Here the poorest boy may rise to the highest position in the nation. Many have done so; many more will do so in the years to come.

From what source, and from what distant time, had this thought come to my mind? At once I remembered. These were the words of Judge Solomon Gitlitz, spoken to me, as they have been spoken to thousands of others, upon the occasion of my American naturalization. I stopped playing Mendelssohn then. I stood on my feet. Murmelstein, nearby, pulled my clothing.

"Don't make trouble. Sit. Sit down."

I thought of myself as I had once been, young, proud, with the thick lips of a woodwind player. 1943. Dark days for the United Nations, and for International Jewry. But the spectacles of Solomon Gitlitz were shining, shining like coins, and so, too, were each of his words:

For you, policemen walk the streets, firemen are always ready to save you, doctors are trying to make the land healthful, brave soldiers and sailors are guarding the coasts.

The song of the temptress had ended. The black automobile drove away. One by one the other members of the Quintet put their instruments down. A. Baer alone continued silently bowing. Everything was still. The only sound to be heard came from the lips of the despoiler. Panting. He had his hat on. And therefore Leib Goldkorn, a citizen, a person who had for forty years every benefit, every blessing, he stepped off the platform and went to the Puerto Rican.

"Listen, young man, you must not do this. You have a fine tenor voice."

But it was as if I were addressing a figure of stone. No person spoke a word. The eyes of the woman in purple stared up into mine. Two small lines, signs of anguish, appeared on her brow. What were the possibilities in such a situation? I tapped the shoulder of her attacker, who slowly turned toward me his head.

"You are dragging the flag of your country in the dust."

Still, he did not respond. A film was over his eyes. His trousers dropped by themselves to his knees. Little time to lose. The younger assassin was staring out of the Steinway Restaurant window, with his hand up, extending the brim of his hat. In a few steps I stood before him, this child, with the wisps of hair for a beard, with his nearly pupil-less eyes, with his dreams of an airship, of stars, clouds, and sky.

"Young man, I believe I understand you and your companion. I was young once, like you. I, too, wore a moustache over my lip. Nor was I always a city dweller, a cultured man; no, I once spoke in a country accent that no one about could easily understand. It is an error to think I was born in Vienna. The truth is I first saw the light in Iglau, which is more than one hundred and fifty kilometers distant. There was in this town no resident opera. Is there not a similarity in our destiny? Both of us colonial peoples? I came to the imperial capital when I was twelve, holding my sisters' hands. The sun at that time was setting. People were sitting in cafés. Drinking drinks of a raspberry color. The glass of the shopwindows reflected the evening lights. Everyone in this rosy world read from a newspaper. I saw a man in a turban."

For a moment, I confess, my own words carried me away. Thus I was shocked to hear gasping. Behind my back Jesús had risen on all fours. The foot of the woman had lost a shoe. It was at this moment not possible to look longer.

"Young man, one thing more. My dream on that day was to ride on a tramcar. These went through the streets of Vienna, throwing out sparks, and each was equipped with a musical bell. The conductors bowed to each passenger wishing to ride. If you work hard, if you learn to speak American English, you will be able to ride in a silver airship. I guarantee this to you! We have here a land of opportunity. Do not commit this terrible crime. Stop your colleague! It is nearly too late!"

"Oh! Oh! Oh!"

The second shoe of the lady came off. Each of her legs was now forced into the air. What happened next was that Leib Goldkorn, I myself, had knocked the hat of the tall Puerto Rican from his head to the floor. Not only that, vigorously I was pulling his hair. Success! The man rolled aside, and the lady—she was missing her collar of pearls—began to adjust her purple clothing. The degenerate then clutched my throat with his hand and narrowed his wolf's yellow eyes.

"*¡Vas a morir! ¡Judío sucio! ¡Judío cabrón!* Chino, tell him. Say what I say!"

But it was not his colleague, it was A. Baer who translated: "The Jew is going to die."

"*¡Sí! ¡Sí!* Going to die! All Jews! *¡Judíos sucios!*"

This Puerto Rican, the one with the pomaded hair, then put the end of his pistol underneath Leib Goldkorn's chin. At precisely that moment, upon the point of my death, the telephone, with its wires shooting in all directions, rang. No? Not possible? But it rang.

Mosk got up from his roll-mop salad. He picked up the receiver.

"Hello, Steinway. You don't need no reservation. He ain't here. Kaput. Some kinda heart attack. Yeah, they're here. You wanna speak to them? Yeah. Hang on a minute." The old Lithuanian shuffled over to where the killer was pressing his weapon's trigger. "It's for you."

Jesús took the pay telephone and began to shout into the

mouthpiece. "Kill! Ha-ha-ha! Kill all! Sundown! I kill them myself!"

"Look, Goldkorn. There." The youth was pointing outside, across Rivington Street, toward Allen, where a phone box stood with a dome of snow upon it. Inside were two men, crowded together, wearing brown hats and brown coats. "It's them. Yeah. The Hostage Squad."

The tall fellow, still hatless, continued screaming into the receiver: "¡*Pantalones! Pantalones de* silk! You bring it! Ha-ha! By sundown. ¡*Pantalones!*"

"Goldkorn, you gotta make the negotiation. You know what we want, the plane, the money. I got six clips, Goldkorn, six shots to a clip; Jesús got the same. Enough to shoot everyone here through the eyes, man, and the ears and the mouth. I see anyone move on that snow, anywhere from Eldridge to Allen, I open fire. You say anything wrong, like mentioning names, like giving descriptions, I fire, too. That's square business. Tell them tonight we got to be out of the city. Tell them we got to be high in the sky."

The boy raised his pistol to a spot near my heart. I looked again through the Steinway Restaurant window. The officers of the Hostage Squad were speaking earnestly into the public phone. I walked then to the back of the room and took the other end of the line.

"Hello? Hello? This is Leib Goldkorn speaking, former graduate of the Akademie für Musik, Philosophie, und darstellende Kunst."

"Hello? This is Officer Tim of the Hostage Squad. I'm sorry, but we don't speak Spanish."

In the background, a different voice: "What are you sorry about? This is America. English is the common tongue."

"Officer Tim again. Are you a hostage? Or one of the bandits? I want you to know we will meet every reasonable demand. You'll be calm? You won't get excited?"

"Give me that. Hello! Officer Mike! You won't get away with this. You're surrounded. If you don't come out we'll come in and get you. And it won't be with kid gloves! We're going to smoke your black butts!"

"Yes, hello! I am the artist on pianoforte for the Steinway Quintet. A Bechstein grand. I am not—"

"Goldkorns! ¿Qué pasa? ¿Qué dice?"

"Goldkorn, what do they say?"

"One officer asks for calm. He has promised to meet demands. But I believe the second officer intends soon to attack."

"Aha," said Doctor Fuchs, who was seated nearby. "That's psychology! The gentleman and the bully. Carrot and stick. Superego and Id. Very clever, very sophisticated."

"Hello? Hello? Señor? Are you there? This is Officer Tim. Have you ransom demands? Name a sum, so we can discuss it."

"I will say what in my opinion is needed. A medical doctor. There is a sick man here, a man aged in his nineties. It is a case of brain fever. Also warm blankets because of the cold of the night. For the same reason a bottle of cognac. Of French manu—"

Through the receiver of the telephone the second man, Officer Mike, was screaming: "Outrageous! Do you hear me, Bechstein? Those are outrageous demands!"

Chino took the instrument from my hand.

"Listen good. I am a stone-cold killer. You don't do what I say, just like I say it, a lot of Jews are gonna die. We got to have a plane to go to China. We got to have a 'copter to get to the plane. We want one million dollars. You two cats got to personally bring it right up to this door. In tens. In twenties. In fifties. Anybody else comes near this building we open fire. Get here by sundown. That's a non-negotiable demand. What do you say, huh? Yes? Yes or no? Hello! Hello!"

Through the Steinway Restaurant window I saw the two officers, like men who had lost their senses, first pull inside out each one of their pockets, and then begin to crawl about in the snow. Looking, it seemed, for a coin.

"¡Chino! ¿Qué pasa? Dígame."

"¡El teléfono! ¡La operadora! She cut us off!"

"Ay! Yids will die!"

A patron—pitchai appetizer, kidney grill—came up to Jesús. He had black curled hair and a rumpled shirt. "I think I now intend to be going. This is not after all a Greek restaurant. I made a simple mistake as I was passing by. Anybody could make it. I am not a Jew. I am a Greek and speak in a dignified manner. Well, farewell!"

The patron at once went through the tables to the front of the room. Mosk, the waiter, walked toward him at an angle.

"Hey, Printzmettle, you forgot your coat."

"Yes, yes, foolish, of course." The gentleman—after all, it was a well-known Avenue B merchant—put one arm through a Chesterfield garment and arrived at the door. His way was blocked by the corpse. He stopped a moment. V. V. Stutchkoff was warm and somewhat maroon. There was a slight odor, too. The shoulders of Printzmettle dropped. His nice coat dragged. He sat at the base of the wall.

Pop! I believe everyone jumped. Then the sound, *pop!* again. The two desperate men had opened each a can of Ballantine beer.

5

Greetings, friends! Leib Goldkorn returns! Look, ha! ha! my hands are shaking! This tremble is in part explained by chill weather, for landlord Fingerhut enjoys making economies on currents of heat; but in greater measure it has a different cause. Not in decades have my fingers displayed such a palsy, not since a youth in green trousers took from me my Rudall

& Rose–model flute. Here is a bottle of Mission Bell, a wine of California manufacture. For this half of a pint the price is forty-nine cents. I have been, only moments ago, upon the premises of the all-night Shamrock, a tavern from which it is my habit to purchase brandy from plums. For the first time they would not allow me a drink on the premises or permit the purchase of a bottle to go. No credit! From the Shamrock! With its welcoming cloverleaf sign! It was this humiliation which, as I removed from my pocket a quarter, together with several Roosevelt dimes, caused my hands and fingers to begin to shake.

There is in this wine a strong taste of sulfur. *Mein Gott!* It is nearly opaque against the light of the sun! I would not drink it if I had not suffered, only one hour ago, a particular shock to the nervous system. What was this shock? It was a fright brought on by the former Clara Litwack, my wife. I do not know what it was that indicated to me that something was wrong. When you live for many years with another person there develops intuition. I am speaking to you from a chair next to the kitchen window. From this position I am able to see through an open doorway the back of the Admiral television and the end of the sofa. All seemed normal, except that in her dozing Clara had kicked the coverlet to the floor. Somehow the sight of her bare feet disturbed me. I stood and went through the door. The cap and the nightdress had been thrown off, too, and the bedclothes bound her body like ropes. Her mouth, lacking dentures, was open. Her eyes were open as well. A coma? Death? Death, then? For some reason, on a mad impulse, I turned about to watch for a moment the adventure on the TV. A motion picture: men and women driving in an automobile, while speaking to one another. However, the horizontal and the vertical controls are on this appliance poorly adjusted, causing the deformed heads of the actors to rise to the top of the screen and appear again at the bottom. With a terrible sound Clara took a breath. It was like a person drowning in air. With this rattle she breathed again. Croup! A case of croup! I am not a weak man. I carried my wife to the bathroom and turned the hot water tap of the tub. In a moment the room was filled with steam, and the crisis, which is caused by a kind of dryness in the membranes, eased.

On Columbus Avenue the trucks are following one after the other and I cannot easily hear my own words. The wine is burning my larynx zone, too. Of the events of some months ago I shall speak no longer. Why continue? What more do you wish to know? There are not any surprises. How could there be surprises when I am here, alive, a survivor, speaking to you? The suspense element is gone. To listen to more is simply *Sensationslust.*

At the Steinway Restaurant time is told by the bells of the nearby First Warsaw Congregation, which chime in polka rhythms the hours away. *We* did not know the end of the story; for *us* suspense existed: Thus we believed that each passing hour brought us nearer to our doom. Terrible! During the night we prayed for the morning, but when the morning came, with its threats, its insults, its fierce demands, we prayed again for the night.

At the middle of the day A. Baer took a turn for the worse. He spat on the floor. His tongue developed spots. *"Naronim! Idiotin! Zei vellen tsushterin yiddishe gesheftin. Reissen yiddishe bord. Farnichten yiddishe Kultur. Loifts! Behaltzich! Doss iz a toit lager!"* I am a non–Yiddish speaker. I read in my youth K. May yarns and then the risqué fables of Schnitzler. Still, anyone familiar with the German tongue could grasp that the aged violoncellist had confused these Hispanic intruders with members of the Nationalsozialistische Deutsche Arbeiterpartei. Now defunct.

The condition of others had deteriorated also. Do you remember that Salpeter had been forced to spend the night without his waterproof cloak? He now periodically sneezed, and there was a clear drop of rheum at the end of his nose. A definite catarrh. The neck of Tartakower, moreover, had

locked into the position of a violinist supporting with his chin
his violin. Patrons, even Doctor Fuchs, were forced to visit
regularly the water closet for men or the water closet for
women. A still sadder affliction had struck the woman in the
purple dress, the same person who had that morning come
so close to being the victim of an unmentionable act. Now
she sat for long periods upon the zinc of the bar, with her
hands touching, or seeming to touch, the pearls that were no
longer around her neck. One leg was crossed over the other,
and moved up and down; a shoe hung by only a strap from
her foot. She smiled with her large, bright, strong-seeming
teeth; she giggled; and—does this not wrench the heart?—
made inviting moues in the direction of Jesús, whom, under
the stress of the moment, she took to be her former gentleman companion.

Still, the worst decline of all occurred not to the living
but to the dead. The corpse of Vivian Stutchkoff now un-
mistakably smelled. It was not hot in the room, although it
had grown uncomfortably warm. The problem was the air-
lessness. Not a fresh breath came to us from the world outside. The smoke of Tartakower's, and others', cigarettes hung
in layers over our heads. And with every inhalation, even when
done through the mouth, came the smell of—it is difficult to
put the experience of one sense into the language of another: It was a thick, sweet smell, and a tangy smell, too. Like
boots, partly, and partly like cashew nuts.

"He stinks!" said Mosk, the Lithuanian waiter. "P.U."

Also, he was for some reason swelling. Large already, an
impressive man, Stutchkoff had begun to bulge even further—not dramatically, not all at once, but steadily, like bread
that is rising. By two o'clock his buttons were straining, and
several had burst. But perhaps the most painful of these
transformations was the way in which his skin altered its color.
It had been, that morning, pink and rosy, as if through some
miracle he had been frozen alive. Think of the pain for

Hildegard Stutchkoff, seated nearby at the window, as that complexion deepened to purple and then turned an absinthe green. He had become like a statue of V. V. Stutchkoff, with a statue's patina; and on this green figure the only tone that resembled life was that of the little patch of auburn fox fur that still clung to the lips of the restaurateur.

And what of this Hildegard Stutchkoff? Alas, the stout beauty was also subject to the process of disrepair. Her blond hair was no longer curled on top of her head. The red lips on her mouth had entirely vanished. Her gown was torn in many places, and anyone's eyes could see, upon her shoulder, the white strap of her undergarment. Under her own eyes were blue semicircles, and blue running paint. Slowly, not according to any plan, the staff of the Steinway Restaurant gathered around her. Although the chimes of the Warsaw Congregation had not yet struck the hour of three, her face was already in shadow. Moment by moment—how quickly this happens in winter—the light was leaving the visible part of the sky.

"And after?" This was Ellenbogen, a waiter, speaking.

"Hildegard," one of his co-workers added, "what about after?"

The cashieress lifted her lids from her blue-ish eyes. "Mister Margolies, what is 'after'? Is already 'after.' Is the finish already." She raised an arm toward the body of her former husband, and dropped it again in her lap.

"But the Steinway Restaurant, Madam. Over eighty years at a single location. Leon Trotsky ate here, what about that? And the Attorney General of the State of New York."

"Also champion boxers. B. Leonard. B. Ross."

Hildegard blew for a moment cool air down the front of her bosom. "Steinway Restaurant is finished, too."

"Wait a minute!" cried waiter Mosk. "This is a money-maker! A gold mine!"

"Is losing seventy-five dollars, in cold weather eighty-five dollars, Mister Mosk, each day, this gold mine. Is five hundred each week, in American dollars, is each month two thousand—"

"That's all right, lady! Don't worry! Please you don't worry! Everything is all right! I make beef broilings!" There were real tears on Martinez's cheeks.

In a soft voice Margolies said, "We are old men here. It is not a good time in our lives to go on the street."

"I wish to remind everyone that music is an aid to digestion. Schiller writes that harmony is a feast for the ears. A feast for the ears!"

"Also, music is, according to our own great national poet"—here, of course, I referred to H. W. Longfellow—" 'The universal language of mankind.' "

"My good, dear friends! Mister Martinez, Mister Salpeter, and all. What am I to be doing about modern times? About American peoples? Broilings? Pitchai? Who comes in such an expensive taxi so far for pitchai? They want Gershwin? Gershwin is on the radio, the TV, the movies—is not necessary to make a request from the Steinway Quintet."

"Look, I am going over here. Attention, everyone, please." Margolies called to us from a table by the wall. "Who sat in this chair? This very chair? Here is where her elbows were on the table, and she put her chin on the back of her hands. Do you remember who sat in this pose, Mister Mosk?"

"Yeah. Sarah Bernhardt."

"Yes! It was Sarah Bernhardt who sat in this chair! And smoked a cigarette in a cigarette holder! Never mind if I am crying. It is not important. Never mind."

"Is to pay Mister Margolies no money. Is no time. Is no more downtown Jews."

"Zei vellen arois reissen unzere tzeine! Zei vellen arois nemen de gold!" A. Baer was spitting onto the floor. "Yes, and make lamps out of our skins!"

All at once Ellenbogen—he was the sort of Jew who had hair tufts in his ears—sank to his knees and grasped his ex-employer by his black suspenders. "What will become of us now, Mister Stutchkoff? What are we to do?"

Everyone gasped and looked round at our captors. The tall one, Jesús, was seated at the bench of the Bechstein, where he played one note, two maddening B-flats over high C, a shrill note, over and over again. Chino, the youth with the immature beard, stood at the window, with his hand on his hatbrim, shading his eyes. Outside there was a black crust, soot, shadows, on top of the white of the snow. The sun was falling like a stone out of the sky. Along Rivington Street the bars of the fire escapes were lighting up one by one, like filaments in a lamp. How long until the end of the day?

All the others now joined Ellenbogen next to the corpse.

"What to do, Mister Ellenbogen? Once I saw a grown man ask Mister Stutchkoff precisely that question, and Stutchkoff—this was nineteen twenty-three; he was only a boy—he said, 'Floor coverings,' and this man went on to invent some kind of linoleum that made him rich. In those days he told everyone what to do."

"A coincidence," said Mosk.

"Once is a coincidence," Margolies went on. "But not twice, not three times. A woman came—this was even earlier, nineteen twenty-one—and she had a certain cancer. The doctor wrote a prescription which she brought to Stutchkoff. It had two items on it. Stutchkoff said, 'Take this but don't take that.' A month or two later the cancer was gone. Another time when a man was sick Stutchkoff told him to buy medicine, fill up a spoon with it, and pour it into the sink. This person also got well."

"It's a lotta hooey," said the Lithuanian. "What about when they dropped dead?"

Salpeter was shaking his head. "No, Mister Mosk, what Margolies says is true. I will tell you a thing that occurred in nineteen twenty-eight, when I was in the position of Murmelstein—that is to say, when I was second violinist in the Steinway Quintet. I was not then the leader. Perhaps for that reason I would arrive early at the Steinway Restaurant in order to practice. Even before you would arrive, my dear Mister Margolies."

"I remember. Ragstadt was the first violin."

"One afternoon—I recall the bright sunshine—I was playing the Hebrew Rhapsody of Ernest Bloch, when a man walked by in front of the window. 'Quick! Stop him! Bring him to me!' Rarely had I seen young Stutchkoff so exercised. I put down my instrument and ran into the street. I caught the stranger and brought him inside, and Stutchkoff, who was then barely sixteen, asked him where he was going; but the man would not say. Stutchkoff then refused him permission to leave. O'Brien, our cook, and I restrained him by force. At last the man began to weep and said, 'Rabbi, I want to confess. I had the intention of committing a sin. I was about to be baptized. But you held me back and now the evil hour has passed.' This same person went on to become a very pious man and a lover of music."

Tartakower said, "But that is a miracle!"

"Unbelievable! Amazing!"

From an inside pocket the Litvak took out a cigar and lit it. His face seemed perplexed. It was difficult indeed to reconcile the tales we had heard with the sight of the green giant that lay before us. Even I, from Vienna, a free-thinker, found myself, in the mounting excitement, struck with wonder.

"Baloney," Mosk said.

Margolies then spoke:

"I came to the Steinway Restaurant in the summer, nineteen nineteen. This Stutchkoff was then aged seven or so. Mister Mosk, I advise you to listen and not blow disrespectful rings in the air. One day M. P. Stutchkoff, his wife, S. Stutchkoff, and their child, Stutchkoff himself, sat down with me to a meal of Roumanian broilings. He was then a thin lad, with a thin face, a long face, and he had black eyes and black lashes. It's true, he never ate much; but on this occasion he would not even touch the food. In addition, he said we must not eat either. Everything was getting cold. A delicious platter of broilings. But Stutchkoff, with that thin face, insisted; he would not budge. On the other hand, he would not give a reason. Nothing. It was like a test. So Mister and Madam Stutchkoff, and myself included, we decided, All right, we'll eat by ourselves. Attention, please, everyone: You have not heard a thing like this before. The meat was on my fork, not an inch from my mouth, when Premisher, the butcher, rushes in screaming and waving his arms. 'Stop! Stop! It's not kosher!' It turns out there was a mix-up with a side of a cow. An inch, Mister Mosk! An inch!"

"Oh! Ah!" said Tartakower.

"A Rabbi! A Prince!"

"Blessed be His name!"

The staff of the Steinway Restaurant began to rock back and forth. Suddenly I was knocked rudely to the side and someone rushed by and fell on top of the dead man. It was Murmelstein, second violin.

"Boss! Boss!" he cried. "I'm asking a favor! I got a kid in school! In college! University of Wisconsin! Boss! You hear me? Boss!"

What could one think, but that young Murmelstein, in the course of this night and day of terror, had lost control of his senses? An act of a madman. We cried out, of course. We took hold of our colleague's shoes. But Murmelstein only wrapped his arms more tightly around the mound of the corpse and clung there, as if to the top of a wave.

"¡Ay! ¡Ay!" the Hispanics cried. "No talking! No talking! ¡No hablen! ¡No hablen!"

The tall Puerto Rican grasped the back of Murmelstein's jacket and pulled upon it. The string player, with the strength of his mania, held on to Stutchkoff's waist.

"No talking! Talking not allowed! This is dead individual! Talking to ghost? Ghost? Ha-ha-ha! No such thing! Ain't spirits! Jew, listen! Ain't anything! Ain't anything! Ain't anything!" With the gun in his hand, Jesús was striking Murmelstein, a parent, on the back of his head.

"Hey, cut it out!"

"You are striking a trained musician!"

"No! No more blows on the head!"

The staff of the Steinway Restaurant had become agitated. Someone restrained the hoodlum's arm. Someone else—this is a true fact—began to strike him on the hip. Let people say what they wish; let them even deny it. We acted, friends! At that hour we fought them back!

There was then a gunshot and a cry of pain. A second shot; but no cry came after. Murmelstein rose from the body of Vivian Stutchkoff. He had an unusual smile on his face. "Hee-hee-hee," he said, and walked away.

"I warned them, the mothafuckas! I told the mothafuckas I'd shoot if I saw anything move." Chino was standing by the window, from which two panes were now missing. He rubbed the mist from the rest of the glass. In the snow, between the two curbs, was the tan-colored spaniel. There was enough light from the low sun to see the blood on its fur. From this sight I turned away. I went to the rear of the room.

"Psst! Look! Look here!" Murmelstein was waiting. He had a thing in the palm of his hand. "Hee-hee-hee. I got it out of his pocket. The key! The back-door key! Hee-hee-hee. It was all a plan!"

6

Yass! Yass! Goldkorns here! At the kitchen table. And the window is just over there. A moment, one moment, while I breathe in some air. I am a vigorous man, but the flights of stairs are now a problem. Breathlessness? No, no: fatigue. A *flight of stairs*—is not this a strange way to say it? For three months I have been unable truly to sleep. Goloshes, M.D., gave me tablets in the month of February. With these tablets it is like falling down a long staircase with something dark, a black thing, at the bottom. In English you say *falling asleep.* Ha! What a language!

The reason I have mentioned Doctor Goloshes is that a short time ago I was speaking with him directly on the telephone. That is why I have gone down and up once again so many stairs. He told me he would come by for a visit after his dinner. Clara is not well, after all. I thought it was the croup, but she is making a sound as though she meant to bring up her phlegm. There is also incontinence of the bowels. We treat this as a little joke between us, but if I dared, if I could find the words, I would request that she wear rubber pants. Am I not speaking of a disgraceful human condition? What a scandal! And to what end? What purpose? Tell me! She does not even know that she is alive! "Am I living or not?" she once said. A better way to treat old people would be to kill them. Kill them off would be better! Like the wily Eskimo! There is no mind in her. No spark. And when does Doctor Goloshes eat his dinner? Already it is growing quite dark. But where was I? Yes, I remember. I would accept any employment in the woodwind area, even the saxophone. In the percussion group I have played glockenspiel, and both the Bösendorfer and Bechstein pianos. Is this a thing you already know?

Four flights. Four. Tartakower, with his yellow fingers, would be unable to do it. Have you ever attempted to make a call from a phone box in this city? The kind where you insert silver coins? We have not here the spotlessness of Vienna. Remember, this was an emergency situation. A call to a doctor. I went to three kiosks, first one, then another, and each time the earpiece hung down, yes, like the neck of a butchered goose. And then, while speaking with Goloshes,

M.D., a respected man, my feet were in a person's urine! There was for me a moment of fear in that place. The darkening sky. A wind springing up. All phone books torn. I then saw myself as if I were outside the transparent glass, as if I were a second caller impatiently waiting: fearful to see the light bulb exposing my hands, my shoulders, my large ears, my hairless head. *Hello, hello, Doctor Goloshes? Clara is having an attack!* What is that telephone ringing? We have here no telephone. I see that already there is a full moon. What a joke! And stars! Do you know what I think? These are simply holes, just pinpricks, in a black cloth. Do not tell me they are proof of a vast universe. In the American language: do not force me to laugh. But what is that ringing? One month ago the Bell Telephone Company came and removed from our flat the telephone. Ringing, however. Still ringing. Yass! If I remember correctly, Doctor Fuchs, in tweeds, picked up the Steinway Restaurant receiver.

It was the friendly Officer Tim. I was at that time examining the mural of Feiner and listened with only slight interest to the conversation. Of course there was a shout of joy, an outburst, when it was announced that both officers would soon arrive with the money, that all demands would be met. Before my eyes was a skillful depiction of the death of Aeschylus: an eagle, according to Professor Pergam, of the faculty of the Akademie, dropped a tortoise upon his head. Thinking the latter was a stone. The telephone rang once again. Naturally—this was their plan—it was Officer Mike. An assault was about to be launched. All hostages must at once lie on the floor. Here was the philosopher Anaxagoras, whom Feiner portrayed as middle-aged, explaining the theory of atoms to a boy with a squint. Socrates?

You would like to ask, perhaps, why I showed such little interest? Such small concern? It was my belief that the specialists of the Hostage Squad, even if they were serious men, and sincere in what they said, canceled each the position of the other. I mean by this that the ransom funds would not be paid and there would be no airship to the People's Republic of China. Equally, there would be that night, or the next day, upon the Steinway Restaurant, no armed attack. The hour had by now struck four. The deadline was approaching. The only question was, what would, at sundown, our captors do?

The tall kidnapper, the one who had stepped through the back of A. Baer's violoncello, was at that moment throwing a pill into his mouth. Somehow he missed; it flew over his shoulder.

"Benny! My last benny!"

He fell to his hands and his knees and began inspecting the floor. The roomful of Jews watched without a word as he threw down chairs, upended a Steinway Restaurant table, and knocked a cart of desserts onto its side. But the little red capsule had rolled into a crevice, a crack. Not to be found. Jesús was weeping. He uttered curses and cries. He pounded with his fists, his forehead, his shoe tips, upon the floor. It was surely a dangerous moment. All at once he sat up, with his back straight and his legs crossed underneath him. His eyelids came down. His chin struck his chest. His hat fell into his lap. Sleeping? No soul dared move. Then he said, perhaps in a dream already, "Ah! Ah-ha! *¡El jefe Mao!*"

Chino, the youth, was no longer at the Steinway Restaurant window, whose panes were now partly rose-colored and partly gray. He was instead behind me, with a cognac glass in his hand.

"For you, Goldkorn."

"This is a very fine cognac. Imported."

"Turn on the lights, man. It's dark in here."

"Dark? On the contrary, young man. It is quite light in this room. The overhead chandeliers do not go on until five o'clock. It is too early."

"Don't be punk-hearted, man. It ain't personal. We ain't

gonna do this because of you. It's just the way the thing broke down. Hit the lights."

"Please. Take this. I am not after all thirsty."

I myself put the cognac glass, which was mostly full, back into his hand. I turned from him to the wall. Why? I do not know why.

"What are you looking at, man? What's this painting called? The one all over the wall."

"This is a mural by Feiner. Considered his finest work. The title is 'The Golden Age.' "

"Yeah. Uh-huh. Which is when a country is at the top, right? Number one. At the peak of its glory."

"Yes, at the peak of its culture and influence. You have, for example, Vienna at the turn of this century. It was then that the directorship of the Imperial and Royal Hof–Opern-theater was in the hands of Mahler, who spent also his boy-hood in the little town of Iglau."

"What place is this? Is this a country? Is it Greece?" The youth with the pitiable moustache pointed to a spot on the wall, where the mount of the Acropolis was depicted.

"Yes. Correct. I believe the man sitting there is Pericles, the leading citizen of Athens. He encouraged art, literature, and philosophy, in addition to music."

"And what's that building? The one on the hill?"

"The Parthenon. It is where the Greeks worshiped Ath-ena."

"Magnificent. Right, Goldkorn? Magnificent."

The temple rose above the individual men. Its columns were fluted and gleaming. The bright marble shone.

"Feiner was a well-known artist."

"You know something funny? I needed two hundred dollars. I owed a couple of dudes."

At that moment, as if it had plunged into a pot of water, the burning ball of the sun went out. Indisputable darkness.

Before I, or the youth, or any other person could locate the switch for the chandeliers, the shadow of Salpeter appeared on the musical platform. With a pencil he rapped sharply the lid of the Bechstein.

"I ask the members of the Steinway Quintet to take their places. Quickly, please! Gentlemen, quickly!"

From different parts of the room the musicians emerged. A. Baer could not by himself climb onto the platform. We gave him assistance by holding his arms. Through the cloth of his coat his skin was hot to the touch. Salpeter, with a handkerchief to his nose, continued speaking.

"Ladies and gentlemen, as you are certainly aware, our concert last evening was unfortunately interrupted before it had reached its conclusion. How long ago that seems, and not merely a matter of hours! However, in spite of the vicissitudes that have crowded upon us, we are still alive, and still here together. Therefore, I am pleased to announce that the Steinway Quintet will present at this time a special program. Our selection is dedicated to the memory of our colleague and co-religionist, V. V. Stutchkoff, a true friend of the arts."

"Play anything by Irving Berlin."

"Thank you, Mister Mosk, for your suggestion. But I am sure you agree that tonight is not an ordinary occasion, and for that reason we shall not entertain the usual requests. The fact is, throughout the long years of its existence, our little orchestra has numbered among its members many distinguished composers, some of whom, like S. Romberg himself, or Maximilian Steiner, the film-score artist, are known and loved all over the world. Yes, Romberg played at the Steinway Restaurant the viola for nearly one year. Other members of our Quintet are appreciated more by connoisseurs. I am thinking, of course, of Rubin Goldmark, K. Goldmark's nephew, whose difficult *Samson* was composed between these walls; and also of our dear friend Joseph Rumshinsky, creator of the two-act *Ruth,* and replacement artist on the Bechstein whenever the late and lamented Schneebalg was indisposed. It is the work of these colleagues that we shall play tonight, beginning, for artistic reasons, and for morale also, precisely at that point at which our concert was suspended. Ladies and gentlemen, *The Student Prince*, followed by 'The Indian Love Call'!"

Murmelstein took his seat. Tartakower took his seat. A. Baer had his damaged instrument propped between his knees. And I, Leib Goldkorn, Schneebalg's successor, slid onto the bench of the Bechstein. Salpeter sat, too. Then everyone noticed that there was a bare music stand among us, and one extra chair.

"Oh, yes," said Salpeter, and rose to his feet once again. "I have placed here the chair of the late Albert Einstein, the recreational violinist, who once, in nineteen forty-nine, joined our little orchestra for a musical evening. In the history of the Quintet, he was the only guest soloist allowed such a privilege. However, he supplied his own instrument, and of course to such a world figure it was not possible to say no. And it is a pleasure to announce that he played quite well."

Salpeter sat down a second time, and picked up his bow. But for some reason Tartakower was standing. Because of the sprain to his neck he had to walk sideways. He came over to me.

"I'll sit here, if you do not mind, and you take, please, my chair."

"But what are you suggesting? What can you mean?"

Tartakower held out his instrument. Yes, he was holding it out to me.

"Here, take it. I want you to play it tonight. I shall attempt the piano. I know the chords."

His metal flute was in my hands. It was a Powell model, only thirty years old, of American manufacture. But it was light, was balanced correctly, and rose easily toward my lips.

"Short of breath, Mister Tartakower?"

"No, no, please. You are the older man, a woodwind specialist. I beg you not to argue."

The first violinist rapped with his pencil the edge of a

music stand. Tartakower abruptly sat down and I, I stood up, I walked to his place, I eased myself onto his chair.

"What's this? What's this?" Salpeter wished to know.

"He—it is his neck, his neck, you know."

Salpeter looked at me closely. He wiped, with a white handkerchief, his nose. Then he dipped his shoulder and we started to play.

I have remarked that it was dark in the room. The music on the music stand was obscure and difficult to read. The instrument, after so many years, felt strange to my hands, my lips. It was as if I were again speaking German, a dear but in part a forgotten tongue. I made many mistakes. My breath seemed to whistle. And soon it became necessary, for a moment, to stop. I looked about me. The revival of the Romberg selection seemed to have brought A. Baer to his senses. He had no bow, but he hummed his part softly, and the violoncello produced a pizzicato in spite of its broken back. The Bialystoker, meanwhile, with his chin on his clavicle, had mastered the pianoforte. I could rest no longer. It was time for the "Indian Love Call," whose melody is played exclusively by the flute. The Powell model now felt weighty. It nearly fell from my hands. Salpeter nodded. I believe that Murmelstein encouragingly smiled. I played a wrong note. A second wrong note. Something was smarting my eyes.

"Stop! Stop!" Salpeter cried. "We shall begin once more."

This we did. From my instrument there came at last—as had happened on one other occasion, the Graduation Day Concert of the Akademie, at which both my parents and my two sisters were present—a series of perfect and lucid and golden-throated tones.

I cannot say how long our concert lasted. Less than one hour, perhaps. The light in the room soon faded completely. Between selections there was no applause. Yet in the eight decades of the Steinway Quintet there had not been such music as this. I am struggling to find words to describe it, and I fear I shall fail in this task. Not, however, because music is, as some critics say, an abstract art. I have never believed such modern, twelve-tonish statements. Each note corresponds to a nuance of feeling, just as every word of a poem does, or any brush stroke of a painting. Very well. I must then simply describe what these feelings were. This is taxing. Difficult. Yet my emotion that Wednesday night was not in essence different from that which I regularly experience upon hearing a broadcast—perhaps of Halévy—on station WQXR. Only sharper. It was what we used to call *Zusammengehörigkeit*, a feeling of connectedness. Connectedness, in the first place, to the man whose music I was at that moment hearing or playing. In that final hour at the Steinway Restaurant I felt nearest, I think, during his Concert Suite and the score from *The Life of Émile Zola*, to M. Steiner. The reason for this is perhaps that he was Viennese. And a former pupil of Mahler. Indeed, I soon felt this connection not only to the film composer but, behind him, so to speak, the whole world of the imperial city, its broad streets, its river, the k.k. Hof-Operntheater, and even at light moments, when I, myself, was executing a difficult trill, the Wienerwald, with its trees and its birds.

As our program continued, this feeling of closeness— better to say an absence of division, of divisiveness—grew to include those with whom I was playing: Murmelstein, Tartakower, A. Baer, Salpeter. It was as if the Steinway Quintet were a single person, giving a solo performance; as if invisible threads bound us one to another, so that when Salpeter moved his arm upward I felt myself pulled so slightly in his direction. And at last there grew to be a similar bond with those who were listening below. We could at that time hardly see them—only the shine from a pair of eyeglasses, a white shirt collar, the napkin on Margolies's arm. Like heads bobbing in an ocean of darkness. Then I felt myself to be not this Leib Goldkorn, no longer the separate citizen, but also a part of that ocean, like a grain of salt, no different from those other grains, Mosk, or Ellenbogen, or the woman, Hildegard Stutchkoff, or the lifeless corpse of her spouse; yes, even— do not feel alarm at what I now say—even the two murderers, for they were a part of that ocean, too. That ocean. That darkness, friends. We know what it is, do we not? And this is my feeling concerning the nature of music: that it connects those who have died, Stutchkoff and Steiner, and before Steiner Mahler, with those who are merely waiting to do so. All in a similar boat, as Americans say.

The last notes of our concert sounded. The violoncellist plucked three times—C-sharp, E, A—his violoncello; Tartakower removed his foot from the foot pedal; both violinists drew simultaneously their bows across their strings. The flautist sealed his lips. There was a pause of a single moment. Then the lights came on and the world fell to pieces.

The elder Puerto Rican, still cross-legged, cried out in a voice of despair, "Oh, Chino! The dreams! *Un sueño. ¡Estuve en China, con dragones y el jefe Mao!*"

The youth helped him to rise. "I know. Come on. The time is up."

"In China! Eating lemons! Only a dream!"

The men stood under the chandeliers and put bullets into their pistols. Several of the patrons began to whimper. A woman was weeping. Then Chino told us what we should do.

"All right! Okay! Listen! The deadline is over. The stars are already out. They ain't coming. Understand? They ain't going to come. I want everybody down here. Everybody in the middle of the room. Quick! Quick! Move quick!"

"Mister," said Mosk. "I ain't electric."

With his arm Chino motioned to the members of the Steinway Quintet. We climbed down—A. Baer had now practically fainted—and stood with the others, in the center of the restaurant.

"Okay. Now, don't argue, don't think, just do it: You people take off your clothes."

Immediately Printzmettle, the Avenue B tobacco dealer,

went to the sad-eyed killer. "I am Greek. Greek! Bouzouki! Metaxa! You must let me go!"

Jesús, with his free hand, ripped the patron's shirtfront, from top to bottom. Each button was gone. "Off! Shoes! The socks! Everything! Off!"

"Put your stuff in a pile. Pile it up in the middle."

Printzmettle did this. We all did this. There were for some moments only the sounds that persons make when they are removing their clothes. Not then even weeping. Not even sighs. I, myself, felt embarrassment at the great amount of hair upon my shoulders, which showed so clearly under the twelve bulbs of the chandelier. Murmelstein, in his boxer shorts, was helping A. Baer out of his shirt.

"Is it you, Mister Murmelstein? *Lust mir iber mein bord.*"

Slowly there grew a mound of coats, trousers, and, shame to say, ladies' blouses, stockings of nylon, a fox-fur boa. Shoes of all types stuck out everywhere. We were not at that time, however, entirely naked; before this could be demanded of us a shout went up, I believe from Margolies, who was standing nearest the window.

"Here they come! They are bringing the money! I can see them!"

"We are saved!" Everyone started to shout this out. "We are saved! Hurrah!"

In an instant the taller of the two gangsters was at the window, rubbing the mist from the glass. "Goldkorns! Goldkorns! *¡Ven acá!*"

I went to where I was summoned, and looked out. It was dark on Rivington Street. Light fell through the panes of the Steinway Restaurant window onto the snow. On Allen Street the lamps were already burning. From the other direction, still in the shadows, two figures approached. They were of the same height. Both wore brown trench coats and, it seemed, brown-colored hats.

"*¡Sí, sí! Son ellos. Tienen todo el dinero.* The money. Ha-ha!"

As they came nearer the rectangle of light we could see that one of these men carried, upon his shoulder, a large sack of some kind, and the other man had a pail in each of his hands. They walked steadily toward us, lifting their feet high out of the inches of snow.

Chino shouted from the center of the room. "Tell them that's close enough, Goldkorn! Tell them to leave the money and go!"

But before I could respond, the two men walked directly into the light and stopped in front of our window. They stood restlessly, shifting the weight of their bodies from one foot to the other. I crouched low in order to call to them through the panes of broken glass. In that position I looked up under the brims of their hats: I knew them at once from their faces. These were not the officers of the Hostage Squad. One was Sheftelowitz. The other was Pipe.

"Fools! Fools!" I hissed these words. "What are you doing here?"

The two men simply stood there, swaying a bit from side to side.

I cried out once more, "What is it you want?"

Sheftelowitz answered. "What else? Pee-pee."

"We been waiting a long time," said Pipe.

I put my hands to my mouth. "Run! Run for your lives!"

"Run! Ha-ha! Run, you policemans!" Jesús waved his gun in the window.

Both Jews dropped their burdens. They looked at each other. Then they fled into the shadows on the left and the right. Chino, with no more beard on his face than on the previous evening, came quickly over.

"Where's the money? How much is it?"

We three looked out the window. Both pails had turned over and spilled their contents onto the snow. Fish: for the most part flounder. The bag had split open. Feathers.

"*¡Ay, ay!* Ain't dollars!"

"A mockery! Insult to honor! Now everybody will die!"

One of these villains grasped the waistband of my S. Klein's shorts and pulled them, what awful tomfoolery, down to my knees. To my ankles. I then was a naked person.

"Get your clothes off! All your clothes! Yids, move your asses!"

Our antagonists stepped into the crowd of Jews and began to rip from their bodies the last shreds of their garments. Now there were plentiful screams, wailing, and exclamations. But the two men went about their work grimly and pushed us, bare, trembling, and sick with sudden fear, toward the open staircase that led to the floor below. Then they stepped back ten, or perhaps fifteen paces. All of us, musicians, waiters, patrons, were huddled together, as if on the lip of some common grave. Our bodies in the light of so many bulbs were extremely white. Ghosts of ourselves when clothed. Above the prayers, the groaning, the heart-wrenching cries, the voice of Doctor Fuchs—even tweedless, an imposing man—was calm and clear.

"What is the cause of the fear of death? Let us think of it in a rational manner. Is it not in reality the childish fear of losing the penis? Of being cut off from this source of guilty pleasure? Notice how when we recognize the origin of anxiety, it at once disappears. Now we begin to feel joyful."

The alienist went on in this manner a moment longer, but in truth I no longer heard his words. For, as chance had arranged it, I found myself standing next to and in fact pressing against the body of Hildegard Stutchkoff. There was a wrist of mine against the small of her rounded back. She turned about. There were two breasts that depended. Impossible not to feel how life stirred in my member; at the same instant I felt come over me a red wave of shame. The reason for this was not my sudden excitement, for how could one not respond to the proximity of such a sportive figure? No, it was just that at that very moment, for the first time in all these hours of terror, I happened to remember Clara, my wife.

Like a child in a classroom I raised my free hand. "Please! I must call on the telephone! My wife! She needs injections!"

Chino, who had previously offered me cognac to drink, now pointed his gun toward my head.

"Goldkorn, you gonna be first to die!"

I closed my eyes. I shut from my ears the sound of screaming. I prepared for what lay at the foot of the stairs.

However, there was no gunshot. Instead I heard Ellenbogen declare, "Look! Mister Stutchkoff!"

I opened my eyes and turned toward the base of the door. At first I could make out nothing; then I saw, by the head of the corpse, a small, fuzzy blur. Like the head of a dandelion, the fluff of the fox fur had lifted off Stutchkoff's lips and was rising into the air.

"*Ooooo!*"

From the open mouth of the restaurateur there now issued a thin, gray-colored shadow, a mist, a kind of a cloud—impossible to know what precisely to call it. Steam perhaps. Perhaps smoke. Everyone saw it slowly rising, more and more of it, growing taller, spreading outward, almost the size of a person.

"Ghost!" Chino exclaimed, although in a whisper.

"*¡Un diablo!*"

The two assassins were of course standing nearest the dead man; the sight of them was, even to my eyes, to the eyes of their enemies, pathetic to see. They had dropped their weapons and thrown their arms about each other. Their mouths were open, their eyes rolled about, and, strangest of all, their legs kept moving, in the manner of dream figures who wish to run but cannot. The cloud, now as large as the man had been himself, detached itself from Vivian Stutchkoff and floated toward the two terrified Puerto Ricans.

"Ah! Ah!" they cried, and disappeared inside the mist. Even their hats were gone. Then the cloud passed away: The men were the same, clinging each to the other, except that tears in sheets flowed from their eyes.

Ellenbogen, who had socks on, ran down the center of the restaurant turning all the chairs upside down.

"The Maggid of Mezritch!" the waiter cried. "So his soul won't be tempted to stay!"

And in truth the cloud followed behind him, moving from table to table, like an eager proprietor. At the end of the room, it covered the zinc top of the bar and obscured the rows of glasses and bottles. It rose to the first chandelier, then to the second. It enveloped the Bechstein. It touched all the walls. I was not able to resist the thought that it was in some fashion saying to the Steinway Restaurant farewell. Then it descended onto my head. And onto the heads of the others. When it lifted we were weeping.

"You see?" said Margolies, as he wiped his eyes. "What did I tell you? It's just like Zev Wolf says!"

Mosk, to whom this was addressed, replied in a gasping voice, "Zev Wolf, my eye! It's what you call tear gas. Look over there!" The Lithuanian pointed with a thin white arm to Stutchkoff, or rather to just behind Stutchkoff, where a second cloud was now materializing from under the crack in the door.

The Hispanics saw this as well. They let go of each other and retrieved their guns.

"Pssst! This way! Follow me! Hee-hee, I have the key!" It was Murmelstein, beckoning us toward the rear of the room.

"Nobody move!" the cruel youth shouted. "Freeze!"

However, the gas had already grown thick in the air. It was difficult to see one another. We joined hands and, in this chain, moved slowly between the platform and the bar, toward the door to the kitchen. The second violinist had already gone through and was fumbling with the lock on the back exit. "I got it!" he cried. "Eureka!"

We all moved as fast as possible—Doctor Fuchs had A. Baer over his back—through the small kitchen to where the barred door was just swinging open. But before we went through, a mysterious sound made us stop wherever we stood.

It seemed to be everywhere about us, a kind of a hum, a drone, growing steadily louder. Then the floor under our feet began to shake, the stacked dishes and pans rattled, and the whole building trembled through its foundations. We looked back through the gloom of the Steinway Restaurant proper. Strange lights were descending in beams from the sky. The snow had risen from the ground and was swirling in the air. The noise was now like fists beating upon a rooftop.

"*Ay, ay!* Angel of death!" the pair of doomed men were screaming. "*¡Espíritus malos!*"

"Ladies and gentlemen! Do not hesitate! Go quickly outside!" Salpeter was urging everyone through the open rear door. I, myself, the flautist of the Steinway Quintet, glanced one final time over my shoulder—the shafts of strange light, the thick clouds of gas, our tormentors crying out with their hands stretched high above them—and plunged with bare feet into the alley of snow.

7

This is L. Goldkorn. You do not want Goldkorn. You want to know what happened next. Am I not able to convince you that it is over? Finished? Kaput? Listen: I never, from that moment in the snow until this one—and it is now nearly midnight; Goloshes, M.D., has been here already an hour, more than an hour—set foot inside the Steinway Restaurant again. Not even to retrieve my shoes, my clothing. These Hildegard Stutchkoff sent me, inside of a Gladstone valise, by the public mail. For what seemed a spring day, it has become a winterish night. Wind blowing. No steam from F. Fingerhut. We possess a small electrical heater, and the electric current is still being supplied, but it is plugged into the socket by Clara's bed. What is he doing there? Why is he taking so long?

I cannot describe adequately our journey—slipping on ice patches, feeling blindly the person before us, unable to hear our own anguished cries—through that narrow alley. Worst was the noise. It struck at one. It blew one's thoughts from one's head. It was like the *dum-dum-dum* of waves on the outside of a ship's metal plates. Inside which you are sleeping. The shock of such sounds on my voyage, Lisbon–New York, New York, made me fear for my mind. I have always considered myself a rational man. A child of the modern age. Not one of the violent, even bizarre actions in the twenty-four-hour period I have been describing caused me to doubt for a moment the nature of reality or the evidence of my senses. Everything could be explained. However, as our group of former hostages emerged from the passageway onto Rivington Street, I felt that the familiar world, one of cause and effect, of physical laws, had been left behind. It was like a new planet.

What we saw was that between us and the Steinway Restaurant the snow was actually rising. It was a whirlwind. At the top of this swirling storm, a black shape hung in the air. It neither rose nor descended, but simply remained, roaring, in defiance of gravity, of physics, of reason itself. From the belly of this form columns of light shot downward and played over the surfaces of the snow. In the tremendous thunder it was difficult to hear what people were saying, but Salpeter pointed toward the Steinway Restaurant door. This had swung open. Standing inside it was Vivian Stutchkoff. He appeared to be stuck. He backed up, into the light of the chandeliers, then came forward and once again caught in the doorframe. It was at this point, naturally, that my own sanity came into question. *Dum-dum-dum* came the sound from the sky. The dead spaniel was, I noticed, only a few feet away. On the third attempt, by turning a few degrees sideways, Stutchkoff got through the door. He came then bobbing toward us. Our party retreated to the opposite curb. "Golem!" some person cried. Margolies and Ellenbogen were rocking in prayer. Still Stutchkoff came, enormous in size, rising and falling, skimming the snow, like a balloon that has been filled with gas.

From a spot nearby, four figures, all clothed, in brown trench coats and hats, rushed forward toward the abandoned door of the Steinway Restaurant. Two local merchants. And the two members of the Hostage Squad. They all went inside. Stutchkoff, meanwhile, had glided to the center of Rivington Street. There he paused, bounding about, turning left and right; then he fell face down into the snow. A tall and a short Puerto Rican stood in his place. It had been some kind of trick! Yes! The restaurateur had been their shield!

Some person was pulling my arm. Mosk, the Lithuanian waiter. "Whirlybird," he declared.

Everything, for me, became now clear. I had been guilty of an error in logic, and my confusion followed from that. You must remember how I had thought the promises of the Hostage Squad, so contrary in nature, must in the course of things cancel each other out, that nothing at all would be done. False assumption. In truth both plans had been put simultaneously into effect. The tear gas belonged to the adamant Officer Mike. What hovered above us was the rescue ship provided by Officer Tim. Indeed, I now saw that hanging from the bottom of this aircraft, nearly invisible in the snow-dust around it, was a kind of ladder, perhaps made from rope. Chino had started to climb it, was in fact halfway to the top. Jesús was just getting on.

Then, from the direction of Eldridge Street, a man wearing clothes came running toward us. "Beverly! Beverly!" he cried. It was the gentleman companion of the lady formerly in purple. He was staring wildly about him. "Has anyone seen Miss Bibelnieks?"

It was I who pointed her out. She was standing alone, near to the curbstone. Her hands were clasped under her chin and she was peering into the center of the whirling storm, where Jesús had climbed to the top of the ladder. He paused there. His hat blew away. With one hand he held the ladder and with the other he waved. Then he disappeared inside the airship. The gentleman friend of the lady put his wrap over her bare, damp shoulders. She seemed not to notice, only stared, moving her lips. "Don't hurt him, don't hurt him," she said.

Suddenly the black shape, with an even greater volume of sound, began to rise straight up in the air. I resisted the impulse, an unusually strong one, also to wave farewell. A light came on in the bottom of the craft, winking off and on. In only a moment this was all that we could see. The sound soon faded completely. The air became clear. There was only the single, silent, red jewel in the sky; and then this vanished, too. We remained, not speaking. Not sobbing either. The yellow light poured from the Steinway Restaurant window and door; but it did not quite reach the street center, where V. V. Stutchkoff lay buried under a mountain of snow.

8

Goldkorn. Did you know there was a well-known composer named Korngold? Also Viennese. An artist, like Steiner, for films. These are the tricks that life plays. I could not, that Wednesday, return directly to my home. The police officers insisted we follow certain procedures, and afterward there was a frostbite examination in the emergency room. It was the middle of the night by the time I pulled myself up these four flights of stairs. My wife was, as I feared, on the floor, having suffered a blood sugar attack. Coma. I gave her, as prescribed, her injection; and when she regained consciousness she did not know whether it was Wednesday or Tuesday or

Thursday. "Am I living or not?" was what, as previously mentioned, she said. She is in a bad way, Clara. The day for her is the same as the night. What is the goal of life under such conditions? And I must pay Goloshes, too! How? With what money? I possess only a single savings-type bond. Let him obtain from the government his fee, since it is the government, with its laws, that insists such a creature, with no spark in her, remain alive!

I shall tell you about the waiters of the Steinway Restaurant, which of course has been closed since that night. Ellenbogen's wife has found part-time work, although Ellenbogen himself has not. Still, they manage to live on her salary alone. Margolies was for many weeks quite ill, with fever and a coating of phlegm. Inflammation. But I have recently learned that he has left the hospital and is living in a kind of home for old persons. They say that Mosk has a small sum of money, in addition to a house of his own in the city of Baltimore. I believe this is true. Martinez I do not know of. I thought one month ago that I saw, on Broadway, Hildegard Stutchkoff, the cashieress. The same springy curls, and she had a handbag that swung by her hip zone. I called out, but she did not hear me. Before I could reach her she had gone into the station of the IRT train. It is possible I saw somebody else. It might not have been she.

What of our tormentors? In China? Possibly. But it is more likely that the pilot of the airship simply maneuvered it to the roof of a nearby prison. In my opinion they are at this moment in jail.

I am sorry to announce the death of A. Baer. I saw this in the newspaper only one week after our adventure had been concluded. It was a complimentary story and contained an interesting description of his student days in Hannover and Paris, his Red Cross concerts, and of how his two little pieces, a sonata for pianoforte and violoncello, and a partita for violoncello alone, were once played by masters all over the world. Salpeter is in Lake George, New York. By the shores of the lake. I have lost contact entirely with Murmelstein, as one does at times with younger people. He is in many respects a resourceful and original artist, wrongfully overlooked, and there of course remains the possibility he will yet find a place worthy of his talent. Tartakower. Tartakower has now a position with the celebrated Gumbiner Brothers Bar Mitzvah Band. It is a strange thing, really. Of course he is a pleasant man, a generous person, and I rejoice he has obtained such a prestigious appointment. But does he have the breath control for that type of music? The truth is, when you own your own instrument, such matters as volume of breath and world experience become entirely mute. Stutchkoff, of course, is buried at the Hachilah Hill Cemetery, within the family vault.

I hear noises now, footsteps, from my wife's room. Yes. Goloshes is coming soon. "Well, and how is she, Doctor?" That is what I shall say. I shall smile, too.

This is my address: 134 West 80th Street. By Columbus Avenue. I would appreciate knowing of even the smallest position, on any type of musical instrument. Oboe. Cornet. English horn. Also the percussion group. I have not in this account attempted to hide my shortcomings but, on the contrary, to present myself as I am. You know that I drink sometimes schnapps, for example, and that I do not possess a religious temperament. Yet I am speaking truthfully when I tell you I feel myself to be now the same person who received the gift of a Rudall & Rose many years in the past; and like that young boy I am still filled with amazement that merely by blowing upon such an instrument, and moving one's fingers, a trained person may produce such melodious, such lyrical sounds. You are no doubt aware that with the flute the breath passes over the opening, and not into a mouthpiece, as with other woodwinds. Its music is, therefore, the sound of breathing, of life. It is the most ancient of instruments, and the most basic, too. A boy can make one with a knife and a hollow twig. This is what shepherds did, playing to sheep.

Music
of the
Spheres

Pericles: But what music?
Helicanus: My lord, I hear none.
Pericles: None?
The music of the spheres! List, my Marina.
—Pericles

1

What is it that drives men into the arms of women, and women to the arms of men? Here is a difficult question. As youths, as students in the Akademie für Musik, Philosophie, und darstellende Kunst, we heard the corpulent Professor Pergam lecture upon the theorem of Plato. Once, long ago, primeval man was round, like a ball, with four hands, four feet, and two faces that looked in opposite directions. Four ears. Two private members. This creature, our ancestor, had great mental powers, wonderful physical strength, and in addition was able to roll forward and backward at a tremendous rate. Alas! He used these same gifts to challenge the gods. Zeus, to punish such insolence, split man in two, the way you or I might split an apple, or the Greeks themselves halved an egg with a hair.

What suffering then! Wounded mortals staggering about

on only two legs. The ache from loneliness. In time Zeus took pity. He caused the loose skin to be knotted up, thus creating the navel. He decreed that the organs of generation be moved to the front of the body, so we poor creatures might sow our seed into one another, instead of behind ourselves, like grasshoppers, as had been the case. Ergo, the two halves of man have ever since desired each other, and embraced each other, in the fruitless attempt to recall the time when they were one. This memory we call love.

Love! Love! In my own tongue, *die Liebe*! What laughter from the Akademie students: pale-faced Willi, for instance, or the thick-lipped Leib Goldkorn, or the gap-toothed Hans. "Zeus!" cried the one. "An apple! Slicing an apple!" from another. *"Der Grashüpfer!"* from a third. All together: *Ha! Ha! Ha!* Herr Turpenstein, the choirmaster, was forced to rap his baton on the music stand. Then we put from our minds all thoughts of muscular men, of red-lipped women, and instead threw our arms about one another's shoulders and in high, fresh, shining voices sang our Viennese songs.

Now—and by this word I mean six decades, more than six decades, later—I am less certain the idea of Plato is only a joke. Like other men, I have had hints, little clues, no clearer than blots on paper—inklings, if I may be permitted a jest— that our lives are indeed a continual striving to return to a time when we were part of each other and shared a common fate. These men and women about me, for instance, some of whom hang like bratwurst, or blutwurst, from straps, or sit squeezed on metal benches: Note the glances darting each to each, the knees which touch, the manner in which shoulders, hip bones, contact and rub. All breathe in, then exhale, the same hot, sourish air. Is this car, a single IND unit, rocking, swaying, hurtling through the earth, in any significant way different from the planet itself, to whose crust we similarly cling as it rockets through the darkness of space? You will no doubt ask why, in the press of this crowd, I have a seat to myself, why none of these revelers dares stand near. Could the Manhattanites be fearful of me? My Hiawatha costume: reddish skin, bear-claw necklace, and my bow and arrow, such harmless toys? Friends: I, too, know what it is like to be joined to others. That chorus! The handsome Pepi Pechler, the aforementioned Willi Wimpfeling, L. Goldkorn, freckled Hans: Here was a primeval life form, multi-limbed, with as many heads as a hydra, yet all singing the identical song.

Enough of such talk. Let us instead throw ourselves into the hurly-burly of actual life. One day—*Mein Gott!* I was about to say long ago. But it was only yesterday morning. Fifteen hours. So: on a recent morning, a hot summer morning, Leib Goldkorn could be seen on a street in the upper Nineties, near the Avenue Amsterdam. He pauses in his promenade, he stops, and sets down the Gladstone-style bag he carries in his right hand and the table for cards that has been pressed between his left elbow and torso zone. Next step: to unfold the hidden legs of this ingenious fixture and turn upright its metal, milk-chocolate top. Done! Now unhinge, open, the valise of ersatz alligator. Contents: sandwich of liver pâté; half-pint bottle of Mission Bell, a wine of California manufacture; carrying case, empty, for Rudall & Rose–model flute; a yellow pail, of the sort designed for seashore use; and, carefully wrapped, a set of eight goblets—each with a stem, a bowl, a pedestal foot. Off with the velveteen! Immediately we see on each glass a pink bird standing in blue water, with the word FLORIDA above and the motto *Fountain of Youth* below. Native sons! No need to tell you this was a reference to the twenty-seventh State of the Union, a peninsula bounded by the Atlantic Ocean to the east and, to the west, Gulf of Mexico. Main products: tourism, citrus. Look more closely: Do you see the triangular chip in the pedestal of one of these vessels? This occurred some forty years earlier, in a moment of confusion, of bustling, at the Tivoli Cine Palace, where I had been given the entire set in return for purchasing two tickets to the evening premiere. These glasses L. Goldkorn places upon the tabletop surface, with the chipped one—in some ways his favorite, raised in a toast once to A. Tosca-nini: *The Maestro, friends!*—at the extreme right of the row.

Did I mention the heat? The hot sun of the day? Around the corner, on the Avenue, children dashed through the thick streams of an open hydrant. I took the plastic pail to this spot and attempted to fill it from the vigorous geyser. "No *Gymnasium?*" I said to the young darkies who stood, some scratching their heads, some with one leg drawn upward, in a pose reminiscent of the flamingos. "No studies?" They watched as I leaned into the thunderous spray. My shirt-front soon stuck to my breastbone; my trousers—formerly in the wardrobe of V. V. Stutchkoff, my late employer—grew damp. With both hands on the brimming bucket, I turned to the assembled youth. "Nevertheless, it is wise in vacations to continue one's reading of books. At your age I enjoyed the Wild West adventures of K. May." How many summer hours did I steal from my woodwinds with Old Shatterhand, who could shoot out a red man's eyes at fifty paces, or pierce a coin with a bullet while it flipped in the air? *Hang it all, fellows,* I can still hear the marksman say: *Zum Henker, Kerle!* But these teens, thin of frame, ebony-hued, only resumed their play in the arc of the spurting fountain.

I returned to my goblet octet, which I filled with varying amounts of liquid: from a splash at the left-most glass to near full at the right. Thus, in brief seconds, the plain mute vessels were transformed into—have you guessed it?—a harmonicon, also known as crystalphonicon, or filjan saz. Of course my instrument was a primitive model—closer to the *Glasspiel* played in beer taverns than the mechanical marvel perfected by B. Franklin himself. Nevertheless, I could play the scale of C major, with the C of my right-hand glass, my dear chipped one, producing vibrations exactly one octave higher than the half-empty glass on the left. To think that such an instrument was once banned by the police of Vienna! Public performance *verboten!* Because of animal magnetism. The sounds, they said, drove you mad.

The following question is surely on everyone's lips: Why that empty carrying case? Do you, L. Goldkorn, think your Rudall & Rose, rudely ripped from your arms in June 1963, will be returned to you now? Do not laugh, friends. In the first place, the case itself was also stolen, only to be recovered by quick, friendly policemen—much chastened because the flute was not inside.it. These officers are still on the job. Second, is this box not worth keeping as an emblem, a reminder? Are not we ourselves little more than empty cases, so much cracked leather, awaiting the notes of a missing song? Third: I unsnapped the buckles, opened both halves of the case on the sidewalk cement, and placed within it, so as to encourage others to do the same, a bright quarter, two nickels, some pennies, and an F. D. Roosevelt dime.

The sun, climbing higher, beat on my scalp. Time to begin. The repertoire for musical glasses is not comprehensive. Gluck. Beethoven. Mozart. A bit of Naumann. Café piece by Rumshinsky. The anti-Semite, R. Strauss. I chose the Adagio and Rondo of W. A. Mozart, K. 617—rather, I chose the harmonica section of this ambitious quintet. I dip my fingers into the plastic pail. With tightly shut eyes, I reach for the perfect circles of the rims. One moment. V. V. Stutchkoff was a large man, a sensualist, and before his death a potted-meatball eater. In brief, his gabardines, weighted with geyser water, were slipping. I hitched them higher, under my nipple area, and tightened the tongue of the belt. Also, I took a white handkerchief from the pocket, made knots of the corners, and spread the linen upon my tanned cranium. An important precaution. Traffic went by, west to east on this even-numbered street. Green vans. Yellow taxis. Again, I shut my eyes and placed my moistened fingers upon the waiting rims. At once the tabletop shivered, resounded, like a basso's heaving chest.

Music! What it does to you! No sooner did the first notes ring out than I entered a time machine more perfect than any dreamed of by Herbert George Wells: memory. Here were the leaves, the grasses, the puffy cloud forms—all seen through the wickerwork bandshell of the Wienerwald concerts. This same piece—also for flute, oboe, violin, violoncello—had been on the summer program one half century ago. The artist upon glass harmonica was a woman: small chin, tight hair bun, but full, plump, pinkish arms. What a virtuoso! The tone was not-earthly, eerie; in my own tongue, *unheimlich*. Some say the sound of musical glasses duplicates that of heavenly bodies, whirling through space. Once, in the days before the vacuum tubes darkened within our Philco-brand radio, I heard a WQXR concert of whales as they sported in the depths. The daring diver had descended into the mammals' midst. Those cries, the watery, wavering harmonies, resembling the impressionism of C. Debussy, were to my ear the very notes of the ringing rims.

A lively cry: "Hey, Mister! How about 'On the Banks of the Wabash, Far Away'?"

I looked up. I halted my solo notes. A small crowd had gathered, twelve people, fifteen people, together with the group of half-naked boys. Most of the dark-skinned races. "Is this a top-forty tune? My Philco is now defunct."

"No, no," said a tall, thin, sandy-haired fellow, toward the edge of the crowd. "That's the state song of Indiana."

L. Goldkorn, brightening: "Ah! State of Indiana! An industrial giant. Capital and largest city: Indianapolis. Bounded on the north by Michigan, the lake as well as the state; on the south by—"

"Play 'La Sangre de Mi Corazón'! *¡Melodías cubanas!* Play on the glasses!" The new speaker was a non-Hoosier. Hispanic, perhaps. A moustache wearer.

Another voice: "Come on, Whitey, give us some *sounds*! Some soul!"

"Fellow Americans! Is the quintet of Mozart a non-request? No matter. This composer wrote another harmonica selection. I yield to popular demand. Solo adagio, Köchel Three fifty-six."

But the crowd, eager to hear its own favorites, would not allow me to begin. They shouted the name of one *Lied* or another. I wavered. This was, after all, the twentieth century. The new world, not the old. What if Mozart himself had refused to break new musical ground? For that matter, what about the advances in my own instrument? Were it not for certain bold spirits—Lully, the well-known T. Boehm—my Rudall & Rose would be no more than a pan pipe, or wooden fife. Therefore, I held up my hands. I spread my full lips in a smile. "Very well, friends. Very well. I am a citizen forty years. I, too, take pride in the heritage of our land. Here is a work by a fellow countryman. S. C. Foster: 'Old Black Joe.'"

Again the rims rang, the metal tabletop vibrated, and the notes—slightly off-pitch, owing to the effects of evaporation—rose through the streets, into the ocean of air. What were my thoughts on this occasion? How Foster, not unlike Mozart, had died penniless, a pauper, neglected by the fickle crowd. Then I heard noises—popping sounds, sharp retorts, a thump and a drone. Eyelids up. The crowd, each person in it, was engaged in an act of percussion. Some were strumming their lips with their fingers, while others produced a rude effect by cupping into their armpits their hands. Still others struck their thighs or their buttocks or their blown-out cheeks, which made a sound like auto horns. All the while these people laughed, grinned, leered. How difficult to believe—upon comparing this vulgar band to the chorus upon the Türkenshanzplatz, Willi, Pepi, L. Goldkorn, Hans—that history moves always upward, to greater and greater heights.

Suddenly, a terrible thought. With a beating heart, a spinning head, I stepped to the front of the table and dropped to my knees. There was my carrying case, open like a mussel shell. But inside were only pennies. No quarter! No nickels! No Roosevelt dime! Slowly, I rose. For a moment I stood in the heat of the sun, my handkerchief slipping from the side of my head, my trousers sending up a faint wisp of steam. Still the riotous crowd strummed, drummed, aping my musical art. For these New Yorkers I felt not anger, not resentment, but pity, instead, and concern. *Repent!* That is what I wanted to tell them. *Be good! Not greedy!* I knew how the gods might yet split us again, this time into quarters. What a calamity then! Mankind would hop on a single leg, with one ear to hear with, one eye to see, like the profiles of people the ancients carved upon temple walls.

It required an hour to walk the many blocks southward, the two Avenues east, to my West 80th Street address. The sun was by then well up in the sky, itself as white, as colorless as a snow cone from which the syrup is sucked. Coney Island favorite. Up the stoop, then, still with the Gladstone, the table for cards. The street door was unlocked, wedged in an open position, so that cats, postmen, youths who snatch musical instruments might move with freedom in or out. The tungsten lamp over the stairwell was dim. Dim? Missing completely. I had to grope my way upward by the light which, with the smell of pork parts, cabbage, the droppings of tomcats and tabbies, came from under the apartment doors.

God! God in the heavens! So many steps! You needed more breath than to play N. A. Rimsky-Korsakov, *"Der Flug der Honigbiene,"* or a transcription of Schubert's *Klavierstücke.* I found myself veering, from wall to balustrade to wall, the way a cyclist attacks a challenging hill. My tabletop rang on my kneecap like a gong. *Gong*: an example, like all music, of onomatopoeia. A pause to look into the stairwell. As far down as up! Onward, then! Upward! F. P. Schubert: yet another example of a musician who died in poverty, in neglect, occupying a workman's flat no larger, with less airiness, than any of these about me. Age 31! Think of it: the creator of *Rosamunde*, of the "Ave Maria," dead when he had hardly begun. "The pity of it, friends!" I shouted aloud. "His *life* was the Unfinished Symphony!"

This original thought was greeted with a fierce snarl, a growling, and the sight of a large brown dog of the type known in this land as—as what? Pugilist? Boxer!—descending upon me. He stood, snapping his teeth, barking, lurching forward on his powerful legs.

"Hush! Silence, Bowser. You will disturb with this noise my poor wife."

No avail. The hound hurled himself to the very edge of the landing area, sending a spray of saliva from his yellow, interlocking canines. A red light, such as a trainman waves to signal danger, burned in his eyes. Special measures, I knew, were called for. Quickly—more quickly than usual, for I feared I was already tardy in giving Clara her insulin dose—I leaned the table against the wall, opened the Gladstone, and removed a souvenir glass. This, while the din continued above me, I filled with the thick, opaque liquid from the bottle of Mission Bell.

My wife. It is a fact that men die before women in every country on earth. It is as if Zeus, with his hair, sliced off more to the left than the right. Yet here am I, more aged than Clara, each day climbing these stairs in both directions. A croup sufferer, she. Incontinence of bowels. Much forgetfulness. Diabetes now threatens. More than once she has swallowed her tongue in a fit. Instrumentalists, especially conductors, are an exception. The Maestro himself lived long, as did my contemporaries O. Klemperer, B. Walter, Mister T. Beecham. The wicked Furtwängler, too. No doubt it is healthful to beat one's arms in the air. More important is music itself, the sound of it, the vibrations, which, moving through space, surround musicians the way bubbles surround bathers who float in a spa.

And the charms which, we are told, soothe the savage beast? The boxer, a landlord Fingerhut pet, was in a frenzy. Grinding his jaws. Howling. Biting, in his eagerness, the splintered landing edge. I set the goblet on the step, dipped two fingers in the sulfurous wine, and began to play a *Tannhäuser* Overture selection. It is only natural you wish to ask what has become in our times such a burning question: Can a bad man, like Wagner himself or the collaborationist Strauss, or W. Furtwängler, all of whom performed for the Blond Beast—can a bad man create great art? The answer you see in the hound, the Wagnerite, who, at the first notes began to whine. Wickedness has its charms, no less than music. This is the century in which whole nations, millions of people, have fallen in love with evil. Millions, yes: but not all. We members of the NBC Orchestra, woodwind section, used often to recount the story of how, when the Maestro met the composer of *Der Rosenkavalier*, he said, "R. Strauss, I take off my hat to you as a musician"—and here A. Toscanini removed from his head his famous soft homburg—"but as a man, I put it on ten times again!" Which he did, over and over. How often I think of the Maestro: his smile, his baton, his war bond concerts, the way he would hum to himself the entire score. Was it not perhaps for the sake of this one man out of millions, a firm antifascist, that our own jealous god did not in his wrath destroy the world?

The boxer had lifted his lips from his gleaming gums. A smile. His tail stump was wigwagging. Hurriedly I drank down the wine dregs and repacked my bag. Time to resume my climb to the fourth floor. "Good boy, Bowser," I said to the hound. Not necessary. His eyes were now rolled up well under his wrinkled brow. A dog daze, to use the English-language expression.

Even before I reached the topmost landing I heard music, laughter, voices. A sudden, fearful thought: Was my wife keeping company with F. Fingerhut? No. It was the boom-booming TV. Clara, then, was watching the screen, even though the lack of an antenna and the age of the set made each person on it resemble a Spanish dwarf. In her youth Miss C. Litwack had played small parts in a number of Yiddish-language films, including one—the star, she often told me, was the handsome D. Opatoshu—in which she and other maidens swim in a river, under the illusion of a Pinsk-area moon. They smell floating flowers. They cry hoo-hoo! Cholera follows: because the rich rabbis won't spend their funds on sewers, only on—we see the social element here—their own fancy robes. Imagine those nymphs! Their sportive figures! In my opinion, the reason Madam Goldkorn sits many hours in front of the television is that she hopes still to glimpse herself—splashing, laughing, with firm, virile arms—upon the late night or afternoon matinee screen. Not likely. I myself, however, often drew close to the table-model Philco, in case the overture to E. Wolf-Ferrari, *Il Segreto di Susanna,* on the RCA Victor recording of which I have an audible solo, should by some lover of music be requested. One need not journey to Florida to discover the Fountain of Youth.

I entered the flat, leaving the valise and the card table near the door. A single glance across the little foyer was enough to reveal that Madam Goldkorn had fallen asleep, not on the sofa but on the floor. Red nightgown and lacy cap. One slipper off and, like the lad in the folkish legend, one slipper on. Asleep? Coma? Or death? I moved quickly to her, stepping around the walker made from aluminum tubes. Eyes shut, cheeks pink, and a definite respiration: the bosom rising, filling with air, like the pouch of a bagpipe, an instrument unjustly neglected by Western composers. Not death, then: mild coma. On the TV a pinheaded man was asking a dwarf team to name five foods that make you thirsty after you eat them.

"Pitchai slices," I murmured. You are asked a question, it is natural to answer. "Herring appetizer—"

A man with no forehead, no calves—the kind you see on the amusement mirrors—gave the prize-winning response: "Potato chips, salted peanuts, pretzels, ham sandwich, popcorn."

This was not a true test of knowledge. One merely guessed what the mass of Americans—the bowling element, the duck hunters, and such—had chosen, according to a Gallup poll. Thus is original thinking penalized.

The next words I heard were in Yiddish: *"Rogerle. Ros-*

alie vet vartn far dir bis di milchama vet endiken. Far eibig!" Madam Goldkorn! The last line she ever performed at the Tivoli Jewish Art Theater. *Brava!* I'd cried, on the occasion, throwing my winter hat in the air. The sugar, circulating within her bloodstream, had caused her to dream of the past. The syringe, as usual, was in the vegetable cooler. I fetched it, with the new disposable needle. There was a time when Clara had been capable of giving to herself this injection: no longer. It was now my task to shake up the cloudy liquid and deposit it in some new spot under her flesh. Not once but, according to the regime of Doctor Goloshes, twice: nine in the morning, nine at night. It was, however, past ten already. Almost eleven. I had intended to use my street-concert earnings to pay for a Broadway Number 104 bus, with a free transfer at 79th Street. Who could guess I might have to walk?

Any questions?

One: Why, when any further delay might place my spouse in danger, did I not inject the fluid at once, instead of standing with my fist thoughtfully under my chin, looking first at the dentures within the water tumbler, next at the corns on the sleeper's toes?

The answer: If I turned, if I descended once more the staircase and then strolled calmly to the shaded bench at the side of the Natural History Museum, then after a pleasant hour, maximum ninety minutes, not one but two souls would be released from their pain.

One night, not long before, I had been awakened by the thump of the aluminum walker upon our bedroom floor. Clara was standing at the window, beneath which the Columbus Avenue vehicles were rolling by. Beams from headlamps passed over the wall, the ceiling, illuminating her nightcap, the flesh that hung from her outstretched arms, the bulk of her body. I watched, not breathing, as she struggled onto the sill. The sweet soles of her feet. L. Goldkorn then closed his eyes. No sound, save for the rumble of trucks and the autos, which whizzed by like my own rapid thoughts. To wit: What if some innocent person were walking below? Would there not be a liability? I recalled from my youth a lesson that spoke of a man who throws flax from a roof and strikes a poor Jew beneath him. Guilty! What if, however, two men are throwing flax together? Is the non-thrower, the one who merely watched, culpable as well? Here was an instance close to my own. Oh, hypocrite Goldkorn! The true analogy is to the man who pushes his comrade from the rooftop—or at least cries, *Jump! Jump!* No rabbis in such cases are needed. Clara was looking at me, in the light of the search beams that swept the room. "What big ears you have," she said, climbing downward. "Heavens! I think they're still growing!"

Another query, this time from the TV: *Name five things a woman is most likely to have in her purse.*

"Stupid question!" I said aloud, at the same time lifting Clara's hemline and plunging the point of the needle into her calf. "Why don't they ask what is the name of the Show-Me State? *Missouri!* Bounded on the north by state of Iowa. Eleven major lakes! Or this: Who was Joseph B. Varnum? Don't know? Baffled? Ha! Ha! Speaker of the House! 1807–1811. Citizens must master the story of their country."

At this moment, the former Clara Litwack half opened her eyes. "Ah, come in, Mister Goldkorn. Pepi has told me about you."

Not fully recovered, it seemed. Still on that snowy night in the past. I leaned down to pull her onto the comfortable couch. "We must become acquainted. I have champagne. Please close the door." My heart sank to hear this. I pulled backward. This was a nearly hairless person speaking. A wearer of rubberized pants. A non-attraction. Who would have thought she had the strength to clutch me so tight?

"Clara. Sweetheart. This is not the Tivoli Jewish Art Theater. Not the dressing room. I have an engagement. An appointment. You must release my chest."

"What a fellow! And such baggy pants! I have a Victrola. Shall we wind it up? Put on a record? 'White Christmas,' 'Sleepy Lagoon,' 'That Old Black Magic': We will dance to all the hit tunes."

This speech filled me with yet more dismay—precisely because, to those rhythms precisely, we *had* made a foxtrot on her dressing room floor. Her loosened black hair hung by her waistline. "Paper Moon." Believe what I say: We were not two people, a he, a she, a Clara, a Leib: We had become a single four-legged being, a beast with two backs. But the present Madam Goldkorn could not take a step without her walker. Dance? An octopus waltz! "No! Clara, no!" I shouted, jerking out of her grasp. A shower of coins, from the purse in her cleavage, spilled over the floor.

That woke her up. "What is happening? I smell liverwurst. Thief!"

I dashed about, snatching up silver. "No, no, no, no. It is only I. Six quarters only. Carfare. Senior citizen rate."

"Where are you going? Are you going to leave me?"

"Only for a little time," I said, already at the doorway, my bag of ersatz alligator in my hand. "Big news! The Steinway Restaurant has once more opened for business. I shall have there a musical audition."

"Oh, I knew it! He is deserting me! He wants to kill me!"

"Ha! Ha! What an idea! I shall return for your evening injection. This is a great day. No more begging! No need to give concerts in the streets! My darling! Clara! Here is L. Goldkorn, member of the Steinway Quintet!"

2

IRT Number 1 local, free transfer to IND D train—option of B during rush hour—at Columbus Circle, then a wait for the F train at any stop between Rockefeller Center and

Broadway-Lafayette, followed by a brief ride to final egress, Delancey and Essex. A stroll then through the Jewry to Allen Street, turn right, one block to Rivington, turn left. This was the route I had willingly taken each working day—or, more precisely, evening—with a return every night: from the year 1959, when of course I possessed still my Rudall & Rose, a flute of English manufacture, and old Schneebalg was the artist on Bechstein grand, until that night not long ago when the Steinway Restaurant—the first, according to scholars, to offer the Roumanian broiling—was forced to shut its doors. I took it again, stepping onto Delancey Street before the sun— how brightly it danced above, like the disk in a strong-man machine—had started to drop from its high point in the sky. Yet by the time I reached Rivington Street, the shadows stretched well down the block. Much dawdling. Long delay.

Aha! Thus the sharp wits among you exclaim. *Fear of failure!* Was it not likely that, in the weeks since the night spot had reopened, its orchestra had already decided upon its five permanent members? Well, what if it had? Nothing prevented the Steinway Quintet from adding—as, in 1949, when A. Einstein had been permitted to join in on what he called his "humble fiddle"—a sixth, thus including within its repertory sextets by the pious Alcorn, L. Weiner, and others. *Plain fear, then?* Of the sort of non–music lover who had once invaded the dining area and purposefully smashed the back of a violoncello, thereby bringing on V. V. Stutchkoff's fatal attack? Not so. It is true that in this Jewish quarter one might have difficulty among the crowds of Ukrainians and Hispanics and Coloreds in finding—here is another mild pleasantry—even a quarter of a Jew. Yet these masses hold no terror for a man whose head once lay in the jaws of the Blond Beast itself. No: The cause of so many detours, to Seward Park, to Simkhovitch Houses, and even to—named for the imaginary Dutchman of W. Irving—Knickerbocker Village, was no different from the reason I had for some time remained away from the Steinway Restaurant, even though all of New York knew it was once more open for trade. Perhaps a certain letter, written in the loops of the Widow Stutchkoff's hand, will explain. Not for the first time did I remove it from the depths of my trouser pocket and unfold its many squares:

> *I am returning your trousers.*
> *Yours truly,*
> *H. Stutchkoff*

The *H.*, of course, stood for Hildegard, the Steinway cashieress, next to whom I once sat on the bench of the Bechstein, playing an L. Fall operetta. Madam Stutchkoff at that time painted the nails of her fingers and—a sight we saw in summer—the nails of her toes. Blond hair curled up in the manner of B. Grable, G. Rogers, S. Henie. Red lips. Blue eyes. Rouge spots. A fur piece—we are now speaking of winter months—hung around her neck, over her shoulders, depending to either side of her cream-colored bust. A fur piece with the clever little head of a fox!

What was the meaning of her written message, which the postman had brought, along with the gabardines, inside this Gladstone bag? To interpret these words, one must be informed of an important fact: The widow had made an error. This was not my garment but belonged instead to her departed spouse. Aha! But *was* this an error? In my tongue we have the expression: *Die Hosen eines anders tragen.* Translation: To enter the rival's breeches, with a suggestion in the realm of erotics. Therefore, we see that the closing words take on a fresh meaning. Among colleagues, an employer and employee, a simple *Sincerely* would do. But *Yours truly! Yours!*

Do not think that in these deliberations I deluded myself about my personal charms: a shiny scalp, thick lips, ears like the soles of Thom McAn shoes. This billet-doux, if such it was, stood as a tribute to the power of art, expressly the musical muse. A devotee, Madam Stutchkoff, of the Gershwin brothers. I remember once, in the pre-1963 era, demonstrating to this same cash-register expert the proper manner of playing the flute. The fingers so. The elbows thus. And the mouth—"Oh, I see. Like this? Is correct?" And she puckered her mouth, with its second, red mouth painted upon it, into a charming moue. Enough! Enough! The sun, dropping westward, glared into my eyes. I folded the letter and tightened the waistband of the gabardines. Up with my Gladstone! To Rivington Street! *Madame Pompadour*: This was the hit we played together.

The Steinway Restaurant, seen from across the street, at the steps of the Warsaw Congregation, looked just as it had when its owner was still alive: the window, with its many panes; the narrow door, in which that same V. V. Stutchkoff became once briefly stuck; the large Steinway sign, blue figures on a honey background, that hung across the facade. This was an original Feiner, the name of the restaurant enclosed by, on the left, a pile of charred broilings, and, to the right, a dark-haired Greek maiden holding a derma platter. A second look: Here was a new wrinkle. A strip of purple tubing, undoubtedly filled with neon gas, formed a border at all four edges. Another unusual touch: The window, both sides of which were capable of swinging outward, was closed, and the front door—propped open on summer days, with a waiter, or two waiters, Mosk, Margolies, lounging within—was tightly shut. I drew closer, only to find a green curtain, schav-colored, had been drawn over the glass. Beneath street level, the window to the water closet zone was open; modesty, of course, made it difficult to peer there for signs of life.

There was nothing to do but knock on the door. Boldly, I did so. No response. With my firm fist I knocked again. Footsteps. Definite footsteps. A woman's? A man's. The door opened up. Inside the frame stood a giant, a Goliath, some black-skinned genie who had escaped his jug. There was a golden ring in his ear and, strange as it seems, a ruby was stuck in a nostril, like a bone in a savage's nose.

"Yes?" the golem demanded. "May I help you?"

"Fuller Brush?" I stammered, clutching the Gladstone to my chest.

The colossus bent closer, so that his face was next to my own. How the black balls of his pupils rolled in the whites of his eyes! "Of course! You must be the doctor."

"Doctor," I repeated, retreating. "Which doctor?" Would that I could have bitten my tongue! Witch doctor! To an Afrikaner! "Ha! Ha! Ha! *Ein kleiner Wortwitz!* A little pun."

The colored person reached out, seizing my hinged valise. "Here. Let me take your medicine bag. Doctor! There is no time to lose."

"No, no. This is not a medical chest. Return it." But the giant—a six-footer, at least—would not let go. For a moment the Negro and I clung to opposite sides of the Gladstone. Then a second figure, no less strange than the first, appeared in the doorframe.

"Who is it?" he asked, in a nasal tone. "Doctor Botnik?"

The aborigine turned. "Yes, he's here."

"Ich bin kein Apotheker! Nicht Apotheker! Nicht Medizin! Ich bin Musiker! Oboist! Fagottbläser! Mit Flötenspezialität!"

The newcomer—tall, eagle-nosed, wearing a nightcap, a nightdress, and a beard that hung from his chin like Italian noodles—took from the blackamoor my precious valise and motioned within. "Botnik, your patient is waiting."

At that, I lunged toward the stranger, taking hold of his whiskers. "Not doctor! Flute player! Trained in Vienna!"

The fellow jerked backward, leaving the whole of his beard in my hand.

"Help!" I cried. "This is a madhouse!"

"What's going on? What's the hullaballoo?" A third man now joined us, this one in black, except for a white towel over his arm. His face was hidden by the bill of a baseball-style cap.

The mammoth, as big and husky as two normal-sized Jews, responded first. "It's Botnik, M.D."

Said the second: "He won't make a house call."

The third man leaned from the doorway. "Botnik? What Botnik? That's what's-his-name. You know. Used to play piano."

I squinted, the better to make out the features beneath the tricolored cap. "Mister Mosk? Is it you?"

"Who else?"

"My dear friend! What has happened to our restaurant? Who are these people? They think I am a medical doctor. Are they here for auditions? Where are the Quintet members? Tartakower, for instance? A fine flute player, even if, owing to tars, to nicotine, he lacks the breath control for difficult trills. What of our prodigy, Murmelstein, and our leader, Salpeter? The Bechstein I trust is in tune?"

"Salpeter? *I* am Salpeter. Who the devil are you?" The chap in the nightdress, clean-shaven now, handed the Gladstone to the waiter. It was the first violinist.

"Ah, Mister Salpeter. Greetings! Do you not know me? Four years flute. Twenty on the grand?"

Mosk, interrupting: "Sure. Liver pâté. Tea with five sugars. A Slivovitz at the bar."

"Ha! Ha! Just a drop. The livers create a thirst."

"Oh, Goldkorn. No, the Bechstein is not in tune. In fact, it has been removed altogether. And Tartakower does not play the flute."

"No? Then this fellow, the Ethiope: He makes up the woodwind section?"

"Me, you mean? I can't read a note of music."

A foolish mistake on my part. Not to recognize the new cook. "What has happened to Mister Martinez? Can this gentleman slice the broilings with the deftness of the former chef?"

Mosk: "This ain't a chef. This is L. Kleiderman, the professional actor."

"Kleiderman? An unusual name. The *L* is no doubt for Leroy?"

Before the Goliath could answer, shouts rang out from inside the room:

"He's waking. His eyes are open."

"Give him air!"

"Pipe! Can you hear me? Mister Pipe!"

"What happened to Botnik? Where is he?"

"Call Fuchs! Call uptown Goloshes!"

Mosk—because of his cap, he looked like a duck—turned toward the tumult. "Uh-oh, that's Pipe. I thought he was a goner."

At that outburst the Negro stopped, squeezing his massive shoulders through the door. Salpeter, starting to follow, paused on the threshold. "Murmelstein does not play, either. We have reached the end of an era. I am no longer a musical artist. I have put down the violin and the violin bow. You see before you a servant of the people. Yes, a Senator. Brabantio!"

Last, Mosk, still with my bag, disappeared into the gloom. "Kaput," he said, "the Quintet."

"Wait! The Gladstone! Must I play on the street forever musical glasses? Is that a life? A living?" So saying, I followed the others into the restaurant. At once I halted. By the dim light, green and watery, that came through the curtains, I could see that the musical platform had been stripped of our stands, our chairs, and the black Bechstein. Instead, just below the bandstand, there was a boat shaped like a gondola, tied by a rope to a replica of a red-and-white barbershop pole. Behind this dock there was a painted street, with painted buildings, all fading in a realistic manner to a distant point. More: Standing to one side, arms crossed on a striped shirt, a cigarette in his lips, was an Italian-style gondolier. The waiter, Ellenbogen! What was this place? City of Venice? Then I saw the crowd, also dressed as Venetians, off to one side. In tights, a silk vest, and a collar with ruffles, a young nobleman lay next to his sword. Only it was not a nobleman. It was Pipe, a local merchant. Also not young: aged ninety-one. He was trying to sit up. There was pink foam, like that on a cherry soda, around his mouth.

Sheftelowitz, in the fish trade, kept pushing him back. "Lie down, Herb. Don't exert yourself. Botnik's on the way."

Pipe: "Lie down? Is it bedtime? Give me my sword, why don't you? Jews! Don't just stand around."

But the men and women—in spite of their puffy sleeves, their opera gloves, I could see they were Steinway Restaurant employees—did just that, shifting from one foot to the other and wringing their hands. I moved closer to the straw-hatted gondolier.

"Psst, Ellenbogen. Goldkorn here. What is occurring?"

"It's a delay. Pipe had a seizure. Banged the back of his head on the floor."

"But why are you dressed in a tee shirt? That boater?"

"Oh, that's only for Act One. A minor part. But in Act Two I am stabbed. Listen to this: *'Zounds! I bleed still; I am hurt to the death.* Then I swoon, the way Pipe did—except he's not acting. Poor casting, in my opinion. Too old for the part. Fighting duels, making plots, crazy in love. What if he has an attack tonight? During the real performance? He could not even be a Steinway Restaurant waiter. Imagine: a tray of hot soup, hot tea in glasses, and butter potatoes. What then?"

"In love?" I asked. "In love with who?"

"Desdemona. Brabantio's daughter. The one who runs off with the Schwartzer."

Schwartzer: L. Kleiderman. And Brabantio: wasn't that Salpeter's part? Before I could fit these pieces together, a voice rang out from the dining zone:

"All right. Put his hat on. Jews, to your places. Act One. Scene one. Line sixty-seven."

Sheftelowitz looked round, still on his knees. "How put his hat on? There's a big lump on his head."

"Excuse me, Mister Sheftelowitz. Do I sell carp? Meddle in mackerel? Allow me to direct the play."

"I just thought—" Sheftelowitz began.

"Don't think! I think! Not you! You sell your fish!"

What a voice! A thick accent. *Think* sounded like *zinc. Fish* like *fizz*. Old Vienna! I peered out over the murky room, the hardly visible chairs, the shadowy tables, in search of the speaker—in whose mouth, suddenly, the butter would not melt.

"Pipe. Honey Pipe, you darling. Stand up, sweetheart. What a trouper!"

Pipe, pale as pirogen, got to his feet. His tights, on his skinny legs, were as wrinkled as veins. "I feel good," he said. "Is this Wednesday?"

"So. The hat, please, Mister Sheftelowitz," the voice—from where did I know it? from when?—continued. "Will someone kindly hand to Roderigo his scabbard and sword?"

"Yeah. I'm fit like a fiddle." Indeed, the bedding merchant now stood erect, his tights straightened, his vest shining, and a plume from an ostrich in his hat. A gentleman. A dandy!

"Jews! To repeat! Act One! Scene one! Line sixty-seven!"

Immediately the whole crowd—waiters, mostly, and musicians—began to run in every direction. Some darted behind the painted buildings; others bunched before them, as if they happened to be out for a stroll; and two or three, among them Martinez, the wizard of broilings, tumbled into the seats of the cardboard boat, where Ellenbogen posed with a mandolin. Pipe and another chap, in black pants and a cape, moved to the front of the stage, just below the balcony of the tallest building. For a moment everything was quiet, nobody moved. Then the person who accompanied old Pipe made a speech:

> *Call up her father.*
> *Rouse him. Make after him, poison his delight.*

After a pause Pipe mumbled something, all the time looking down at his pointed-toed shoes. Then the man in black spoke up again. I took a closer look: short, pale-faced, with slicked-down hair and a little moustache. M. Printzmettle,

Avenue B tobacconist. He waved his arms when he spoke, as if shooing gnats. All of a sudden he fell silent and turned to his smartly dressed comrade, who stood, looking blank. Printzmettle repeated his words, nudging the feather-bed merchant with an elbow point. Pipe lifted his head and, as if he were amazed to find himself in the city of Venice, opened his mouth: Not a word came out, however.

"Prompter! Prompter! Mister Mosk!"

"Hold your horses," replied the Lithuanian waiter, wetting a thumb to flip through the volume he held on his lap. He did not look like a duck so much as—the black pants and black jacket, the white towel over his arm—a penguin. He held the book up to the neon windmill that was turning and turning next to my Gladstone, on top of the bar. "Wait a minute. Here it is. Okay. Pipe says, quote, *What, ho! Brabantio! Signior Brabantio, ho!*"

All eyes turned back to the nonagenarian, who was tugging at the handle of his sword. His eyes were open, his mouth was open, and the froth, like on a mad dog, was once more boiling at his lips.

"Again, Mosk! Louder! Speak always from the diaphragm!"

The waiter took a breath. With both hands he gripped the visor of his Baltimore Orioles cap. *"What, ho! Brabantio!"* he shouted. *"Signior Brabantio, ho!"*

Immediately the twin shutters at the nearest building burst open and Salpeter, in his nightcap, thrust his head out the window:

> *What is the reason of this terrible summons?*
> *What is the matter there?*

"No! No! Idiot! I will break your neck! Like the neck of a chicken! That was Mosk! The prompter! Not Roderigo!"

Ellenbogen began to strum his mandolin. "I'm not a musician," he said. "The strings are only rubber."

One of his passengers, a woman, let out a scream, pointing to where Pipe stood knock-kneed, both hands on the hilt of his uplifted sword. "He is going to stab us!"

All at the same time the tobacco-shop owner hopped to one side, Salpeter slammed down his shutters, and the passengers jumped from the gondola, knocking over the gondolier. Everyone was shouting, screaming. But the loudest cry came from the swordsman himself:

"*Puchfeder! Farsichert! Hundert perzent!*"

At this, a Yiddish expression, the room grew hushed. We watched as the sword dropped with a clatter and Pipe brought both hands together, like a man on the edge of a springboard. Then he plunged forward, into the bottom of the Italian boat.

Confusion. Uproar. Half the people ran forward, half ran away. Cries for Botnik rang out. The facade of the buildings, the *palazzi*, began to sway, as if an earthquake were striking. Sheftelowitz, weeping, beat on his chest, which made a hollow sound.

"*Signior, is all your family within?*" That was Mosk, still screwing his eyes up to see the dimly lit page.

Then all the bulbs of the glass chandeliers came on. In the dining section, in a jumble of tables and chairs, sat a squat man, nearly neckless, also hairless, with a wide, rubbery mouth: Pepi Pechler, a onetime Austro-Hungarian, known throughout America as the director of the Tivoli Jewish Art Theater.

What a pang went through me when I saw this man. The salt in my tears stung my eyes. It is not difficult to understand why: This was in the course of my life the third occasion I had seen the fun-loving Pepi. First, as you know, in youth, as a colleague at the Akademie für Musik, Philosophie, und darstellende Kunst. There we had laughed together, struggled with ideas, and sung—I a baritone, he a tenor—our harmonious songs. The voice, the round, red cheeks, the golden locks of an angel. *Ein Engel!* Also, *ein kleiner Teufel*, a mischief maker. He knew how to penetrate the balconies of the k.k. Hof-Operntheater, how to lean over the loges, so as to examine in safety the breathing bust points of the ladies below.

Our second meeting: three decades later, only a short time after my arrival at the Port of New York. In the month of November I entered the Tivoli Jewish Art Theater, which, according to rumor, was soon to be converted into a cinematograph. A play in the language of Yiddish was going on: men and women running about, shouting, waving their arms. One performer wore the braids of a girl, but had the fine stout arms of a woman. Similarly, she wept like a child, rubbing her knuckles into her eyes: But her daring skirt was at calf muscle level. I noted her name: Clara Litwack.

At the stage door I waited for my classmate, who had by this time dwelled in America for twenty years. Balding, then, this Yankee, with a barrel chest and warts not visible in youth.

"Pardon, Pechler. Word has come to me you are soon to build here a picture theater?"

"And if the word is true?" said the impresario, in what had become a deeper, more gravelly voice.

"I play in addition to woodwinds the pianoforte. Perhaps you have a need for an accompanist to films?"

"No, no. No jobs. Not hiring," he said.

"This is Leib Goldkorn speaking. *Is not the road to Athens just made for conversation?* Remember? Text of Plato?"

"Listen, we have here talkies. In color! In color the same as life!"

"Talkies?"

"*Ja!*" cried the plump fellow. "*Mit* sound!"

With what subtle thread does the loom weave its design! What if there had after all been such a position? I might never have played for the Maestro! For NBC! On the other hand, had I not sought that spot, I would have failed to encounter Miss Litwack—*Brava! Brava, Madame!*—who a mere sixteen days later became my bride, my lifetime companion.

Let us return to the Steinway, where Mister Sheftelowitz still beat his chest like a tom-tom, and the other Venetians stood wringing their hands. What a cruel thing, thought I, still gazing at Pepi Pechler, to see a man once in his youth, again at middle age, and once more aged eighty. It is as if nature had become accelerated in its course, as in those films where flowers bloom in seconds and clouds go whistling across the sky, or as in the theorem of A. Einstein, where things zoom by so fast they start to go backward: Thus the frog does not turn into a prince; instead, Prince Pepi, the toast of the Türkenshanzplatz, turns into this no-necked toad.

And what, in fairness, did the director think of *me*? No question he recognized his former companion. The heavy lids of his eyes dropped down, then retracted. He was looking right at me.

"Goldkorn," he commanded, "take off those pants!"

There you have it, the old, jaunty Pepi, with his quick wit, his love of humor. "Ha! Ha! You take off *yours*, Mister Pechler."

But the hairless man, without eyebrows even, did not return my happy smile. "And the shirt! And the shoes! You! The rest of you! Why are you moping? Pipe is dismissed! Non-employed. Seize him! Take his costume! Strip him bare! Quick! Be quick! Only two hours to the premiere!"

Poor Herbert Pipe! The players fell upon him, tugging his trousers, yanking his vest, prying away his shoes. You would have thought they were stripping his very flesh—though in fact they left him his stained BVDs. Meanwhile the waiter, Margolies, and the musician, young Murmelstein, approached me with the outer garments. Martinez, the cook, followed, holding the ostrich plume hat.

"I do not understand. Why have you done this? What can I do with such close-fitting breeches?"

Margolies: "What do you think? Put them on."

"But you see I am already dressed. Moreover, I am no longer a hat wearer. It is best not to constrict the blood supply to the scalp."

Murmelstein: "If you act in a play, Mister Goldkorn, you must wear a costume that fits the part."

Margolies: "*A Venetian Gentleman*. That's what it says in the book."

I turned to my old schoolmate, affecting the casual note. "I may be a pipe player, Pechler, but I am not Pipe."

The director narrowed his puffy eyes. "You will not be Pipe. You will not be even Goldkorn. You will be Roderigo."

"Please. Let us be serious. I do not know this drama. I have not heard of Roderigo."

"*Othello* by Shakespeare," put in Mosk, from his prompter's position. "The one about the jealous Schwartzer."

"Do not worry, Leib Goldkorn. It is a simple part." Pechler was purring again. Was it my imagination? Did his skin really seem greenish? "You are a man in love. All you think of is Desdemona. Her beauty. Her voice. Her skin. Her hair. You would do anything for her. Lie. Cheat. Steal. Kill. Yes, Goldkorn: kill. A single motive! One great cause: *You are a man who is in love.*"

It was, I saw, no joke. The surviving Quintet members, the Steinway waiters, gathered in a circle about me. Surrounded. "I am a woodwind player. I do not know how to act."

Pechler threw his head back, so that his throat, full of veins, expanded against his collar. "Act! You do not act! You are a shell! The shell of a cockroach! A nothing! *I* am the actor! *My* voice comes from your mouth! My will moves your arms, lifts your legs! You! You stand on the chalk marks!"

Up stepped Martinez, on cue: "*Aquí tiene el sombrero. ¡Magnífico! Con pluma de avestruz.*"

Pechler grasped the admiral-style hat and sprang from his chair. "On! Put it on!"

The humpbacked hat, which had fit Pipe to a T, dropped over my eyes to my nose. Laughter. Tee-heeing. I put my arms out. I groped in the dark. Then Pechler's voice cut through the merriment: "Stop this buffooning. Jews! Dress him at once!"

Immediately, I felt fingers groping at my collar, at the buttons of my shirt. Someone was undoing the laces of my shoes. "No. Please. Stop. No tickling!" But the groping, the grabbing continued. My shirt came away, as did simultaneously my Thom McAns. To my horror, I felt a fumbling at my belt strap, at my waistband. Strength then filled me, as it had the blinded Samson. "Attention! Those are Stutchkoff's pants!"

With one motion I wrenched free and lurched toward where I believed the doorway to be. There was a crash from the piled-up tables and chairs. Clutching the loosened gabardines, I reversed direction. Better to spend a lifetime rubbing harmonica rims, or playing a musical saw, than to parade in tights before strangers. Not Leib Goldkorn!

"Watch out!" That was Mosk's voice. "Watch out for the stairs!"

The stairs! The WC! A whole staircase! On one foot I hopped, I veered, and flew across empty space until the edge of the balustrade rail caught me in the abdomen, and the hat, of the sort N. Bonaparte used to wear in his battles, flew from the impact away.

For a dizzy moment I remained doubled over the railing, attempting to regain my breath. The restaurant staff hurried over, with their smooth waiter's glide.

Margolies: "Are you hurt, Mister Goldkorn?"

Ellenbogen: "Knocked the wind out, eh?"

I did not reply. Below, in a long white gown, a bride's gown, with her golden hair piled up like coin stacks, Hildegard Stutchkoff was climbing the stairs. I could not help but look directly down the front of her dickey, where both bosom halves were in unison rising, then falling, then rising once more, nearly hurling themselves over the bodice rim—quite like the hot springs the family Goldkorn used to visit in the Bohemian-Moravian Heights. Of course I at once averted my gaze, but not before noting that her right arm was passed through the left one of the black colossus. What mischief was this?

"Mister Ellenbogen." Oh, there it was, that voice which

had so often mingled with the cheery tones of the cash machine bell. "Please to me explain the reason for dress rehearsal delay."

Kleiderman, in his apish rumble: "It is already a quarter to six."

Ellenbogen, still in his gondolier outfit, moved to the head of the stairs. "We forgot to tell you. We had a little accident with Mister Pipe. We have to start from the beginning again."

Have I neglected to say that Margolies, heat or no heat, was wearing a fur-lined jacket, with a tall hat like A. Lincoln's? He leaned over the rail. "You can wait in the dressing rooms, Madam Stutchkoff. When I say—I mean, when the Duke says—*Fetch Desdemona hither,* then you move to the stairs."

There was a tingling in my body, like a sniff of horseradish. "*Desdemona!* Is that the part of the Widow Stutchkoff?"

Said Ellenbogen, "One and the same."

"And who," demanded the actress, lifting the bridal veil from her painted lips, her sturdy nose, her bluish eyes, "is this?"

"Hildegard! It is I! Look, sweetheart! The pants are a perfect fit!"

Joyfully I threw out my arms, in case the widow should wish to run into my embrace. I never thought this would cause the loosened trousers to fall to my knees. "Ha! Ha! This was not done on purpose! I swear it!"

Just then the door opened up and a short, thin man, with one moustache above his top lip and another, an imperial, underneath the lower, stepped into the room. "I had to walk. No taxis," he said, adjusting the round wire glasses at the end of his nose.

"Another patron! Please, Mister Ellenbogen, Mister Margolies: Explain is our opening night. Staff only. Kitchen is closed."

Here Sheftelowitz came running across the room. "Botnik! This way! It's a concussion at least."

"Do not be alarmed, Madam Stutchkoff. Here is the medical doctor. We called him on the telephone. And this—maybe you don't recognize him without a shirt on, not wearing a collar: That's Quintet member Goldkorn."

That same Goldkorn, in a ringing tone: "No! False! Incorrect, Mister Margolies. You speak too fast!" I turned then toward the figure leaning at the bar, between the Gladstone and the windmill. "Mister Mosk, my first line, if you please."

"Wait a second. I got it here somewhere. You open the show. Oh, yeah. You say, quote, *Tush, never tell me,* unquote."

Next I bowed before the—what should I call her? The bereaved widow? The blushing bride? With one hand I held up the trousers; with the other I attempted to hide the hairiness of my shoulder zone. "Dear Hildegard! You see before you not Leib Goldkorn! No longer a woodwind player. Greetings from Roderigo! A Venetian gentleman. *A man who is in love!*"

3

The time? A dusky traveler has requested the hour. "You got the time, Chief?" were his words. Two o'clock, three o'clock, four o'clock: How in this earth pit can we know? Where am I? BMT? IND? Brooklyn? Isle of Manhattan? Do you know the story of how it was sold to the white man for trinkets? For beads? I have removed my war bonnet, which lies now in my lap. Beneath it is concealed a tequila bottle, Cuervo Especial. This is not a favored form of schnapps. Of Mexican manufacture. Suspect in color. But what choice, after the debacle, had I? One snatched what one could from the Hotel Belmont bar.

My own car is quite deserted—only three Afrikaners, each with a cap, one holding a wireless box, tuned to a station for youth. What, friends, do you suppose would occur if, instead of responding to the request for the time—"No Bulova. Sorry. Watchless"—I had stood up, in my Squanto loincloth, in my vermilion hue, and had sternly demanded of the three Negroes, *Return to me my Rudall & Rose?* There is a pressure on my ears. On the tympanum. Thus we may answer at least one of our questions. Not Brooklyn, not Isle of Manhattan, but under the waters of the river between. East River. Sixteen miles in length. Four thousand feet in width. We hurtle, we plunge, throwing out sparks, like a chariot descending to Hades. Perhaps we shall pass Madam Goldkorn. On her way to River Styx. The taste? Quite like that of a squash pie or pumpkin. Made from a cactus, they say.

We Jews are a modest people. Orthodox believers hardly change their clothing, certainly not their undergarments, and above all not with somebody else in the room. The real zealots, the Crown Heights element, are not allowed to touch themselves in the genital area—though married men may, when making water, support their testicles from below. Do not expect such fanaticism at the Steinway Restaurant. The waiters and musicians, old acquaintances, simply formed a circle about me while I stepped from trousers of V. V. Stutchkoff to Herbert Pipe's tights. It was only then that I became aware of an obstruction, a protuberance, in the crotch zone. Unseemly moment! Even for a man such as myself— born not in the last century but in this one, and educated in Vienna. Once, in March 1921, I attended a performance of a play by A. Schnitzler, in which a courtesan entertained a soldier. I have turned often the pages of R. von Krafft-Ebing and glanced upward from the orchestra pit during the Strauss fiend's "Dance of the Seven Veils." Yet this growth at my groin was, even to a cosmopolitan, a cause for chagrin. "Gentlemen, I beg your pardon. An involuntary action. Such a thing has not happened for years."

"Mister Goldkorn, think nothing of it. Why I myself—"

Margolies broke off, visibly flushed. I followed his glance to where, between his legs, hung a similar pouch.

"I have the same thing myself," said Ellenbogen. "You get used to it after a while."

From outside the ring of men, Printzmettle added a comment. "Not me. It chafes."

I peered out at the tobacco dealer, then at Ellenbogen, at Sheftelowitz, at young Murmelstein: Each showed the symptom of arousal. "Gentlemen, if I am not mistaken, somebody has been putting peppercorns into the broilings."

Mosk responded. "It's what you call a codpiece. It's what the goyim wore in olden days." Just then, the chimes of the First Warsaw Congregation struck seven times. "One hour!" the Litvak announced. "One hour to curtain!"

As if his words had carried outward to Rivington Street, there came a blast from the horn of an automobile, followed by a high-pitched tooting from two or three other cars. Simultaneously there was a knock on the door, as well as a *rap-rap-rap* on the panes of the window. At once the circle of Jews disbanded, leaving me fully attired—from my pinching pumps to the cockade hat which, stuffed with the balled-up pages of the New York *Post,* rode on top of my head like a boat upon the waves.

"It's the uptown Jews!" exclaimed Ellenbogen, peeking through the drapes. "Lawyers, it looks like. Accountants! I can see taxis! I can see yellow cabs!"

Tartakower looked over his shoulder. "A limousine. A sedan. The street is full of tycoons!"

Further confirmation: The shut door opened up and a Jew in a panama hat stuck his head inside. "Steinway Theater? Box office? I want six tickets. Orchestra seats."

The prompter, his cap a gay blend of orange, white, and black, shuffled over. "Too soon. Come back in a while. We got fifty minutes to curtain."

"Wait! You don't understand. I'm a gynecologist. Arnold Lipsky. With offices in three different boroughs!"

Behind this man you could see others, also uptowners, using their elbows to get into line.

Fifty minutes to curtain. That, of course, was a metaphorical expression, since at the Steinway no such barrier between the audience members and the stage existed. *Castles in air:* That is another saying of the folk. But what else was it that hung high up, near the ceiling coffers, if not the walls, turrets, and battlements of a fortress? Suddenly, and indeed for the first time, I realized that the many events of that afternoon, rushing so swiftly by me, were not wisps of imagination, not fancies, but matters of solid fact. Ergo, in only minutes I was going to be standing in these tights, mouthing words I scarcely knew—*"Tush, never tell me"* was all, after a quick glance at the prompt book, I was sure of—before Jews of real flesh, real blood. The impact of this thought made my limbs grow weak, so that my knees clanked against the sheath, so hard, so solid, so real, of my sword. I turned, moaning, to the person closest by. "Murmelstein, can this be happening? Could so many people come these days to the Jewry?"

Murmelstein: "It's the power of the press. You know my son, Stevie? University of Wisconsin? He graduated from the journalism school. He put a word in the Bergen *Record.* 'Revival of the Jewish Art Theater.' The next thing you know, there's a picture of Pechler in *The New York Times.* All the big critics are here. It's history being made. Right, Margolies?"

The old waiter, with his two colleagues, had managed to bolt the front door. These exertions, and the Duke's robes, made him perspire. "This is in my opinion bigger than Adler. Bigger than *Dos Pintele Yid!* It's like the heyday of Jolson, when he painted himself up like a Schwartzer."

The Schwartzer! The colossus! In my excitement I had almost forgotten his existence. I saw him at once, standing with Mister Sheftelowitz near the cash-register station. The latter was patting the back of Hildegard Stutchkoff, while the former, in his saucy manner, was actually holding her hand.

The widow, I saw, was weeping! I hurried over, even though each step was a torture. "Hildegard, has this blackamoor caused you distress?"

"No, not distress, Mister Pipe. Is a nostalgia. The way these Jews press to get in so eager. Banging on doorframes. Arriving in yellow cabs. It is like old days with Schneebalg on piano and Madam Roosevelt standing in line."

Sheftelowitz leaned forward. "Pardon, Madam Stutchkoff. That ain't Mister Pipe."

Margolies: "Once in the war years she had to wait more than an hour. This was the case even though she brought as her guests Queen Wilhelmina and Mister C. W. Beebe."

Mosk: "Herring appetizer. Same for the Queen."

Young Murmelstein: "Was this the Beebe who went in a ball under water?"

Salpeter: "I was not in the war years first violin. That was still the Ragstadt era. But we knew what to play whenever Madam Roosevelt dropped in. 'I Loves You, Porgy,' by Gershwin."

"They stood the same as anyone else. The Jewish restaurant is a democracy." Margolies paused, looking up at the murals of Athens that stretched across the walls. "The same as in the drawings of Feiner."

"Speaking of herring"—here Doctor Botnik licked the parts of his lips that were visible between his moustaches— "I'm hungry. What's the special tonight?"

The six-footer's voice boomed in reply. "Ho! Ho! We eat *after* the performance, not before! That is the stage tradition. Come to the Hotel Belmont if you are hungry. To the Indian Room. That is where we shall eat, while we wait for reviews."

"Hotel Belmont?" echoed the doctor. "That's a fancy place. You need a tie, a jacket. How can you go dressed like that?"

Tartakower, the flute owner, drifted over. "Everything

has been arranged. We change these costumes for others. The rule is: We have to be Indians there."

Said Murmelstein, "Why not join us, Botnik? It's a party. The best costume wins a prize."

"You can wear Pipe's getup," Sheftelowitz said, motioning toward the gondola, where the stroke victim still lay. "He won't be coming."

Kleiderman, still with the widow's white fingers inside his huge dark paw, spoke next. "It's more than just a theater party. There's going to be an announcement. A special event will occur. Eh, Hildegard?" Such familiarity. The wink. The leer. The nudge with the sensualist elbow. It was all I could do not to throw myself upon him, even if he was as big as a policeman on top of a horse. Large, well-developed men: V. V. Stutchkoff, L. Kleiderman. This was, alas, a weakness she had.

"Brabantio, Gratiano, Lodovico! Duke of Venice! Come here!" That was Pechler, calling from his spot in the director's chair. Wherever they happened to be standing— Salpeter, Sheftelowitz, Murmelstein, and Margolies—each stiffened, then walked toward where the director sat. The roll call continued: "Montano, Cassio, Iago! Roderigo, you too!" The last name, of course, was my own. I hobbled after, respectively, Ellenbogen, Tartakower, Printzmettle, until I was standing before the friend of my youth. Next came the names of the two lesser women—"Emilia! Bianca!"—impersonated by Madam Ellenbogen, in private life our cocktail shaker; and by Miss Beverly Bibelnieks, a former Steinway Restaurant patron. Last of all, the principals: Desdemona, Othello, the smooth-shouldered Hildegard Stutchkoff and the hulking L. Kleiderman, his arms hanging down like an ape's. Beauty, in short, and the beast. Correction—not the last. Up came Martinez, holding an armful of hats: a Senator's, a Gentleman's, an Officer's, an Attendant's. All the nonspeaking parts.

The cast of Venetians stood before the director. Behind

him, in the bar-mirror glass, the headlight beams of the taxis glittered and dashed. Mosk had opened the door, and the uptowners were filing in, moving quietly to their seats. Ellenbogen whispered to me behind his hand: "Now comes the pep talk."

In fact, however, Pepi Pechler only raised his large head and asked, "Any questions?"

A thousand sprang to mind. What—aside from a few memorized words—did I know of this drama? Once, as a lad, during the Akademie years, I had read the work in the Schlegel translation; yet nothing remained in my memory save for the scene in which Desdemona floats down the Nile in a barge. On another occasion, the weak-willed Furtwängler conducted the Verdi version at the Vienna State Opera. Thus, like a *Gymnasium* student I raised my hand, clicking together my heels. Is that a wedding dress the widow is wearing? Is she going to be married, or what?

Before I could put this thought into actual words, Printzmettle blurted aloud, "Explain to me this Iago. Why does he do it? What is the reason he makes so much trouble? Sometimes I don't understand what I'm saying."

"That's easy," Ellenbogen said. "In his own words: '*I hate Othello.*'"

But that's what I don't understand," persisted Printzmettle, who had a thin moustache, the kind boys draw on pictures of ladies. "*Why* does he hate him so much?"

Here Margolies thought to solve the puzzle. "It's because he won't give him that job he wants. Because he hires that other fella. Cassio. It's in your first speech."

"No, no, that's not the reason," Cassio—that is, Tartakower—replied. "How could it be? After he gets my job, he goes on with the plot. More than ever."

"You are barking up the wrong kind of tree, gentlemen," Murmelstein declared. "Mister Ellenbogen, I too am capable of reciting the text. '*And it is thought abroad that*'—no offense, ladies—'*twixt my sheets he has done my office.*' Ha! Ha!

Twixt my sheets! He hates Othello for—you know: um, er— with Emilia." Here Murmelstein, a married man, with a son who possessed a B.A., made a ring from his left forefinger and thumb, while thrusting his right forefinger through it.

"I do not understand." Leib Goldkorn speaking. "Why is he making the letter Q?"

Miss Beverly Bibelnieks: "Wrong boat, Mister Murmelstein. It's not the Moor he suspects with his wife. It's the handsome Lieutenant. *'I fear Cassio with my nightcap!'* "

"You mean," said Margolies, "Cassio and Emilia? Together?"

Once again for some reason Murmelstein formed the alphabet's seventeenth letter. "Ha! Ha! Look, Ellenbogen! His nightcap!"

"Maybe he doesn't hate me at all. Maybe he hates Cassio from the start. It's just a thought."

"And a good one, Mister Kleiderman," answered Salpeter. "I recall a phrase from the final act. Wait. Yes. *'He hath a daily beauty in his life that makes me ugly.'* Iago says that about Cassio."

Madam Ellenbogen: "In other words, he's jealous because he's so good-looking?"

Sheftelowitz: "This might sound silly. I'm embarrassed almost to say it. But what if all along he only wanted to kill Desdemona? *'Strangle her in her bed'*—aren't those his words?"

Printzmettle: "Yes—*'Even the bed she hath contaminated.'* But we are back where we started. Why is it he hates *her* so much?"

Sheftelowitz, mumbling, eyes on floor: "To have Othello for himself. I mean, what if he doesn't hate him but loves him instead?"

At this piece of swinishness, which only a fish merchant could think of, there was an outburst of indignation.

"What? A Schwartzer?"

"This is Shakespeare, Sheftelowitz. This is not *Bowery Follies.*"

"*Er ruft im a fagele. Schanda! A fagele!*"

"*¿Cómo se llama? ¿Un pato?*"

"Wait. Wait a minute. I have a quotation. Look at the third act. Scene three. Where they kneel down together to take a sacred vow. Printzmettle, what do you say? Othello may command, Iago will obey. It's like a marriage, almost."

Kleiderman, murmuring to himself: " '*I greet thy love. . . .*' "

Printzmettle, his hair as shiny as his patent leather shoes: " '*I am your own forever. . . .*' "

Miss Bibelnieks: "Everybody is right and nobody's right. The problem, Printzmettle, is not that you don't have a reason. You've got too many."

"I know it! How can I perform? He doesn't know what he thinks himself!"

"All done? You racked your so-called brains enough?" That was our director, taking command. "It's touching to see you. You want to find a reason. An explanation. Even a Jewish waiter wants to have a mind of his own. He's got to understand. What if we had a microscope and could look at a germ, a microbe? If we could listen to its thoughts? *What's my motivation? What am I feeling? I can't act this part!* I heard this stuff at the Tivoli Jewish Art Theater. From Adler, from Kessler, from Satz, and from Schwartz. Now I must listen to waiters, musicians, and women! Everybody wants to be a psychologist. All right. You want Iago. His insides. His soul. I'll show you. Look. Here. Iago!"

The lights had gone out, all except the dim windmill rays. P. Pechler got to his feet in the glow of these wavering watts. He threw his head back and seemed to drink down the air. His body pumped up like a balloon. His round shoulders straightened, his chest flew out, his legs, like elastic, grew longer. He seemed for a moment to be as big as Kleiderman. His face, full of warts, was terrible to see. The nostrils in his nose were moving in and out, his eyeballs popped, and his mouth, when he opened it, was like a pit, a cavern. Somebody reached out of the darkness to clutch my arm. I confess that, at the sound of the director's voice—a creaking, a croaking, like a door on hinges, or a stone shifting on top of a tomb—I clutched this person back, gripping a roll of fat. I noticed the bittersweet smell, like orange peels, of his perspiration. We trembled together at the sound of Iago's words:

"I am not what I am."

Lacking a religious temperament, I am no longer a Torah reader. Nonetheless, I remembered the burning bush, and the voice of the Lord:

I am that I am.

A cold chill went through me. I clung to the one beside me, who pinched me feelingly back. This was God's opposite: the Destroyer, not the Creator. Instead of the one who is, the one who is not. My colleagues, more pious than I, had already apprehended this meaning.

"The Satan," sighed one.

"Angel of Death," said another.

"Espíritus malos," muttered a third.

Printzmettle said, "I see. He's evil. Period. Simple as that."

Next, from the far side of the stage, came the voice of the Lithuanian waiter. "What a lotta hooey! Satan! Angel of Death! Tell it to the Marines!"

That broke the spell. Pechler, once again five feet, five inches, sank back in his chair. From all about us we could hear the sound of people coughing, stirring, crossing one leg on top of the other. The director snapped two fingers. The lights came up over the stage. Venetians began to scurry this way and that: Ellenbogen to the gondola, Salpeter to the balcony, the strollers to the end of the street. The person beside me released his grip. Not his. Hers! The Widow Stutchkoff ran for the stairway. She had given me a sign! I had been permitted to squeeze her waist zone! She liked short men after all! "Hilda!" I cried, watching her veil float in the space behind her. "What a nice orange blossom perfume!"

"Shhh!" said Pechler. "We begin."

Mosk, crouching in the darkness, with the fat book on

his knees, was the substitute for the missing curtain. "Ladies and gentlemen: Act One of *The Tragedy of Othello*. Venice. A street."

"*Tush! never tell me—*" It was Leib Goldkorn who delivered those words. Somehow, inspired by the widow's touch, by the smell of citrus, by the memory of Pipe's performance, I drew my sword and woke Brabantio. When that poor father descended, I slashed my weapon about and told him his daughter—none other than the blond Hildegard Stutchkoff—had run off with the lascivious Moor. Beyond the blinding glare of the overhead lights I could sense the Jews stirring with indignation. Quickly I pulled Brabantio offstage. My own heart was racing, in part from stimulation, in part from the fear that we might be too late to stop this mingling of races. What was that noise to our rear? It sounded like the pop, the hiss, of livers in a pan. Salpeter stopped. He tapped my Napoleon hat. "Listen," he said. "Applause!"

Alas, that moment of exhilaration could not last. There was nothing to do but stand helplessly by, sometimes off the stage, sometimes back on it, while it became clearer and clearer that the "thick lips," as the playwright calls him—in fairness I note that, owing to the need to direct the breath over the air hole of my Rudall & Rose, my own lips have developed a pucker—not only had courted the fair Desdemona, but had already achieved his goal of marriage. Worst of all, not one of those standing with me, in some cases only inches away, intended to intervene. Even Salpeter, once so exercised, surrendered: "*I here do give thee,*" he said to the abductor, "*that with all my heart which, but thou hast already, with all my heart I would keep from thee.*" Meaning, his daughter!

Did I say worst of all? Rash Roderigo! Who has not had a dream in which they wish to run, or walk, but cannot? That was the sensation I had, watching while Desdemona winked, blinked, and made coy movements toward the mammoth Moor—while he, with his nose-jewel shining, held her hand, squeezed it, like some black behemoth trampling on a lily. And I, the stupefied sleeper, unable to utter a word!

A pain broke out at my foot, as sharp as that in my heart. I looked down: Printzmettle was trodding on my pointed toes.

"Iago!" I cried.

"What sayst thou, noble heart?" the tobacconist responded, sweeping his hat from his pomaded head. Only then did I realize the streets of Venice were deserted. Exeunt everybody! Printzmettle and Goldkorn were alone.

"What sayst *thou, noble heart?"* the former repeated.

The latter had not the slightest idea.

"Goldkorn! For heaven's sake!" I recognized, in the wings, Ellenbogen's voice.

"For heaven's sake!" I declared.

"Psst, listen: *What will I do, think'st thou?"* This time it was Mosk, crouching behind the scene. *"Psst. Psst,"* he hissed, like the air rushing from a sports ball.

"Just move your lips," Printzmettle advised.

I did so. *"What will I do, think'st thou?"* The words came out, lisped somewhat, in the Lithuanian manner.

After that, my lips continued to move, my jaw flapped on its hinges; but I no longer listened to what was said. Act One, I knew, was drawing to a close. As I strolled toward the exit, I resolved not to return for Act Two. For what purpose? What point? *She* was already married! And to the Moor! What more was there for me—this mannequin, this ventriloquist's toy—to do? As if in response to these inner thoughts, my companion then said, *"If thou canst cuckold him, thou dost thyself a pleasure, me a sport."*

I stopped in my tracks. "Cuckold him?" I asked. "You mean me?"

Printzmettle placed his hands on the back of my shiny vest and pushed me off the edge of the stage: *"Go to; farewell."*

I stumbled—with age comes lack of spryness—into the

wings. Behind me Iago continued to talk to himself, and then—

Hell and Night
Must bring this monstrous birth to the world's light—

he too dashed from the stage.

Applause. Confusion. Kleiderman and Murmelstein, our youths, were pulling like coolies upon thick-braided ropes. The remaining musicians, aided by Margolies and Sheftelowitz, put their shoulders to the walls of Venice, which began to move. "Costume change," said Ellenbogen, and in front of everybody began removing his gondolier's pants. I pushed through the milling cast, toward the tobacconist of Avenue B. He was directing a spray from an atomizing bottle into his mouth.

"Printzmettle! Did you say the word 'cuckold'? What does that mean? What I think? Hanky-panky?"

"Correct, Goldkorn." He, too, made the Q-sign. "Understood?"

"But how—? When?"

"First things must come first. We will make certain that Cassio is drunk. Then we arrange for him to get in a fight with you. To destroy, you know, his reputation."

"Cassio! Mister Tartakower? What has he to do with the matter? It is Desdemona I love!"

Before the plotter could answer, a whole block of the Grand Canal slid between us. Margolies, sweating like a Turkish bather, looked up from the painted scene. "Attention!" he cried. "Look out!"

A turret of the castle dropped down not a foot from where I stood. I retreated to the first row, where the director was sitting, smoking a cigar. "Pechler, pardon: but I wish now to make a complaint. You said Roderigo was in love with Desdemona. Hildegard Stutchkoff in her private life. But to this moment I have not succeeded in addressing to this beloved even one word."

"Patience," said Pechler. "There are four acts to go."

"Patience? I have shown patience. Desdemona in the meantime has married somebody else. When is it my turn?"

"Soon. Coming up. A little longer. Besides, if you paid attention you'd figure out: Desdemona, Othello—they're not really married."

"It's a fib, Pepi Pechler! I saw them myself!"

"Look, how did they spend their wedding night? Like a man spends with his wife? No: On account of the same day they're married they leave for Cyprus. It ain't a honeymoon. It's separate boats. Then, the first night on the island, what happens? There's a big commotion. He has to right away get out of his bed."

"This commotion—is it because someone is fighting with Cassio?"

"Believe me, Goldkorn, the Schwartzer never shtups his bride. It's no marriage. A non-starter. No consummation. They are only on Cyprus together a total of one and one half days!"

"Hee, hee. Clever Iago."

"Go back to your place. Prepare yourself. When people see you it breaks the illusion."

There was no need to inquire what the former Akademie student meant by that. The lights, which had been dimmed, grew brighter. A sunrise effect. I saw before me a seaport in the realist style. The gondola, through the addition of a simple sail, had become a fishing craft; the thoroughfare of Venice now a wharf. Behind this scene—you could almost smell the tanginess of sea salt and hear the reed-instrument tones of a gull—there loomed the fortress, firmly attached to the ground. Martinez, with a musket, patrolled the battlements. Applause, in appreciation, rose through the Steinway Theater. In my enthusiasm, I clapped too. Why not? *Soon,* the director had said. *A little longer.*

Act Two. First comes a ship with Desdemona, now wearing a summer smock; then the blackamoor's boat. *"O my fair warrior!"* he calls her. *"My dear Othello!"* she says. Then they start kissing. *Eins. Zwei. Drei.* The giant lifts his face, like a buffalo, a hippo, drinking at the Congo. Pink gums, white teeth, lolling red tongue. *Vier! Fünf!* What could I tell myself, at sight of this spectacle, but *It is only a play?* These were not their sincere emotions. *Mein Gott!* What was he doing? Blowing his black breath into the curve, like a violin scroll, of her ear! This was worse than A. Schnitzler! I confess that in spite of my peaceable nature, I was upon the point of violent action. My hand gripped my sword. *Sechs! Sieben!* Oh, I would chop him like an onion! To pitchai pieces!

But Printzmettle seized my arm and, as soon as the other departed, whispered his plan:

> *Do you find some occasion to anger Cassio.*
> *Provoke him. So shall you have a shorter*
> *journey to your desires.*

"I will do this," murmured the crouching Mosk. *"Adieu."*

But I sang out the words, playing them as if they were notes on a woodwind: *"I will do this. Adieu!"* Then I tipped my hat and stepped under an archway—from which spot, though hidden from the audience, I could see what happened next on the battlements and the wharf.

First Printzmettle talked some more to himself, a habit he had; then a Herald, played by the unbearded Salpeter, wearing a red shirt with brass buttons, announced a feast and a dance and a wedding celebration. After that the Moor came back, with his hand upon the buttock zone of his wife—the hot droppings of an animal upon a field of unstained snow:

> *Come, my dear love,*
> *The purchase made, the fruits are to ensue,*
> *That profit's yet to come 'tween me and you.*
> *Good night.*

Purchase? Fruits? Profit? *Good night!* He was forcing her toward the marriage bed! What to do! Ah, punctual Printzmettle! Already he'd gripped Cassio-Tartakower and was calling for—and here I shall quote him directly—*"Some wine, ho! Some wine, boys!"*

Montano—it was Ellenbogen, in his new pants—appeared with a flask. Of course it was only Welch-brand grape juice, a nonalcoholic beverage. But the realism of the color, the purple stains at the drinkers' mouths, upon their shirtfronts, above all the way they soon began to stagger and sing folkish songs—*"His breeches cost him but a crown"*—all this made me lick my own lips, which had gone so long without a drop of schnapps. And how long had it been since Herr Kleiderman and his Frau had retired? Minutes? Hours? I looked up. Imitations of stars were winking. Somehow a moon hung in the sky. Cassio had moved so near to where I stood that I could see the whiskers on his poorly shaved cheeks and the nicotine stains on the fingers with which he played his Powell-model flute. *"Do not think, gentlemen, I am drunk,"* he said, and marched straight under my archway.

Time for action. I drew my sword and, by using two hands, succeeded in raising it over my head. Cassio likewise drew his. Thus we two woodwinders faced one another. "Now what, Mister Tartakower?" I whispered.

"You have to hit me," he answered. "Then I hit you."

This, for a Jew, was easier to say than to accomplish. Hit somebody? With a weapon? And where? Surely not on the head, the seat of reason. But his body was no more than skin and breakable bones. I recalled that in the winter months his topcoat was fastened with pins and with paper clips, not true buttons. A widower, too. Thus debating, my sword grew heavy, like an anchor molded from lead. My arms ached. They trembled.

"But, hark!" This was Printzmettle, who on the stage was cupping a hand to his ear. *"What noise?"* He and Ellenbogen kept glancing around, toward our shadowy arch.

"Goldkorn! What is the matter? You're supposed to hit me." Tartakower's breath, smelling like leaves of tobacco, rushed by.

"My arms! They have frozen! Heavens!" This was true. My limbs, like those of the Atlas at Rockefeller Center, had turned to stone. The joints had locked!

"But, hark!" Printzmettle was shouting. *"What* noise?"

"It's your cue," hissed Tartakower.

"Help! Help!" I cried, and rushed with arms above me onto the stage.

Cassio pursued. " *'Zounds! You rogue! You rascal!"* Then Tartakower closed both eyes and began to strike me with the flat part of his sword. On the shoulder. On the back. On my fleshless nates. What could I do? I bore it, as did the poor Titan, condemned to hold up the whole of the sky. *"I'll beat the knave into a wicker bottle!"* screamed Tartakower. His face had developed red spots, like radishes, and a trail of spittle hung on his chin. Was he perhaps drunk after all? To strike a fellow Jew?

Just then Ellenbogen drew *his* sword, and addressed my antagonist: *"I pray you, sir, hold your hand."*

Off in the wings, cast members began shouting, and some person rang a bell. For a brief period, everyone stood as if posing for one of Feiner's historical paintings, with swords raised in the air.

Then, to Ellenbogen's rear, I noticed old Mister Pipe lift his head above the sides of the fishing boat. *"What ho, Brabantio! Signior Brabantio, ho!"* He stood erect in his buff-colored woolens.

"It's Pipe! A recovery!" cried Botnik, from his seat in the crowd.

Ellenbogen whirled, to face the bedding merchant. Tartakower did likewise, but toward the sound of the doctor's voice. Both their swords struck me broadside, hitting either arm between shoulder and elbow point. My own weapon flew from my hands and fell with the weight of an anvil directly upon my head. Tremendous concussion. I dropped to my knees.

To see the stars: This is an English-language expression, which might perhaps explain the projectiles I saw shooting about me. But no: Those orbs were still overhead, twinkling through the black cloth that represented the nighttime sky. *To knock the brains out:* another Americanism. Was this my own gray matter I saw bouncing about me, in the form of small, colorless balls? Half-fainting, I reached for one of these spheres. Letters, syllables, phrases covered the convoluted surface. For an instant I thought this must be the impression of the millions of words I had read in a lifetime, indelibly etched upon the cortex of my brain. Then I realized that the rolled-up pages of the New York *Post* had spilled through the rent in my admiral's hat.

"What is the matter here?" Kleiderman's voice. I felt the earth shake, heave, from his approaching tread. Called from his bed, then! Disturbed in his amours! Success! Then the night, with all its planets and stars, fell in earnest.

4

We have been discussing, have we not, the ideas and myths of the Greeks? Ancient Greeks. Not the short, dark drinkers of licorice-flavored schnapps. The gods, the heroes. A little-known fact: Athena invented the flute. Hermes, of course, the lyre. Who was that fellow so skilled with traps, with puzzles, with mazes? My memory function is not at this time near its peak. Daedalus: inventor of sails, the ax, the winkle, and flight. It was he who devised a wooden cow, inside of which the Queen of Crete was able to satisfy her abnormal passion for a bull. Fanciful, you think? What then of Catherine, Empress of Russia, who suffered a rupture because of a horse? Oh, these women! These women! Consider the Corybantes, wild maidens, who cut off the head of Orpheus, who charmed the inhabitants of Hades with his lyre. "Eurydice! Eurydice!" that severed organ cried. This drink is made from a cactus! Thorns! Sharp needles!

What a dizzying journey! F train in the wrong direction, east, to Brooklyn. BMT RR to the Times Square Station; transfer to Number 1 Broadway–7th Avenue local. So many circuits and tunnels and switches! The detours! The shuttles! The transfers! A labyrinth for Daedalus himself! "Fiftieth Street," the amplification horn speaks. "Five-oh." Then Christopher Columbus Circle. Look! An IRT rat! Journey's companion! Soft eyes! Whiskers! Intelligent nose! Have I cheese?

I have withheld until this moment a vital fact. I have not on my person either my alligator-skin bag or the glasses within it. No instrument! No harmonica! How am I to charm, upon the staircase, the soul of the savage beast? Pluto's pup! I cannot fly like Herr Daedalus on wings of wax! Yes, pumpkin meat is the proper description for the taste of this yellow beverage. A Thanksgiving Day treat when baked into pies. Recipe of Indians. 66th Street—Abraham Lincoln Center. 72nd! Heavens! 79th! Time to exit! To depart. The squash is not native to Europe; it came, that annual herb, from these shores. On the other hand, the rat, bringing plague, bearing pestilence, moved from the old world to the new. 86th Street! 96th Street! We rise, like mercury indicating a fever, into the lower one hundreds. The lyre of Orpheus became one of the heavenly constellations. There was a man who loved his wife.

Was I alive? I collected the evidence of my senses: a purple glow in the air; the odor of orange peel; a taste of metallic salts—either blood from the head blow or schnapps, the absence of which will produce in time the sensation of a penny upon the tongue. Sense of touch: an ache in the crown of the head, accompanied by tenderness in the nerve tips, as if a breeze were constantly blowing over the skin. Awake, then? Let us test first the faculty of memory—born, town of Iglau; graduate, woodwind section, Akademie für Musik, Philosophie, und darstellende Kunst; American citizen, 1943; NBC Orchestra member—and then the faculty of reason: How may a moving body reach a particular point, since it must first travel half the distance to the goal, then half the remainder, and so on forever? This is the theorem of Zeno, not Zeno the stoic but Zeno the logician. Professor Pergam: *The fleet Achilles will never catch the slow-moving tortoise.* Yes, awake. But what was that sound all about me, like the crackling of flames? Hellfire! Hellfire for Goldkorn! This foolish fear lasted only an instant. The sound was of course made by clapping hands. Applause. *Othello!* The end of the act! Time for Roderigo's return!

I sat up. At once a hidden woodsman, or perhaps executioner, struck my head with an ax. The applause grew fainter, until at most seven or eight old Jews were beating their palms together—as much to keep warm, thought I, in my lumberman's coat, as to show their appreciation for the players before them. November 1942: the Tivoli Jewish Art Theater was not steam-heated. On some nights no more than three or four lovers of drama could be seen on the benches, the straightback chairs. Why pay for heat, for cushions, when the edifice was soon to be transformed into a cinematograph? I returned six nights in a row. *Brava! Brava, Madame Litwack!* I cried, throwing the soft hat I wore in those days into the air. A non–Yiddish speaker, I knew nothing of the melodrama, save for the fact that this child-woman, woman-child—full breast development but hairs in a braid—had fallen in love with a Yankee. The way she wept! Real tears spilled over her fingers. *Rogerle. Rosalie vet vartn far dir bis di milchama vet endiken. Far eibig!* Those rabbis! Medieval monsters! Make way, gentlemen, for love!

Sixth performance. Outside, a seasonal snowfall. Inside,

the bittersweet ending. Roger, in a G.I. Joe uniform, was about to sail across the Atlantic, to defend these same rabbis against the Hun! I stood alone, in the pit of the orchestra. "Brava! Congratulations, Madame!" The actress bowed. She smiled a coy smile. Then she saw my hat. It was upside down on the stage, like that of a begger for alms. She stooped—a hand on her bosom—and held it out toward the stage-door Johnny. For the briefest of instants we grasped it together, on opposite sides of the brim. I am still able after countless years to feel in my fingers the electrical thrill. She made her exit, and when I put on my hat—in that era a small patch of fuzz remained in the dimple of my skull, in addition to the hair horseshoe which persists to this day—a slip of white paper fluttered out.

> *Mister Goldkorn. I await you in my dressing room.*
> *(Miss) Clara Litwack*

A roar, like a lion, came from above. *Pish,* I heard. *Noses, ears, and lips.* The sounds of a chamber for torture: *Is't possible? Confess! Handkerchief!* Had I been mistaken? Was I after all thrust into the hell pit? For my sins? My lusts? *Oh, devil!* came the agonized cry—followed by such a tremendous thud that the ceiling above me trembled and cracked.

I swear by the memory of the Maestro I will never again desire possession of Mister Tartakower's flute! In stressful times we will say who knows what. Silence. I opened my eyes. All was as it had been before. Only now I knew precisely where I was. The purple light was the illuminated gas tube on the Steinway Restaurant sign. It poured directly through the open cellar window. That meant I was in the dressing room of the Widow Stutchkoff! A room filled with her orange perfume! Also, her knickknacks! Even her clothes! From the davenport sofa I lay on I could see where, over the arm of her wing chair, she had thrown the white gauzy gown of her wedding dress. That voice, that bellow: surely L. Kleiderman in a fit, tumbling down. Here was the moment for a Venetian gentleman to take his place. If not now, never! Once more I sat up and once more the woodsman, not nodding, struck with his ax. I fell back on the couch springs, a bruise of plum-colored light before my eyes.

Was there such neon in the Forties: to be specific, June 1943? Yes. The dome above the Tivoli Cine Palace was ablaze with Christmas-like trim. Bulbs of the incandescent type had sprung up like—what is the word? *Die Champignon.* Mushrooms!—like mushrooms upon the facade. A great effect was made by the search beacons that shot, at the angle of cocktail straws, into the sky. The very clouds were lit up, like the shades of enormous lamps. A double premiere! First, *Happy Go Lucky,* a film with the theme of non-Jews upon a holiday cruise. In colors of an ice parfait. The musical score—*Typical, Topical, Tropical Hits!* said the gay advertisement; a *Musical Cruise That Chases the Blues!*—was not of the quality of the work of M. Steiner, my compatriot, or the oddly named Korngold, E. W., also a composer for films.

Second, this was the premiere of P. Pechler's kino-theater. "Tivoli!" exclaimed the happy owner, approaching myself and my wife in the crowd. "*I lov it* spelled backward!" Oh, yes, my wife. A certain Rabbi Rymer—his nose was flattened into his moustache, a Pechler acquaintance—married us only sixteen days after our first encounter. Horses, if this is the proper expression, could not draw from me the description of what occurred behind that closed dressing room door. Her hair, no longer in the youthful braid, had been allowed to flow over her shoulders, her back. Also, barefooted. "Ah, come in, Mister Goldkorn," she said, holding out both full-size arms. "Pepi has told me about you." An incense stick burned in an incense holder. Corns on the toes, I noticed, was a thing we had in common. A Victrola. A pile of disks. Dance tunes. Hit songs. Her form—waist identation, hearty bosom, thigh tissue—was like that of a violon-cello. Hush! No more words. Do not believe those cynical persons who tell you there does not exist love at first sight.

Through the limousines, lights, mounted policemen, we two entered the lobby. Corn, and flash lamps, were simultaneously popping. An usherette handed me a matched set of glasses. Then we walked down the aisle to our velvet-covered seats. Tangos came from mechanical speakers. The curtains swayed like Hawaiian skirts. The chandeliers gradually dimmed. "Florida! Look, Clara: capital, Tallahassee!"

I do not remember in detail the plot of this brightly colored film. The fact is my mind was concentrated upon the difficult examination I was soon to take in the chambers of Judge Solomon Gitlitz—in preparation for which I had learned not only the capitals of the forty-eight states, but many further facts about the Federal Republic, including routes of La Salle and De Soto, the latter the discoverer of the River Mississippi, M-i-s-s-i-s-s-i-p-p-i. I fear that these preoccupations, however praiseworthy in a citizen candidate, caused me to overlook more than this—I quote once again—*Tropical Trip That's Really a Pip!* I did not give my bride the many attentions all lively women crave, nor did I note how her narrow waist had grown outward into definite plumpishness. With such a distracted husband, is it just to criticize her coolness or the fact that even through the night she failed to remove her garter trolleys? You will thus understand my pleasure when, to the sound of marimbas and bongos, Madam Goldkorn put a grip on my arm. *William Whipple, William Williams, Francis Lightfoot Lee:* I had been in silence reciting the names of the original signers, Declaration of Independence. But my spouse squeezed ever more tightly and breathed at my ear. I turned, so that her rounded features became visible in the projectionist's beam. "My sweetheart! Want a kiss?"

No wonder so many citizens flock to the motion picture theaters. The darkness, the music, the packaged malt balls—

all this is a stimulus to romance. Not to mention, so much larger than life, the lips of D. Powell and B. Hutton, which were at that moment contacting upon the screen.

The former Miss Litwack now clenched my arm with a two-handed hold. Her hot breath flew from her mouth. Panting. Panting in a manner reminiscent of the previous November, within her dressing room. I lip-kissed the ear-lobe that descended from the bun of her hair. She moaned, thrusting her hips and her buttock zone out of the seat.

"Perhaps we should go home?" I whispered. "We could take a taxi."

Here she whipped her head about and, releasing my arm, began to pull at her bloomers. I felt a tremor of alarm. Even in the shifting light I saw that her face had turned the bright red of a tomato. Sweat beads stood on her brow. With the tips of my fingers I gave the hot skin of her cheek a caress.

"God! Oh, God!" she groaned, in a voice audible throughout the orchestra section.

"Shhh!" a viewer admonished.

"Down in front!" another patron insisted—perhaps because Clara had half risen, as if she meant to move down the aisle. Instead, a number of nearby spectators quickly departed, while Clara dropped heavily back onto her seat.

"Wait, sweetheart. Be patient. We'll look at the film. Then later. Tonight. When we are alone." I pointed up at the screen, where all the stars—M. Martin, R. Vallee, B. Hutton, D. Powell—were singing and dancing on the deck of a boat. *Ta-ra-ra*-boom-*de-ay*: That was the refrain of their song.

"Somebody go for a doctor. Is there a doctor in the house?"

"No. No need," I said, turning toward where that voice had rung out. "We are newlyweds."

But there was a need, after all. My sweet spouse screamed and slid from her cushion, which sprang upright, like a snapping jaw. It was at this moment that one of our goblets suffered a minor chip. As for Clara, she lay wedged on the floor, with her shoeless feet in the air. "God! God! It is the end of me!"

Two rows behind, one of those Jews you sometimes see, robust, redheaded, stood at attention. "I'm only a medical student, but perhaps I can help?" With those welcome words, Goloshes, M.D., entered our lives.

Meanwhile, a square of light had formed at the rear of the theater. Pepi Pechler, with two usherettes, was tramping down the aisle. "What's the idea?" he demanded. "We are having here a Paramount Pictures premiere!"

"It is my wife, Pechler. My wife! She is having a catarrh or something."

Goloshes looked up from the angle of my wife's spread-out thighs. "Ha! Having a baby, you mean!"

I stood, stunned, counting months on my fingers. On the screen a chorus of Caribs, all wearing zoot suits, were striking steel barrels and shaking dried gourds. *November, Dezember, Januar.* . . . Was such a thing, with human beings, possible?

Forward stepped the usherettes, aiming their torch lights down. I saw Madam Goldkorn's face, wide-eyed, perspiring. What was she saying? *My Pepi? My baby?* I could not draw closer, because the theater owner was at her head. I tapped his shoulder.

"Please. Pechler. I have paid for a ticket."

Just then, Clara uttered what is rightly called a blood-curdling ejaculation. Even the mote-filled movie beam seemed to blanch in response. Then up spoke the ruddy medical student: "Wait. All right. Ah, ha! Where is the father? It is a girl!"

"Ha! Ha! It is definitely I!" My friends, what joy. Tears washed over my expanded pupils. Through this glistening film I could see a wavering doctor hold up a fuzzy child by the ankles and give her nates a smack. Dark hair, she had! Little curled-up hands! An eight-pounder at least!

"Fellow Americans! We shall call her Martha! My Martha! To honor the wife of a man who, unfortunately child-less himself, was nonetheless the father of our country. Here is a little-known fact. The name Martha is from the Aramaic. A Semitic tongue. Madam Washington herself was not, how-ever, a Jewess. Another fact: A Martha Washington descend-ant, a great-grandaughter from her previous marriage, was wed to the well-known R. Edward Lee, the Confederate gen-eral. Well, I am not speaking with strict logic. Everyone here is my guest! Schnapps for everyone! Look how darling she is! So much hair! Not like the papa! Ha! Ha! *Martha,* you know, is the name of the opera by Flotow."

I blinked my damp eyes. I shut my chattering mouth. Everyone in the row—Goloshes, Pechler, the patrons and usherettes, Madam Goldkorn herself—had fallen silent. The only sounds to be heard came from the singers and dancers and musicians upon the screen. It then dawned on me—oh, my thick, lumpish skull!—that while Goloshes had indeed struck smartly my newborn daughter, she had not made a cry in response. No! Nor any movement! Only hanging sus-pended, her darling arms, like plump sausage links, dan-gling down. "Doctor! Doctor!" I shouted. "Doctor!"

"Don't look," said Pechler.

The usherettes, in their stiff-shouldered uniforms, started weeping.

"Dead? Martha?" I asked. "Not living?"

The medical student turned about. I could see only one small foot—to my eye fat, healthy, with admirable toes—sticking from the folds of his bundled jacket. "I am sorry," he said.

I dropped to my knees. "Clara! Clara! Unhappy Clara!"

She did say something in reply. I saw her lips moving. But her words, whatever they were, were drowned out by the Caribbean chorus and by the cheery, pink-cheeked stars, who repeated the same syllables over and over—*boom-de-ay, boom-de-ay*—as if the heat of the tropics had caused them at last to take leave of their senses.

* * *

The poor soul sat sighing by a sycamore tree
Sing all a green willow,
Her hand on her bosom, her head on her knee,
Sing willow, willow, willow.

This was not a Paramount Pictures song. The notes came
not from the screen, but from above.

The fresh streams ran by her, and murmur'd her moans;
Sing willow, willow, willow:
Her salt tears fell from her, and softened the stones.

I knew my location. Downstairs. Stutchkoff's old office. Now
the dressing room. And I knew the voice of the singer:
Widow! Widow! Widow! The lament soon ended. Swelling
applause. Another act done. Time running out for Roderigo. Poor Goloshes! His flat feet prevented his service in the
Coast Guard or Army. My examination proved less difficult
than I had feared. No request to recite either "Paul Revere's
Ride" or, also by Longfellow, "The Miles Standish Court-
ship." A citizen! I wore in celebration a new pair of shoes.
Excellent, 1943-model Thom McAns!

My reverie ended at the sound, the *click-clack*, of footsteps on the stairs. The next thing I knew, Hildegard Stutchkoff came through the doorway and began to take off her
own high-heeled shoes. There were two possibilities: Either
she knew I was in the room, or she did not. In the latter case,
any gentleman would at the least clear his throat—*ahem,*
ahem—particularly as the former cashieress was already pulling at the zipper of her smock, which had apparently stuck.
Zipper? Surely there were no such lightning fasteners in olden
Venice. Anachronism. The former case: Assuming the employer knew the whereabouts of her employee, she must have
come to pay him a visit. Get well. Cheer up. The show must
continue. A zipping sound. The smock divided itself, fell from
the slopes of her shoulders, and lay, like foam at the feet of

Aphrodite, upon the floor. Did she mean to join me on the davenport couch? It was hardly big enough—why, my feet protruded from one side, my head from the other—for one normal person. But no: She merely stood at the high window, while with each inhalation her body swelled from the ends of her corset tube.

There was a third possibility—namely, that in a dream I was transporting the events which had occurred in Clara Litwack's dressing room to the Widow Stutchkoff's. This hypothesis was supported by what happened next. My companion lifted her sizable arm and removed from her head the sheer wisp of a snood. At once her curls fell to her neck, to her shoulders. For a moment the various premises—that she knew or did not know of my presence, or was not even present herself—went round in my mind like the tigers in the folk tale of Sambo. Then, with a sound like a clock spring, her corset flew from her body. Two breasts, which had thrust skyward, now hurled like boulders down. What is the name of the armless statue? Venus of Milo? Here was a more virile portrait. The purple light made her skin glow, like that of an aubergine. With one hand at her curls, the other akimbo, she turned in my direction. What a torso, my friends! Chest, hips, thigh flesh, kneecaps, mighty shins. Still she revolved, until there came into view the handsome buttocks, each with its own dimple above it, like a slot to deposit a coin. *Widow at Window.* Artist unknown.

"Ah-ah-ah," I sighed, not only to show appreciation, but because the sensation of breeziness on my skin had created the need to sneeze. I was saved by the sound of—not distinct words, but voices, which came through the half-open door. Printzmettle's first, oily and smooth; then the squeak of Pipe's reply. They were having, these two, a conversation. Hildegard heard them as well. She moved to the wing chair and picked up the ladies' nightgown that lay over the back. Instead of putting it on, however, she sank slowly to the cushion and broke into tears.

What now? I wondered. No more than an American yard separated the widow from me, with no sofa back rising between us. She held the silk scarf—I saw it had a strawberry pattern—to her eyes. Her soft shoulders shook with emotions. "Oy! Oy!" she sighed sweetly. "Miserable me!" This was more than a man could bear. Poor darling! What had he done to her? Kleiderman! Animal! Beast! Slowly I stretched out my arm, at the end of which, trembling, was my hand. One after the other her tears fell upon my fingers and knuckles and wrist. What a smell of citrus! Heat waves came from her body. Ahead, only inches away, her breasts hung down like the holiday stockings that pious Christians attach to their mantels. Bulging! With bonbons! With toys!

"Greetings, Hilda," I said.

I do not believe she heard me—in part because the words came out in a kind of strangled croak, but also because Madam Ellenbogen, in her servant's costume, was standing in the doorway, shouting out loud: "Not dressed? You'll miss your cue! Put on your nightie. Dear Madam Stutchkoff, hurry!"

The widow looked up, still sighing. "Ah, Vivian! Vivian! What a thing, Pearl Ellenbogen. So soon, this marriage. With Mister Stutchkoff only just passed away."

The waiter's wife stepped into the room. She was standing almost on top of where I lay. "But it's all decided. How can you think of changing your mind? The rabbi's already in the Indian Room."

"I have in my head no room for a mind. Here is nothing but opening night, wedding night, memories of Vivian. Is a torture for me."

"Listen!" the barmaid exclaimed. "Do you hear?" Above us the actors were shouting: *Help! Hark!* and *Murder!* There was a banging sound. Feet ran hither, thither. "The cue! We have to go! Slip this on! It's the future of the restaurant. What else is there for us? We will be unemployed Jews!" So speaking, Madam Ellenbogen slipped the lingerie over the widow's shoulders. The two of them stood, casting their dim shadows upon me. Just then, there was a new outburst above, shouts, curses, cries:

Oh, help me here!
That's one of them!
Oh, murderous slave! Oh, villain!

The two women, one shoeless, the other with sandals, dashed round either side of the sofa and disappeared through the door. I lay still, shivering in spite of the fact this was the summer's height. Something was floating in the purple air. It was the silky snood. Slowly it dropped, furling, unfurling, like a dandelion tuft, or a tiny parachute. I followed its downward course until, slipping and swaying, it fell directly upon my member, which stood, I saw, over my naked body the way the spire of a cathedral stands over the ruins of a medieval town.

Nothing changed. Nothing altered. The footsteps went on clip-clopping over my head. The voices murmured and buzzed. A breeze from the window gave me a chill.

And Roderigo dead.

Those words darted toward me like hornets from a hive. And stung, too. What an eerie sensation, like reading of one's own death in the newspaper: *L. Goldkorn, the well-known NBC Orchestra flautist, was found today in an alley. Cirrhosis of liver suspected.*

Alas, good gentlemen, alas.

By the time that lament was spoken, I was already, two or three at a time, climbing the stairs. Alas, indeed. No more

Roderigo! What would become of Desdemona now? My head broke above floor level and, as luck would have it, the first thing I saw was Mister Pipe, lying not five feet away. He was wearing my clothing! From toe to top: the pointed pumps, the Napoleon hat with the feather. A dagger's handle protruded from the armpit area, inches from the heart. Dead!

No time for pity, however. At the back of the stage, in a room lit by a single candle, I saw a heart-stopping sight. The Schwartzer, bare-chested, was approaching on tiptoes the bed of his bride. Not only that, she, with her dear curls uncovered, and a foot and an ankle visible at the corner of the bedsheet, was in it. Was this the dread moment? Consummation? But what of Pechler's promise? Something, someone, would intervene.

"Put out the light, and then put out the light," said the dull-witted darky, repeating himself. Then—like all members of his tribe, insensitive to pain—he placed the pink palm of his hand over the flame, and quenched it. There was just enough light to see how he bent down to kiss her. *Mein Gott!* His thick lips on her thin ones! He did it again. Ha! Look there! The toes of her foot were curling in anguish. A third time he kissed her. Look at that! She stretched, she yawned: *"She wakes,"* said the brute, discovered in the act.

"Who's there? Othello?" my darling demanded, rubbing her sleep-filled eyes.

"Ay, Desdemona."

The hair which covered my shoulders crackled like electrical wires. I waited for the scream, sure to come. However, when she opened her mouth—such pearly teeth, like Chiclet-brand gum—these words, precisely, came out:

"Will you come to bed, my lord?"

The black beast reached forward and began, with both hands, to caress her white throat. At the same instant I sprang from the stairwell, and like a youth leaped the corpse of Herbert Pipe. A frightening growl came from my throat.

Moving my knees, swinging my elbows, I crossed the stage and fell upon the foe.

"What's this?" Kleiderman asked, whirling to face me. "What are you doing?"

Mosk: "Where are we? This ain't in the script."

"Uncircumcised dog!" I shouted, and sank my strong teeth below his rib cage, at the flank.

There was a disturbance. In the audience, females screamed and chairs fell back to the floor. From behind scenery, waiters and musicians came running. Some person, Margolies perhaps, pulled on my leg. Still I clung to his flesh. I wished only that my teeth contained venom, so that I might inject the poison into his blood. The house lights came on. Martinez was shouting in Spanish. All to no avail. Over and over we two enemies rolled. Kleiderman came out on top, breaking my grip, winding his fingers around my neck, my windpipe.

In desperation, gasping, choking, I buried my hands in his Afro-style hair and pulled downward with such force that—even now I feel numbness, a chill, at the thought—the entire top of his skull came apart. I screamed, dropping my gory prize. He toppled forward upon me. I pushed him back. That was worse: His very skin came off on my hands. I leaped to my feet, staring wildly.

"Curtain! Curtain!" The voice of Pepi Pechler. "Curtain!"

"But there is no curtain," Margolies replied.

Madam Stutchkoff rose from the bed. She approached me. "Mister, ah—"

"Goldkorn," said Pipe, resurrected.

"You are in the Steinway Restaurant no longer employed. No more the flute, the Bechstein piano."

Even these fateful words made no impression. I could not take my eyes from my wounded rival. Was I dreaming? Had I gone mad? All too plainly Kleiderman's chest, his arms, and even his face were now the color of a white man's, while I—hands, arms, the whole of my torso—had turned the color of mud.

"Watch out! Madman!" I cried, jumping from the stage and running as fast as I could toward the Rivington Street exit.

Mosk, the Lithuanian, blocked the door. "Where's the fire?" he asked. I halted, but only long enough to snatch the linen napkin from the crook of his arm.

"I have lost my mind!" I shouted. Then, wrapped in that loincloth, I plunged into the dark streets, the dark alleys, of the Lower East Side.

5

Dawn, almost. Already the alarm clocks are ringing on thousands of clocks. Busy people. A shave! A shower! So many jobs to go to. So much useful work to do. Did you think this story was over? Humiliations quite done? That barrel, friends, has no bottom. You can always plunge your arm in for more. The Hotel Belmont, then. Green canopy. Red carpet. A doorman with a whistle and a muscular chest. Midnight. The bold fellow, he looks like a general, peers into the gloom. Who approaches? An Iroquois. What a magnificent bonnet of feathers! And a bow, arrows, slung over his rubicund shoulders. "I beg your pardon," he says to the uniformed guard. "Which way to the Indian Room?"

"One Hundred and Tenth Street, one-hundred-ten," announces the loudspeaker system. The masses crowd in. Cheerful in the morning. Doleful at night. These Americans are in my opinion as industrious as the ants. They do not know the pleasures of life. In Vienna we used often to sit in the cafés. A newspaper. A conversation. Schnapps from plums. The populations of Mediterranean countries avoid the heat of the day with siestas. Why hurry, Manhattanites? Sisyphus will roll his rock forever. The sea that tempts Tantalus is infinite in depth. Unlike, it seems, these spirits of Mexican manufacture. Look: only a drop. One drop! Finished!

Have you heard of the Chinese torture? Drip-drops on the head until you go mad? Between Orchard Street and Ludlow Street, near the First Roumanian American Congregation, there is an iron hydrant in all respects similar to that upon the Avenue Amsterdam. Except one: From this nozzle there came, instead of the gush, the geyser, the barest trickle. I sank down beneath the fixture and—what had I, insane already, to fear?—allowed the drops to strike my whirling head.

Where's the fire? asked in a rhetorical question Mister Mosk. *In the center of the universe,* Pythagoras, so far ahead of his time, replied. This Greek was the first to believe in the transmigration of souls. Thus he spoke against eating either meat or beans, holding that the latter were formed from the same type of matter as man.

The square of the hypotenuse in a right triangle is equal to the sum of the squares of the two sides. Could a man able to grasp the philosopher's theorem be truly mad? Reason intact. And memory? I recalled how, owing to obesity, Professor Pergam delivered his lectures sitting down. His heavy head was propped in his hands, so that the young academicians could see the bald spot where the brilliant thoughts rushed in and out. Suppose, the Professor once told us, that Pythagoras is sitting in a field, humming idly upon a blade of grass. He plucks another, longer stem. The tones are deeper, lower. Next he takes a shorter blade, half the length of the first. The note is—

"Twice as high!" exclaimed the gap-toothed, dimple-chinned Hans.

"An octave higher!" from Willi, whose growth seemed to have prematurely stopped.

"It is the invention of pitch! Of harmony! Of music!" we variously cried.

Pergam turned his face up, revealing his chins. "All notes are mathematical numbers, and all numbers—that is, all things that exist—are notes. Thus music must be always about us, within the smallest blade of grass as well as the solar system itself." We sat, spellbound. Here was the pinnacle of Pythagoras: the music of the spheres. The closer the planets to the central fire, the more slowly they circled about it, then the deeper the note they produced; whereas the farther and swifter planets give a higher tone. What was the sound, we wondered, of this cosmic chord? In my opinion—remember, please, this was before the discovery of the new planet of Pluto—the heavenly harmony must be in the key of C-major, that same perfect octave, C D E F G A B C, to which I had tuned my eight glasses.

My glasses! I sat bolt upright, sending the water droplets off in a spray. My instrument was still at the bar! Beneath the turning windmill! How could I live without my *Glasspiel?* Literally live? I could not walk by the hound in the hallway. Could no longer play for pennies. Not to mention the sentiments which, for reasons you know, the glasses themselves produced in my breast. Goldkorn's occupation gone!

It was only two blocks, across Orchard Street, across Allen Street, to the Steinway Restaurant. But the building was deserted by the time I arrived. Neon light extinguished. Front door locked and barred. The window of the dressing room had not, however, been touched. It was a simple matter to step over the sill and drop to the floor. I did so and—with hardly a glance at the three white costumes, gown, smock, negligee—moved upstairs.

I saw at once my Gladstone was gone. The blades of the

Dutch-style windmill turned and turned above the empty bar. With a cry, an oath, I began the search: upon the stage, on top and beneath the chair seats, behind the drapery, in the wings. Nothing. Back again at the bar, I threw from their shelves the lined-up glasses: tumblers and tankards, stemware and steins, jiggers and cups. Alas, no goblets. No Florida souvenirs. There was, however, upon the cushion of a revolving stool, the thick volume of the prompter's book. Open to the last page of the play. I seized it and moved toward the platform, where something was glittering in the glow of the spotlight. A blade! The dagger! And here was the bed, the foul nest, where the dark deed had been done. The stained sheets still upon it!

"Oh, Desdemona!" I cried, and raised the shiny steel blade.

Jews have been known in spite of the rabbis to take their own lives. The Zealots on Masada come to mind. All hope being lost. Well, friends? Had I not seen with my own eyes how the blond-haired Hildegard Stutchkoff invited the Ethiope to her bed? Had I not only been robbed of a Rudall & Rose–model flute, but lost in addition what the French call the *instrument de Parnasse*? Consider the example of Socrates, who refused to escape after his jailer had been bribed. Where flee, he asked of Crito, when the sentence of doom has been passed upon all mankind? Thus, with firm hand I raised the dagger. My words came, as advised, from the diaphragm:

> *I kissed thee ere I killed thee. No way but this,*
> *Killing myself, to die upon a kiss.*

I plunged the sharp steel into my breast.

What happened, I believe, is that the blade of the weapon somehow collapsed within the handle. I looked toward my thorax. Not only was there no wound, and no blood, but— and this was the fact I found most astounding—my flesh was white once again! I examined my arms, my hands, my abdomen zone. Wherever the hydrant had touched me, there the sable skin had simply washed away. Indeed, my loincloth was covered with the drips and runs. Paint, then! Greasepaint! A trick to make L. Kleiderman—in all likelihood a sallow Sephardi—look like a Moor! I dropped the knife. The playbook tumbled from my hands. Two could play at that game, I reasoned. What would work for one Jew would suit another.

My skin? Its ruddy hue? This was accomplished in the Steinway Restaurant kitchen, where, in the icebox cooler, Mister Martinez keeps always a large kettle of borscht. This soup I splashed over my limbs, onto my hairless scalp, and rubbed into my torso. For authenticity I applied the cold beets under my napkin, which hung almost as far as a Scotsman's kilts. I looked, when done, the color of brick—or like an iron statue, long since rusted, which has by a miracle returned to life. The feathers came from Essex Street; the bow, the arrows, the necklace of genuine bear teeth and bear claws from Avenue B. In other words, from Pipe's shop and from that of Printzmettle, the tobacconist, where an Iroquois Indian stood grinning just inside the door. I knocked that portal down with a shoulder thrust; the window of the bedding merchant's I broke with a rock. The owners, I knew, were out.

It took almost an hour to attach the goose quills, the turkey feathers, to the strip of mattress ticking. Wearing that warrior's bonnet, I glared at myself in Pipe's counter glass: had I, or had I not, that same evening removed the scalp of a living man? The bow was in the grip of the tobacco-shop brave. One by one, without remorse, I broke off the firm fingers. The rest was a simple matter of transferring the quiver and arrows from the redskin's smooth shoulder to my bushy one, and slipping the gleaming fangs around my neck. Was it a fancy that I then felt the strength of that grizzly now flow through my limbs, my sinews? Never mind the midnight hour. What did it matter that Jews were sleeping? I threw back my head and, with the power of tooth, of claw, let out a roar.

Then, all silence, all stealth, I moved on the pads of my feet along Houston Street, westward, until I came to the First Avenue.

"Far side of the lobby," says the doorman, his chest swelling against the double row of buttons. "Turn right at the palm trees and left at the bar."

"Danke schön," the Indian mutters, and steps onto the cold marble tiles of the hall.

The name, INDIAN ROOM, was spelled out in false rubies above closed double doors. Before I reached that entrance, however, a tall, pale Jew came from behind the pots of palm trees and turned at the bar. He was wearing a white hospital gown and had a large bandage on his head. Automobile accident victim. Then I looked again. L. Kleiderman himself! Hee-hee. I tittered, behind my hand. What a wound I had caused him. What a swelling! He approached the doors. They opened. The keeper, with a curved sword at his side, made a bow, ushering the invalid within. I moved forward then. The double doors opened again, as if controlled by an electrical eye. But the wielder of the scimitar stood before me, blocking the way.

"Sorry. Private party."

"Ha! Ha! I am a cast member. Role of Roderigo. It follows, then, I am a welcome guest."

"Nobody goes in without a costume. What kind of getup is that?"

Before I could answer, two more cases, also with head wounds, with baggy ward trousers, came strolling toward us. Margolies! And, with his duckbill replaced by a ball of linen, Mister Mosk! Poor fellows! Hit by a truck! Both patients walked by me, over the threshold. Again the guardsman bowed over his curving sword; and in that instant—"Iroquois!" I shouted; "Tribe of Hiawatha!"—I dashed past, into the Indian Room.

What a sight greeted my eyes! The entire cast of the play were seated along the far side of a banquet table, their heads wrapped in tourniquets or, in the case of the ladies—the widow; the waitress, Miss Beverly Bibelnieks—their faces hidden by wisps of sterile gauze. The smell of medicaments hung in the air. No time to speculate upon the nature of the calamity that had befallen my colleagues. The man with the saber—bare-chested save for a little red vest, and wearing puttees—was already striding toward me across the floor. I whirled, taking refuge behind one of four tree trunks, whose thick bark, gray and wrinkled, resembled that of the cork trees I'd seen in Lisbon. Crouching within this grove, I saw my pursuer turn to intercept a nice-looking young man; white shirt, herringbone jacket, spectacles with tortoiseshell rims. The younger Murmelstein, it soon developed.

"Pop! Hey, Pop!" he shouted, as the sentry bore down upon him. "I've got the reviews! The *Times*! The *Post*! The *Daily News*! It's a hit! A sensation! Look at this! They say the Jewish theater has been reborn!"

At the table, Salpeter stood, lifting his wine-filled glass. He was wearing, undoubtedly because of injury to the neck, a stiff Nehru-style collar. "Ladies, gentlemen, a toast to our success!"

Ellenbogen also rose. "And to our bride! Our groom!"

"Hurrah!" cried the others, looking toward the table center, where the widow and Kleiderman sat. One after the other the musicians, the waiters, and finally old Sheftelowitz, old Pipe, stood to raise a glass.

"To the Steinway Restaurant!"

"The Steinway Theater!"

"Long live our employer!"

"To Leopold Kleiderman!"

"Success! Success!"

Then Mister Salpeter drank at one gulp what looked like a Burgundy red. The empty glass had a pink bird painted upon it. The flamingo! Tartakower finished his potion. His glass was the same! Murmelstein likewise! Here was my harmonica! The entire octave intact!

Sheftelowitz was the last to drain the dregs. Then he turned and—from what source in the fish business did he learn this Gentile custom?—threw the goblet at the base of the wall, where it smashed to uncountable pieces. It was as if one of my own arrows had pierced my heart.

"Ho! Ho! Bravo!" said Murmelstein *père,* flinging his glass after the first. Ellenbogen next. Then Margolies.

Did Sebastian, the saint, suffer more from sharpened shafts than did I? Each glass, crashing, exploding, was a new torture. At last only Mosk, the Lithuanian, was left. "What's the big idea?" he asked, holding the ultimate vessel, the one with the pedestal chip. Then he added that goblet to the pile of shards.

Dust, a cloud, dropped over my eyes. How long did I remain there, motionless, crouched? Only moments. Yet I felt older, by decades, by ages, than when I had entered the room. My skin withered, my brittle bones creaked. It was as if, with the smashing of the glasses, the Fountain of Youth itself had dried up.

Across the floor, at the table, a man was speaking in a nasal tone. You could hardly hear, because of the way his nose lay flat on his moustache. I knew him! Rabbi Rymer! The one who had wed Clara and me so long ago. I took the bow in my left hand and with my right I fit an arrow to the string. Where aim? The head, from which issued the empty phrases, or the wicked rabbinical heart? Ha! Here was the groom, Kleiderman, standing next to the bride. He reached through the slit of his hospital gown and took out something small, something shiny. The ring! I pulled taut the bowstring. Here was the target. Old Shatterhand would not miss at sixty paces.

Closing one eyelid, narrowing the other, I let the metal-clad arrow fly. In that instant, while the shaft covered, in accordance with the laws of Zeno, first half the distance to the goal, then half the remainder, Kleiderman handed the ring to my old classmate, Pepi, who slipped it over the darling white finger of the former Widow Stutchkoff. He kissed her. Pepi Pechler!

"Ouch!" cried Doctor Botnik, who had just come into the room. The arrow had gone right through his turban.

"What's this?" said Pipe. "Cossacks?"

"No! No! It is I!" I stepped from behind the tree trunk. "Look! L. Goldkorn here! Winner of the costume prize!"

Margolies began the laughter. A giggle first. Then a titter. Then an outright guffaw. "An Indian! An Indian!"

Ellenbogen held his hand up, in the manner of a traffic policeman. "How!" he declared, and began laughing too.

"Woo-woo-woo-woo!" This war whoop came from Printzmettle.

Murmelstein's face had become suddenly as red as my own. "Tartakower!" he spluttered. "Tartakower has won the costume prize!"

I turned toward the flautist. He sat cross-legged, with rags draped over his gaunt, fleshless bones. You could see his rib cage, and the skin beating over his heart. He took his Powell-model flute and began to play—what was the selection? Featured at the last Steinway Restaurant concert. S. Romberg: "Indian Love Call." To my amazement, a snake came out of the basket he held in his lap. It swayed back and forth to the tune.

"He's got a wire," said Mosk. "Right on the end of his flute."

"This is the costume winner? He is not a Navaho. Not a Sioux."

The whole room echoed with laughter. Pepi Pechler wiped a tear from his puffy, lashless eye. "Idiot. You always were a *Dummkopf*! This is India! In Asia! We are Hindoos!"

I looked about, more closely. The tiles on the floor had,

it is true, an Oriental flavor. The smell, which I had thought an antiseptic, was incense. The tree, the four tree trunks: these were the legs of—I gazed up, and up—an elephant! A giant tusker. Skillfully stuffed.

"I have made an understandable error," I said, backing toward the doorway, where the fierce swordsman, with fat, folded arms, stood waiting. "The same one made by C. Columbus, except in reverse." But none of the Asiatics, doubled over with laughter, heard my words.

No need for beet coloring now. My skin burned crimson with shame. Above the cascade, the crescendo of merriment, like the clear tones of a glockenspiel above a noisy brass band, or perhaps a triangle—percussion instrument, equilateral in nature, having thus angles of 60 degrees; in English language, when any two persons are in love with a third, as when two men desire the identical woman—there rang out the pure bell-like laughter of the new Madam Pechler. With my hands to my ears I dashed through the doorway, pausing only long enough to snatch from the bar top the square amber bottle, Cuervo Especial—two thirds full, one third empty, depending upon an optimist's or pessimist's assessment. Then, with the swordsman behind me, I ran from the Hotel Belmont, through the streets, until I came to the steps of the F train, IND.

6

A question, a riddle: What do the sufferings of Sisyphus with his rock, Tantalus in the water, Ixion on his wheel have in common? Their eternal nature. Atlas, old friend, must hold the world on his back forever. And Prometheus, Atlas' brother? How long was the eagle commanded to attack his internal organs? Thirty thousand years. Thirty thousand! The IRT Number 1 local runs between 242nd Street–Van Cortlandt Park and the terminus at South Ferry. Let us simplify, saying each round trip will require in theory one hour. Thus we shall make 24 circuits each day–night period, 720 in each lunar cycle, or 8,760 in every year, for a total of more than— Ha! Ha! Not so drunk as you thought, not so tipsy—260 million complete journeys, Bronx–Manhattan–Bronx. Damned! Forever! Goldkorn in Hades. The purpose of the Prometheus legend, according to the rationalist argument, was to demonstrate the regenerative power of the human liver. The eagle devours it and devours it, but it is not consumed. The Greeks never drank Mission Bell! Cirrhosis of liver causes nonreversible damage. I may yet—for what else are these sharpening pains in the abdominal section?—cheat my fate, joining the former Madam Goldkorn.

Free will? Do not, as Mosk states, make me laugh. Here we are, 116th Street. Why not get off, cross the platform, return to my home? Only think! Even if I should, lacking my musical glasses, mount past the boxer, what sight would await me behind the closed fourth-floor door? Perhaps, after all, she called Doctor Goloshes? Or put into her thigh flesh the proper injection? Impossible! Not to be dreamed of. Our telephone was, by the Bell Telephone Company, removed long before. So. Moving. Speeding like a bullet. Somewhere in the crowded car I can hear the schnapps bottle tumble and roll. Why the horror of death? As Socrates proved, it is either a sleep from which we do not waken—and who among us would not choose a peaceful as opposed to a restless, dream-filled night?—or a removal to the upper world, where we may converse with the noble spirits of the past. Happy Clara: in the company of that good-looking D. Opatoshu, or with Adler, Kessler, and other leading men. Pipe dreams! Childish wishes! Pain, we fear, and the darkness. The loss of talent. The unknown.

What is this sudden light? All about me shapes are glowing, illuminated by fire. Blinding! Painful! Not to be endured! We slow. We stop. What is that music? Listen! Like chimes! What is this tintinnabulation? Why is the world aflame? Dear Professor Pergam: explain once again the theorem of Plato. Man, dwelling in caves, sees only his shadow, hears only the echo of his voice; but the soul, brought into the light, sees true beauty, and hears the music of the spheres. Am I dying? Dead, then? Has my soul traveled from the lower to the upper world? Where is Mendelssohn-Bartholdy? Meyerbeer?

"One Hundred and Twenty-fifth Street. One-twenty-fifth!"

I shade with my hand my bedazzled eyes. The sun, round, red, ablaze, rises in the east. To the west, the mighty Hudson, three hundred miles in length, its source in distant lakes. Below, the streets, the rooftops, of Harlem, filled with Harlemites! Ha! Ha! I had forgotten what I had known. The IRT local rises above ground, to travel for a time in the light and air. Listen: Someone is whistling. A youth on the platform. Someone else, a woman, is somewhere practicing arias and trills. Below, from every window, the tuneful sounds of the Philcos float onto the air. What a musical people! As a lad, in the Wienerwald, I would lie on my back, watching white clouds pass overhead, like the busts of great men. In the trees, invisible songbirds were singing, while moving from branch to branch. Friends, do not fear. Even the songs of birds, even these whistlings, are not lost. All the melodies ever played rise, according to laws of energy conservation, into the ether, where they make a ringing in the bowl of the sky.

The Magic Flute

Musicians, O, musicians, "Heart's ease, Heart's ease"!
—*Romeo and Juliet*

I

TIME: *11:58 PM*
DATE: *1/9*
TEMP: *34 F—1 C*

This information I obtain not from my Bulova watch, long ago exchanged for a pawnshop ticket, but from the illuminated sign upon the shores of the nearby state of New Jersey.

Drink Coca-Cola.

Excellent with Barbados-type rum.

Even that pawn ticket has been taken from me, together with the other portables within my Gladstone valise: half-pint bottle of Mint Cream, H. W. Longfellow volume, assorted heel lifts and selection of laces. Did they think with this last item I might hang myself? Soon comes the dawn! Let them do that work for themselves! Meanwhile, an hour of life is an hour of life: time enough to tell my tale.

About me, in the shadows, on meager pallets, men are sleeping. Snoring in the pitches of organ pipes. One cries out: *Mama!* he says. The others, some dozen black men, toss and stir. Poor sufferers! Even in sleep pursued by woes. Again the dreamer, his skin coal-colored, a youth of forty, perhaps, utters his cry: *Mama!* Inside all men, even octogenarians, the child exists, running from fears—a lightning bolt, a tiger's jaws, the hooded hangman—to his mother's bosom. Silence now. The not unpleasant water leak in the johnny. Fading steps in the corridor. Outside, twenty stories below, the hoot of a horn: from a taxi? An ice-bound harbor boat? A mighty ocean steamer? What an odor here! The unsponged men. The hosiery. The bubbling, stool-filled bowl. Now a man's teeth begin to chatter, perhaps from fear, perhaps from cold. My own fingers, in this heatless chamber, are numb about the pencil stub. The glass in the lone window is shattered, admitting the wintry blast. Look! At the opening! The pale face of the moon, like that of a prisoner, is pressed against the bars.

Correct: pencil stub. An item which, inserted behind the ear, was overlooked in the search. A trick learned from Steinway Restaurant waiters. Others are not so fortunate. For them no pencil points, no lunar illumination, no parchment of tissue rolls. Chained, in the dark depths of dungeons, they write in blood their tales. Let me delay no longer, but plunge to the very moment—that is, less than twenty-four hours ago— when I happened to hear, after a two-decade silence, the sound of my Rudall & Rose–model flute.

After all, one further delay: in order to warm in my armpit my frozen fingers. In this brief pause the moonlight patch has moved inches over the floor. Soon even this little light will be gone. Why is it that now, after men have walked on its surface, one hears the opinion the moon is made from Limburger cheese? More evidence, in my opinion, of the child, and childish notions, in the body of the grown-up man. Consider my own thoughts, when little more than a weanling: the moon, I believed, was no larger than a *Krone,* with the round-cheeked, pleasant features of His Majesty, Franz Josef, stamped upon it. Yet try as I might, reaching through my narrow crib slats, the silvery coin eluded my grasp.

A similar error, a confusion of perspective, repeated itself when, age three, or age four, I sat with my sisters watching the steamship *Leopold II,* a vessel of the Kaiserlich und Königlich Kriegsmarine, come round the bend of the Iglawa. Even now I am able to form a picture of the sight: the tawny river; the steamer, rust-colored and blue, black smoke pouring from the black smokestack; and the shiny barrel of the cannon, on either side of which stood a sailor in white. Then, the scream of the whistle, followed by the definite sound of music: marches, waltzes, three-eighths-time mazurkas. The ship drew closer, revealing, at the stern, the naval band: blue pants, red tunics, and a bandmaster with a silver-fretted staff. What did I do, friends? I hurled myself down, kicking my heels, beating my little fists upon the promenade: *Gib mir! Ein Bootchen! Gib mir!* Some trick of the light, the shimmer of water and spray, had made the warship seem no larger than a toy. "Want one! Want one!" I cried. Alas, the *Leopold II,* named for that earlier Hapsburg, steamed onward, its paddle wheel beating the yellow river to a white, foamy froth.

Yes, the Iglawa, not the Danube. From this alone one may deduce that Leib Goldkorn, although Viennese, was not born in Vienna but—the date is the second day of November, 1901—in Iglau. This is not—difficult to resist in the English language these amusing word plays—an Eskimo ice hut, but the old town at the Bohemia-Moravia frontier where I spent the early years of my life. November 2: also the birth date of the composer Karl Ditters von Dittersdorf, by coincidence a member of the k.k. Hof-Operntheater Orchester, and the creator of the symphonies on the *Metamorphoses* of Ovid, in which, through skillful orchestration, the listener can almost see the poor peasant folk turned into frogs. 1901. Life begins for little Leib but ceases for Victoria, Queen of Britain, Empress of India, and for G. Verdi, the non-Wagnerian master. Also in this year we find the construction of the first Mercedes-brand motorcar; the debut at the Royal and Imperial Opera of L. Slezak, the tenor; and the completion of the Mombasa Railway. Do I ramble? Digress? More theme, Leib Goldkorn! Fewer variations! Brief conclusion: I did not cease crying; my fit of weeping continued until Yakhne, the older of my two sisters, consoled me with the gift of a whistle—not a true flageolet but a sort of pan pipe, capable of producing six notes, the last a hair-raiser, like a kettle, or a locomotive, or—the most heartfelt wishes are on occasion granted—a steamship blast. Thus I whistled my youth away upon the streets of Iglau, its cobbled byways, from the promenade, to the old silver mine, to the Ferdinand Column; while at my heels, constantly baying, strode a number of schnauzers and dachshunds and spitzes.

2

Last evening, when my tale begins, was bitter cold, colder by far than tonight. At dusk, with Gladstone in hand, I left my home in order to earn my daily fare. Such weather, friends! Have you ever seen anything like it? The mighty Hudson has utterly frozen, allowing daredevils on foot to cross from the New Jersey shore. A cold wind blows unceasingly from the north. Pipes burst; automobiles, lacking a spark, fail to start; and water from firehoses freezes before it can reach the hungry flames. Even corpses, strange to say, must wait to be buried, until a thaw softens the ground.

And the living? Landlord Fingerhut is at this season in Miami Beach, Florida, sleeping upon the sands. The foam washes around him like linen sheets. No answer on his personal or his office phone. Is your Washington quarter returned from the Bell Company box? Ha! Ha! How often I stood within the clear cubicle, as cold, as colorless as an onion within a cocktail glass, beating with fists on the instrument, even as Fingerhut, with fatty breasts like a woman's, basked in hot sunshine, drinking the milk of a coconut. What a name! As if, in English, you would call a man Mister Thimble. Therefore the Admiral television has been moved to the spot next to the kitchen sink formerly occupied by the non-popping toaster, and Madam Goldkorn passes each day on the mattress spread before the oven's open door. That was how I left her, the darling, the mouse, at dusk: in nightcap, in mittens, in clean rubber pants. Warm as toast.

"Off to work, sweetheart!" I called, clutching my valise. "Off to the Steinway Restaurant!" How the flames danced gaily, in and out of the broiler, and leaped with a snap from the burners on top. Like gazing upon the hearth, into the fire, a custom the Gentiles enjoy. Who can say? Clara may be there still, unless she has in these thirty hours failed to take her injections, or the gas flames—such misfortunes sometimes happen—have caught the corner of the coverlet.

"Mister Goldkorn!" she cried, as I stepped over the threshold into the cat-and-dog smell of the hall. "Bring meat! Red meat! A beefsteak! A broiling!"

It took, owing to the ice-covered streets and the many delays of the IRT/IND system, two hours to reach the corner of Allen and Rivington streets. By then the sky was black, save for the bright, twinkling stars and the nearly full moon. The light from the Steinway Restaurant fell through the windowpanes in a parallelogram upon the ground. I followed my muffler, blowing before me like words from the mouth of a comic-supplement figure, to the steamed-over glass.

Let us pause to note the cheerful scene within. There are the waiters, Mosk, Margolies, Ellenbogen, gliding over the floor like skillful skaters on ice. Uptown Jews, with red, glowing faces, dip their egg bread in gravy and clasp in their fists their spoons. The two violinists, Murmelstein, Salpeter, draw their bows over their violins. Tartakower fingers his Powell-model flute. And the double-bass strings are plucked— even outside, one can feel the reverberations—by Doctor Julius Dick. At the register sits the Widow Stutchkoff-Pechler, no longer in black. Lipstick color: red, and red fingernail polish, with red rouge on the cheeks. Feet and toes crowded in an exciting manner into tight, pointed shoes. Behind the bar, Madam Ellenbogen is squeezing winter lemons into soda-whisky. Miss Bibelnieks passes hither and yon, selling mints. How normal, how like uncountable other evenings this lively tableau! Look: Over the double doors of the kitchen one can see the top of Mister Martinez's hat, puffed up, airy, like a Yorkshire-style pudding. The windmill sign turns and turns atop the bar. Incandescent bulbs glow in the former gas chandeliers. Never, not in a thousand years, would a non–English reader, let us say a visitor from China, guess that the sign in this very window plainly says: UNDER NEW MANAGEMENT.

The men's water closet and ladies' water closet of the Steinway Restaurant were in the days of the Stutchkoffs pleasant spots for the passing person to move his or her bowels. At any time of the day or night Jews could be found there, lingering in discussion, warming their trousers on the steam-heated pipes, or, in the deep handwashing basins, soaping their shoulders, rubbing a shampoo into their hair. A coin telephone was provided, and chairs; there was even, according to Mister Margolies, a table for chess. No need to list the living legends who were dazzled by the—here I speak exclusively of the gentlemen's facility—gleaming stalls for the passing of water, or who breathed freely the spearmint-scented air.

On this frigid evening I entered the Rivington Street door, and at once descended the stone staircase, following the footsteps of—after all, let us name a sample number: F. Kreisler, S. Romberg, G. Mahler, K. Kyser, the well-known Rumshinsky, all from the musical realm; also, the champions B. Leonard, B. Ross; from the world of diplomatics, Trotsky-Bronstein, Mister Ho Chi Minh; C. W. Beebe, the undersea explorer; Abbadabba Berman and B. Baruch, financial wizards; T. Herbert, of the Chicken Pullers Union; the half-Jew C. Zuckmayer; A. Einstein, onetime guest artist with the Quintet; and, turning right at the bottom of the staircase, not leftward, E. Roosevelt, S. Bernhardt, Wilhelmina of the Netherlands, and the belletrist, P. Sydenstricker Buck. Such were the notables whose steps I followed—also the Gershwin brothers—into the porcelain depths.

Not a moment too soon. A crowd of anxious patrons were milling before the locked rest-room door—proof, if any were needed, that the Stutchkoff era was over. A lock! A bolt! This change in our hospitable customs had occurred immediately after the death of P. Pechler, some nine months before. One day everything was normal; the next day, not only had a lock appeared on the door of the comfort station, but a coinbox had been placed upon every privy. Pepi Pechler, it seemed, had choked on a shad bone. Of a sudden the staff of the Steinway were employed by a gentleman named H. Schwartz.

I removed my thumbless mittens and took from my Gladstone the key set, with which I unbolted the door. Then I followed the eager crowd into the WC and hung up my muffler and lumberjack coat. Three patrons, I noticed, had formed a line at the high, wooden shoeshine chair, and a fourth, Lipsky the gynecologist, was already settled upon the air-filled cushion. I paused, surveying the busy scene. Several uptowners stood at the stalls. Another was—I do not mean here a euphemism—washing his hands. Inside one of the private johnnies a Jew, the owner of worsted trousers, was humming a tune from before World War II. Setting down my double-hinged bag, I fell to my knees before the throne-like chair.

"Any requests?" I asked.

Lipsky, in gum-bottoms, cocoa-colored uppers, grew reddish in the face. From embarrassment. "Offenbach," he said, in little more than a whisper. And then, leaning toward my cocked ear: "You know, 'Cancan.' " My face blushed, too. Not from shame at this risqué selection, which, after all, was sometimes played in public, and even appeared upon the famed NBC Orchestra "Beloved Opera Bouffe" disk. No. My distress was caused by the demanding nature of the work, its complex rhythms, full orchestration, breathless tempi. *"Ja! Ja!"* I said, forcing—was not in America the customer always in the right?—a smile. "Selection from *Orpheo in die Unterwelt!"*

Quickly I spilled out the contents of my ersatz-alligator valise: varieties of cloth, calico, woolens, rag pieces; various brushes; tins of Kiwi-brand polish, also polish in bottles and spray-type cans. Sideline accessories: lifts, laces, corn pads, Doctor Scholl–brand odor eaters, skin of moles. Last, a hand-held shiner, double-rotor design, upon the principle of the egg-beating machine. Opera buffer! Ha! Ha!

There was a brief pause while the chap near the basin—it was, I noted, Maizlish, D.D.S.—noisily pulled down paper towels. More sounds from above: treading feet, a dinner-ware tinkle, soft strains from the Steinway Quintet minus one. Then, crouching low, rubbing a soft cloth over the size-seven vamps, I replicated the rustle, the hiss of petticoat layers; next, with smart slaps of my open palm, I created the *click*, the *clack*, of the young ladies' stiletto-style heels, as they formed them-selved into the chorus line.

There are some at the Steinway Restaurant who insist that I am the one who invented this form of musical art. Not so. At most we may say that L. Goldkorn has somewhat refined a technique that is centuries old. Indeed, such rhythm accompaniments to labor go back to the dawn of man: rock striking rock, bone striking bone, the beat of tom-tom, of jungle drum. Why stop there? All nature is song, and every orchestra instrument is nothing more than the clumsy attempt to capture by mechanical means what occurs freely in the wild: The call of birds one to another we hear in my own specialty, woodwinds and flute; the breeze in bare branches, the insects' hum, the babble of the trout-filled brook—enter the various strings. Hear: The stormy brass echoes Jove's thunderbolts, as well as the roar—do we not speak of the elephant's trumpet?—of mighty beasts. Percussion? Note the sharp slap of the beaver's tail, the clam shell dropped from a height by the hungry bird onto a rock, and the majestic redwood falling to the floor of our California forests.

Alas! The longer man's tenure on earth, the further he moves from his roots in nature, then the less attuned he is to the great symphony of onomatopoeia about him. To wit, the croaking of what to my shame is the Vienna School: A. Schönberg, the twelve-toner, and pupils Webern, Pisk, Berg. What cacophony! Caca-phoney, if I may be allowed one further jest. Nothing to whistle, to tap the toe to, to hum. Not to mention the current fad: work composed for, if not by, machines. Here, in these blips, beeps, bloops, we reach the ultimate estrangement: sound not occurring in nature. *Ping!* Ha! Ha! Ha! *Pong!* Madness!

No. We must find inspiration, and rediscover our musical roots, in more primitive folk. Thus I came one day in the Morningside Heights quarter upon a black fellow tunefully shining a pair of shoes. His cloth popped, his rosy palms smote the leather, and his lips smacked together—all in skillful syncopation. So from the humble shoeshine boy and his tattered cloth we derive the words "rag" and "ragtime," a polyphonic form that I, a modern Viennese, a twentieth-century man, am doing my utmost to carry on.

At long last, the finale. About me stood the occupants of

the Steinway Restaurant Gentlemen's WC, breathing strenuously through their noses. Lipsky's face, and not only Lipsky's, was crimson-hued. "This," said Maizlish, still by the towel machine, "is where they kick their legs."

It was indeed. Hurriedly I spread the Kiwi paste round and round upon the leather. A sharp jet of pressurized polish duplicated in uncanny fashion the frenzied bloomers of the female dancers. Now I snatched up my cotton cloth and began to flick the frayed end at either toe box, just as we lads at the Akademie für Musik, Philosophie, und darstellende Kunst used in mock anger to hurl our bath towels at our fellow boarders' bums. The snapping rag brought to mind once again the staccato rhythm of the high-heeled French shoes. The jaws of the uptown Jews dropped downward, as did, from exhaustion, my own. The maintenance of this dance-hall rhythm required, in addition to musicianship, athleticism of championship caliber. The sweat soon stood on my brow. My spine made popping sounds. My arms, as the chorines kicked their calves immodestly skyward, thrashed in a blur, like those of a Hindoo icon. Then, just as I experienced such a painful liver-zone spasm I felt I could no longer continue, the occupant of the cabinetto flushed his private johnny, creating a thunderous roar. Crescendo.

I announced, in the Maestro's manner, *"Finito."*

The audience applauded. Up stood Lipsky, flush-faced, fumbling in his pockets. His gum-bottoms gleamed.

"Ha! Ha!" I laughed, holding out my empty hand. "Non-salary basis. A non—wage earner."

Here the worsted-wearer threw open the privy door. "I'm next," he announced. "That's my place in line." Naturally, before such a figure—here was the type of Jew whose ears stuck out at an angle and whose hairline began little more than an inch above his eyes—the others gave way.

"It's H. H. Levine!" the gynecologist exclaimed, dropping a dime and a nickel into my palm. Then he moved to the exit door. Fifteen cents!

"Mister Lipsky. A word. Please. I am starving. Yes, that's what I want to say. A starving man!"

"Starving?" echoed an uptowner, the half-Jew, Apt. This real estate baron had a wad of tissue in one of his nostrils. "Don't tell me a Steinway Restaurant employee doesn't eat like a king."

"This is, Mister Apt, a myth. It may have been true in the Stutchkoff era. And Pechler, there is no denying, permitted Mister Martinez to fry in a pan an onion half, some liver strips, and a tidy broiling. Now we have a new management. Scraps! Leftovers! I speak of oddments! Protein content nil! And even these peelings do not find their way to my mouth. Each morsel is wrapped in—how do we say this? *Ein Hundpaket.* A pooch pouch. This I take to my darling spouse. A diabetes sufferer. Non-continent. The sweetheart! Look! Do you see? I am holding my gloveless hand to the source of light. One can see the bones in the skin!"

Hurriedly, heartlessly, the uptowner passed through the rest-room door. The man he had called H. H. Levine settled onto the elevated chair and thrust forward a pair of oxblood bluchers. "Make it snappy," he commanded. "I got a job offer tonight."

"One moment," I said. "Brief intermission." Taking with me a bottle of Camel Tan polish and expending my new Roosevelt dime, I secluded myself within the cozy boundaries of the nearest booth. In order to create what we Viennese call the proper gestalt, I faced outward and dropped my voluminous gabardines. Jews in the outer world would have no choice but to think I was attending the summons of nature. In truth, however, I removed the cap on the polish bottle and drank down the amber brew. Do not be alarmed, friends. This was only a barley mixture, the appropriately named Johnnie Walker. Alcohol content: forty percent. Another? One more? How else to perform through the remainder of this evening, and all the bitter evenings to come? A shad bone! Who would have thought such consequences, such suffering, could be contained in such a small, insignificant thing?

Poor Pechler. All the Steinway Restaurant waiters, the musicians, attended the funeral service at Hachilah Hill. His skin, outside the stone mausoleum of the Stutchkoffs, was red, boiled-looking, as if the former Akademie student had just stepped from his bath. The plot of the family Goldkorn was not far from that pyramid-shaped tomb. A brief walk in the April breezes. After the ceremony, I stood there alone.

She sleeps!
My lady sleeps!

Words of H. W. Longfellow, still visible upon the small, curved stone. Also, *M. Goldkorn, 6/7/43–6/7/43. M.*, of course, standing for Martha. Here is a little-known fact: The Longfellow bust is placed at the Poet's Nook, Westminster Abbey. Unprecedented honor for a Yank. Fortunate fellow. Three daughters. Three! One day his wife, while inside their house, burned up in a fire.

I burst through the door, accompanied, for realism, by the cascade of the Niagara. Levine was still in the chair, his face pale as his shirtfront, through the buttonholes of which sprouted the manly hairs. I sank before the worsted-covered knees.

"Any requests?"

"Yeah," the customer responded. What a big jaw he had! What a big chin! " 'Slaughter on Tenth Avenue.' "

The hours of employment sped quickly by. Maizlish, the novocaine expert, requested the *Negro Rhapsody*, a work by R. Goldmark, onetime Steinway patron and nephew of the world-famed Carl. Large range of dynamics. Breakneck tempo. And all to be managed upon the dentist's slip-on pumps. What else? Some Zemlinsky trifles. The D. Milhaud *Kentuckiana*. And, from the realm of popular culture: *Most*

Happy Fella overture; theme from M. Steiner's *Gone With the Wind*; and the *Lied*, "Happiness Is a Thing Called Joe." Little wonder that in the course of this concert I finished Camel Tan and was forced to open Cordovan, whose true contents, of California manufacture, were the perfect shade of purplish-blue.

It was past midnight by the time the last uptowner departed in a Checker-style taxi and the waiters, as well as the Quintet members, trooped down the stairs to do their business. One after the other, or in small groups, they strode to the stand-up stalls, at the bottom of which ran an encouraging brook. Mosk, the skeptical Lithuanian, made a few drops, which for the most part fell upon the vamps of his two-tone shoes. Dick, Ph.D., possessed a contrasting technique: a single vigorous jet into one stall, then—still carrying his instrument with him—a powerful burst into another, and sometimes a shot into a third. Prostate sufferer. Bane of contrabassists. Salpeter, amazingly, used no hands. While a silky haze spread over the locked compartments—the result of Tartakower, puffing in private upon his Pall Mall Virginias—I counted my taxable income: one dollar, eighty-six cents. Hardly enough for the IND/IRT passage to work and home! How was I to avoid starvation?

"You hoo!" sounded a high female voice, followed by a rap, a knock on the door. "Mister Goldkorn!" Waiting for me was Miss Beverly Bibelnieks, who each night at this hour brought from the kitchen my meager scraps. A well-favored, fortyish lass: frilly tutu, strong teeth like the keys of a Bösendorfer, a tray with mints and, for me, a covered dish. Imagine my delight when I lifted the uppermost of these plates and saw, amidst a swirl of steam clouds, a genuine Vienna cutlet covered with bread crumbs, from which had been taken only a single human bite. A schnitzel! A six-dollar item! So dizzy was I with the meaty aroma that I could barely suppress the impulse to pick up the darling, to waltz with it, to hug it to my bosom.

Instead, I clapped the two plates together, so no one could spy the treasure within, and returned to the shoeshine chair, where I whisked the prize between the air cushion and my buttock zone. Then, in a nonchalant manner, I looked about. No waiters. No musicians. All quiet within the private johnnies. Still I sat, until the last dull thud of the chairs, as they were being upturned upon the dining room tables, ceased above me. A muffled shout. The slam of a distant door. Alone, then! At that thought, a thick syrup drained from my mouth, over my quivering chin. No one to see me! No person to know! Even a dog is fed once each day. He is permitted to sharpen his teeth on a bone. How long since I had eaten a liver pâté? Tasted a pimento roll? Weeks, dear friends! Very well! With caution, I drew the covered dish from its secret place, where the warmth of the entrée had penetrated my gabardines with the forcefulness of a sitz bath. Slowly I tipped upward the topmost plate. *Mein Gott!* It was no dream! The cutlet existed! What a fine one! The pretty protein had been hammered flat into the shape of California, our thirty-first state. To snatch up this calf's flesh, to grip it in my jaws, grind it, gobble it down: All that was the work of a moment. So!

Fear not. Be calm. We are men, speaking to men, and not brutes. No canine, at such a moment, would recall the parting words of its bitch: *Meat! Bring meat! A broiling!* Clara! Her little lace cap. Her dear feet inside the athletic hose. The pinkness of her gums. To rob this blood-sugar victim of protein would be like passing a sentence of death. Might as well throw her—ha! ha! ha!—out the window, into the street below. There are other laws beyond those of nature, where only the fittest survive. *For better or worse:* Those were the words of Rabbi Rymer, spoken in a nasal tone in the winter of '42. Also, *In sickness or health.* Such an oath, for a citizen, is surely binding. *Wedlock!* That is the expressive word for it. Wedlock! *Until death do you part!* Thus the husband will chew the cutlet, grinding the meat with his molars, until the firm, healthful flesh is no more than a mash. Not swallowing. Taking no taste. This pulp, with a little warm water, he will spoon into the spouse. What beast in the jungle would perform such a task for its mate?

Just then the bell towers of the Warsaw Congregation broke into the first cheerful chords of "The Beer-Barrel Polka." A pause. A silence. Then a single, sour B-flat. One A.M.! One in the morning! I abandoned the double dish and hastily swept the tools of my trade into the Gladstone, which I set beside the closed door. The switch for the lighting fixture was just above. I flicked it off. Pitch blackness, save for the foggy glow of the nightlamp in the high, street-level window and the narrow strip of light that showed through the gap where the interior wall came just short of the ceiling. I moved gropingly in the latter direction, stopping at the leftmost compartment to feel for another F. D. Roosevelt dime. One dollar and *seventy*-six cents, then. The tissue roller was on the right hand wall, at the height of a standing man's loins. I removed the complete roll, using a pad of the paper to lower the seat cover in a sanitary fashion onto the mouth of the potty. Then I stood upon the sturdy lid and paused for breath.

The water box for the convenience was attached to the rear wall at a height of more than five feet. The only means of reaching it was to move from the seat cover to the steel prongs of the dispenser and then, all in one motion, hurl a leg over the top of the partition that separated this cabinetto from the one adjoining. From there, one might grasp the cold-water pipe that ran the length of the room, and so swing to the ironclad, water-filled box. This was a maneuver that might cause even a youthful gymnast—not to mention a flautist of the Franz Josef era, toiling in darkness—to think twice. "Hoopla!" I cried, nevertheless, and sprang upward, from foothold to handhold, hauling myself higher, still higher, until, with one final step into the void, over the abyss, I found myself in what is known as the Schneebalg position: one leg planted upon the square top of the flushing box, the other braced against the rear wall of the booth. By bending the trunk, by leaning forward, it was possible to view, through the crack between the stucco wall and pressed-tin ceiling, the entire brightly lit interior of the Steinway Restaurant Ladies' WC.

Schneebalg, the Quintet's original Bechstein artist, had constructed this stance, the better to remark the form of S. Bernhardt, still in her costume from *Frou-Frou,* upon the first of her many visits to our Roumanian grill. Appetite for rare broilings. For herring fillets. For cigarettes in a holder. In the winter of 1919–1920, however, the pianist ran from the comfort station, two and three steps at a time up the staircase, and threw himself upon the first person he saw. Young Margolies. Apprentice waiter. "Help me! It's a disaster!" Even now, if requested, Margolies will repeat this tale. "She's got a wooden leg!"

Thus I stood, my tendons aching, hardly daring to take a breath. Below me, at the center of a private booth, Hildegard Stutchkoff was engaged in either number one or number two. Her greenish dress was drawn up about her like leaves around a bud. The flossiness, the fluffiness, of her butter-colored hair! Her fox fur hung round her neck, so that the bushy tale covered one portion of her bosom, and the little triangular head, once filled with clever thoughts, depended upon the other. What else in this portrait? Stocking rolls at the calf zone. Two sturdy knees protruding from one end of the New York *Post,* upon which the checkerboard of the word puzzle was printed, while at the other end, upon the plump, rosy band of human flesh, that is, upon her thighs, there lay in plain view—*Gott! Gott im Himmel!*—a scattering of garter trolleys.

At that instant there was a thump on the door of the gentlemen's WC, which opened, and the light bulbs, hundreds and hundreds of watts, blazed on.

"Hello! Anyone is here? *¿Es el baño desocupado?*"

Martinez! The broiling chef! I froze where I was, in the

exact posture—a sculpture by Feiner, perhaps—of a thrower of the discus. The Hispanic leaned into the room, peering leftward, peering right. Then he turned, reached once more for the light switch, and, to my horror, stumbled against the alligator-type surface of my valise.

"Ah!" he exclaimed. "Goldkorns! ¿Estás aquí? ¿Dónde estás, Señor?"

A simple glance upward would supply the answer to that query. Luckily, the cook bent downward and swept with his gaze the area beneath the compartment doors. Seeing nothing, he lifted my valise and flicked downward the switch for the lights. The broiling wizard had gone. But just as I was about to relax my difficult pose and take a welcome inhalation, I heard a sound—a bang, a click, a thud—that went through my body as a skewer goes through a shishkabob. The door. The latch. The bolt. Locked, then! And my key set: friends, you remember. Inside the Gladstone bag!

3

Is there a youth who does not dream of one day becoming an Arctic or Antarctic explorer? With what eagerness did we lads on the Türkenshanzplatz turn from our studies, our woodwind drills, to devour the accounts of those daring dashes to the Poles: to the north, the toeless Peary and his faithful Negro; and, southward, the ill-fated Scott, killing his ponies one by one. Compared to such dangers—the ships crushed by ice, grampuses that rose from the depths to seize unwary huskies, the yawning crevasse—what had I, enclosed within the Steinway Restaurant lavatory, to fear? Here was my red-

and-black lumberman's jacket, here my thumbless mittens. Let us share a secret: Beneath the air-filled comfort cushion, inside the seatbox, the shoeshine chair contained a polish reserve: four bottles cordovan-colored and a fifth neutral, clear, colorless, of Soviet manufacture. In extremis, I possessed an entire Vienna cutlet, whereas the famed Sir Douglas Mawson, the discoverer of Magnetic Pole South, survived for month after month on a raisin packet, the meat from the last of his dog team, and cupfuls of boiled snow.

These comforting thoughts lasted no longer than the little bottle of potato schnapps. The steam heat had already shut down for the night. The temperature was plummeting. Before my eyes the tiny tumbling brook at the bottom of the stand-up stalls grew sluggish. In the bowls of the privies, crystals of ice began to form. My own breath came in a vapor. Splinters of wood, metal pins, needles, were being driven by a hidden torturer under the nails of my fingers, the nails of my toes.

"Help! Help!" I cried, pounding on the locked and bolted door. "Definite signs of frostbite!" Indeed, the fatal symptoms, so familiar to the readers of Scott's last journal, grew rapidly worse. A weight seemed to be pressing downward on my head, my shoulders, and a lobster, or so it appeared, had taken hold of my nose. Suddenly I experienced an elastic sensation as, with a twang, my manly parts vaulted upward in search of what little warmth my belly could provide. Belly? What belly? The hard shell of a walnut. A pebble. A rock. With a growl in my throat like a wolf's I fell upon the double dish and clamped my jaws upon the meat. Not even the drill of Dr. Maizlish, the bicuspid expert, was as powerful as the electrical volts that shot then through every tooth. Better to chew on the porcelain, gleaming, glacierlike, all around me, than to attack this frozen veal.

Thus tormented, tired, I sank to a sitting position. I knew well that this bone-weariness was the most dangerous symptom of all. No drowsing! No dreaming! Rule number one for the Arctic or Antarctic explorer. This was the sleep from which no man awoke. Up, then, Leib Goldkorn! A jig, that's what we want. A pep-filled rigadoon! Alas, the weights pressed downward from above, while from below a thousand little hooks, each attached to my clothing, pulled and pulled. I went from my knees flat to the floor tiles. My legs drew upward, my fist curled under my chin. Danger! Danger! Woodwinder, shut not your eyes!

D. G. B. D. B. Three eighth notes; a strong quarter note, triple forte; the eighth note again. Key of G major. A bird call! In winter's depths! *Da-da-da-dee-da!* Auditory hallucination. The common sparrow, the robin with gaudy vest, the chaffinch, had all, like Frank Fingerhut, gone south for the season. Yet the call came again, the same five notes—light, lilting, larklike, a burst of gay laughter. Mockingbird? *Ein Kuckkuckvogel?* No! No bird! A flute! And not any flute. No pennywhistle. A Rudall & Rose! Instantly my eyelids flew wide. My frozen heart began to pump. Thus I lay, straining to hear that instrument's distinctive tones. They came at once, from a spot beyond the high, frost-covered window, near the Steinway Restaurant door: not the five-note call but a slower, more rhythmical song. Now I was stunned, indeed. I knew that timbre, knew it better than the sound of my own voice, or the familiar pulse that beat within my ears. Some fellow on Rivington Street was playing my Graduation Day prize!

Have I, I asked myself, gone mad? Impossible, beyond all laws of probability and chance, that the instrument I heard was the same one a green-trousered youth, a Harlemite, had plucked from my arms. Broad daylight. The busy Avenue Amsterdam. 1963. No. More likely I had succumbed to that delirium that seems to afflict with special savagery we Austro-Hungarian musicians: H. Wolf, for instance, forever flinging himself into water; or B. Smetana, who ended his days in an asylum. You know of the mass delusions of the twelve-toners, some of whom seemed to believe they were producing tuneful melodies. And what of K. D. v. Dittersdorf, born under the same star as myself, also an instrumentalist in the Royal and Imperial Opera, who in the last years of his life suffered from the misconception that he was a horse? A tear, hot, salty, spilled from my eye. Had it come to this? Hearing things? Twitterings? Warblings? Birdsongs? Now the entire three-part sequence, all the notes, sounded again, with a shift back to the tonic, forming a lively, invigorating chord. Friends: No madman is speaking. A pox, as the Americans say, upon odds! This was the very instrument that had been awarded to me at the Graduation Day Concert, 1916, upon the recital stage of the Akademie für Music, Philosophie, und darstellende Kunst.

"Now we come to the wind students. Is that correct? The wind students." The speaker had paused, squinting through his nose-pinchers at the parchment he held in his outstretched arms. A tic made it appear he was screwing a monocle into his eye. "Where were we? Percussion graduates? No! Winds!" Those of us on the stage, not least we in the woodwinds and brasses, sat eagerly forward. The aged figure licked his whiskery lips. His hands, holding the prize scroll, constantly shook, as did the knees inside their flower-white trousers. The only sound in the room came from the little gold chain that was attached to his sword and scabbard. The same sad thought at that moment passed through many heads: There would be no more Graduation Day concerts at which His Kaiserlich und Königlich Apostolischen Majestät, though aged a mere eighty-six, would appear. A more immediate question was: Would he live through this one? Sweat streams had begun to run on his brow. The tic twisted his cheek flesh, above the white muttonchop of his beard. The scabbard itself started clanging. A Gentleman of the Household stepped forward, together with a military aide. But the Emperor of Austria, King of Hungary, resumed: " 'First prize, for his flute artistry, is awarded to—' " What happened next—my account is not as precise as it might be, since the phrase I had just heard, "flute artistry," caused me to swallow the multiflavored sourball I had been passing from cheek pouch to cheek pouch: Still, we all saw the award list slip from Franz Josef's fingers, fly on air currents over the first rows of faculty members, and, in spite of choirmaster Turpenstein's tremendous leap, land in the lap of my younger, more fleshly, nonbespectacled sister.

" 'Goldkorn, L.,' " she read, completing her sovereign's sentence.

A gasp, as if from other citrus drop swallowers, came from many throats. Lajpunger, Professor of Woodwinds, turned round in his seat. "This is nonsense. An example of country humor. Majesty, allow me—" Here the expert, his own beard was full of creamy wisps, like a *spanische Windtorte,* seized the parchment from my sibling's grasp and handed it upward to Franz Josef the First. The aged ruler stood upon the lip of the stage. His whole head, quite bald, we saw, without its plume of parrot feathers, was abob. With how many cares was our poor Papa, as thousands called him, burdened! Eleven ships of our German comrades lost off Jutland, and the remainder of the fleet trapped in harbor. The British, so it was rumored, were building a new sort of movable cannon that could be fired first at one spot, then another, through the employment of caterpillar traction. And, as the whole nation knew, here was also a human being, one who had lost through violent death a wife, a brother, an only son.

Only? They used to say, what with the actresses he befriended, the k.k. Hof-Operntheater singers, that His Majesty had fathered a good many more. Indeed, one proof of this sensualist strain—and surely the reason why His Highness, the Hapsburg, should honor, in the midst of world war, our modest concert—was little Willi, that is, W. Wimpfeling, who only moments before, in spite of tone deafness, had taken top viola honors. Our *proud* Papa, then, looked now over the list top, into the fourth row, to where my sister—she had a beauty mark on one bosom that on the previous day she'd worn on the side of her nose—was slowly rising.

"From the country, was it?"

"Yes, Excellency. We are from Iglau."

"And the name was—?"

"Goldkorn, L. My own name is Goldkorn, M."

Franz Josef, with a simple head motion, caused one of the Hungarian Guard to step forward with a box: the prize. "The winner on winds is Goldkorn, L.," the Monarch declared.

I stood, foolishly grinning. Utter silence in the hall. Except, next to the chair where I had been seated, young Hans, my fellow flautist, gap-toothed, with black, wet-looking, slicked-down hair, was making a noise with his lips and tongue. It is probable that fine fingerer considered himself the more deserving recipient of the prize. And what, I wondered, *was* that reward? A medal? A citation? A decoration with ribbon attached? Boldly I moved to the stage front, where the Guardsman was holding the long, black box; the Emperor himself, with his palsied hands, forced it open.

My dear friends: the Rudall & Rose. The instant I saw it, silver, shining, upon its bed of velvet and plush, the swallowed *Sauerball* shot upward and lodged like a second Adam's apple in my throat. There I stood, in my checkered suit, with mud-guard puttees, gasping, red-faced, directly in front of the Annexer of Bosnia and Herzegovina. The Hungarian Bodyguard member—he did not lack for medals and ribbons and stars—took the instrument and placed it in my hands. I remained motionless, staring at the Golden Fleece Order, which the Emperor wore at his throat, at his red sash, his blue, twinkling eyes. *"So,"* said that kindly soul: *"Hier ist ein kleiner Jüdischer Musiker."* With those words he gave me a sharp, friendly swat on the shoulders, propelling the candy to its point of origin in my mouth. I raised the instrument: no! So buoyant was it, so light and balanced and bursting with life, that it bounded on its own to my thick, puckered lips.

"It is a mistake, I tell you," Lajpunger called from the crowd. "He is not a true Graduate."

"Ha, ha!" laughed Hans, though his face had a frightening look. "Let him play. They'll hear something! *Ein furzender Hahn! Ein schreiendes Schwein!*"

I took a breath, a second breath, then expelled from my lungs a flow of air which, in spite of the rolling sourball and my own trembling fingers, became the first lilting notes of that season's success, *Die Rose von Stambul.* What rich, golden tones! It seemed to me that the Akademie rooftop had parted and the strong summer sun was bathing us in its liquid light. Where had such an instrument come from? Surely this was the very flute that Athena, its inventor, had discarded because she saw in the fountain of Ida how the action of blowing upon it distorted her face. Look, you gods, who had it now! Not, as Professor Pergam believed, the unhappy Marsyas of legend! No! L. Goldkorn! In the words of his Emperor, the little musical Jew!

I paused, while the last note trembled and faded, like a dew upon a flower. Complete soundlessness. Not a movement. Then the Emperor leaned out over the audience, which—guests, family members, professors of the Akademie—sat as if struck by lightning.

"Did you say *M*? The letter *M*? M. Goldkorn?"

My sister's chest zone heaved upward. Her mouth made a moue. "Yes," she responded. "For Minkche."

No sound now but the wind. Had I been dreaming? No matter. The sound of the Rudall & Rose had pulled me from dread Morpheus' grasp. My eyes had been opened, and my gaze, skimming along the floor tiles, darting beneath the privy doors, came to rest upon a welcome sight: a matchbook. Dropped by Tartakower, the Steinway Quinteter, while smoking in secret his Virginias. At once I crawled to the booth and seized the cardboard booklet. On the cover was a photo image of a he-man, a well-developed torso zone, together with the name of a five-borough spa. And inside—again we see, as with the shad bone, what a small thing may stand between death and life—a single crimson-tipped match.

It took but a moment to fill to the brim the rubbish container with paper hand towels and streamers from the tissue rolls. Yet even this effort left me trembling, with hardly the strength to pull off my mittens. My frozen fingers fumbled at the stem of the solitary match. Like the last leaf on a twiglet, a final party guest, it would not without reluctance quit the spot. Impossible to get a grip on the tiny torch, much less strike it with precision on the diminutive strip the spa had provided for that purpose. Time and again I failed at the task. Bits of strawberry-colored phosphor began to crumble against the grainy flap. Worse: After a few such feeble strokes I found it difficult to raise even this featherweight stick. Protein deficiency! Starvation attack! Fortunate the explorer who could depend upon the red meat of his sled dogs! Gathering my energies for a last attempt, I flung the hand with the match toward that which clutched the detonating pad, only to watch in horror as both items spun away to the floor. There was the cover, in tatters. But where the willowy wood, my slim reed, the darling redhead?

The answer came swiftly. A smoke wisp rose from the heap of papers, followed by a puff, a *whoosh*, like the sound made by a trombonist blowing saliva from his mouthpiece, and at once the entire basket burst into fire. Success! Quickly I whisked the Vienna cutlet from between the double dishes and with my bare hands thrust it, barbecue-style, directly into the merry flames. What a sizzling! Such thick, black smoke! Deftly I turned the veal, so as to ensure an even roast. The tongues of fire danced higher, licking, searing. The molten meat bubbled in the blaze. That aroma! The little leaping balls of fat! Coughing from the billows, with scorched fingers protruding from my singed lumberman's cuffs, I lifted the cutlet high over my gaping mouth—the way an Englishman lifts an asparagus or a mother bird feeds her nestlings. Then I clamped my teeth on the flesh of the schnitzel and in bliss started to chew.

What a taste! Horrible! Like celery stalks! Like a carrot!

This was milk kosher, not flesh kosher. A meat imitation! With a single exhalation I spewed the ersatz veal over the floor tiles of the comfort station. Carrots! Celery! Squash! Even the dread soya! "Martinez!" I cried aloud. "Turncoat! Traitor!" Yet even as I spoke these words, the sound of coughing, of choking, continued. Not from my own lungs, then. From someone else's! I whirled about. The smoke hung in black coils beneath the ceiling. Through the oily clouds, in the space above the dividing wall, I saw a human face, with watery eyes and a tongue hanging out.

"What's going on?"

Mosk! The Lithuanian waiter!

"That is what's-his-name? You know. The shoeshine boy."

Another one! Salpeter! First violinist!

Three different emotions fought for supremacy within my breast. Amazement, of course. Joy next, at my salvation, my rescue. But above all irateness, and stern indignation.

"Gentlemen," I said, in an admonishing tone. "I must inform you that you are standing inside of the Ladies' WC!"

4

For all the dangers of the Arctic and Antarctic circles, crevasse falls, snow blindness and the rest, the common cold is not among them. This is because the germs that cause catarrh, grippe, and unsightly gumboils are frozen in a nonactive state.

"Ah-choo!" It was I who made this ejaculation. "Ah-*choo!*"

"*Gezundheit,*" said Mister Mosk.

No sooner did the rescue party, led by the cook, Martinez, bring me to their redoubt in the women's rest room, than my nose began to drip with rheum. Shivering fits. A feverish brow. Dizzy, weak-kneed, I sank onto an empty chair and looked around.

The room was warmed by two electrical fires, whose glowing rods provided just enough light to make out a circle of chairs—the same ladderbacks I had earlier heard being upended upon the dinner tables. Seated on them were the Steinway Restaurant waiters, together with the female barmaid and the surviving members of the Quintet. Also, as mentioned, the Hispanic cook. Nor were these the only familiar faces: Sheftelowitz, the fish merchant, and the featherbedder, Pipe, were seated as well, on either side of M. Printzmettle, the Avenue B tobacco dealer. A dozen Jews then, not counting one—a whistling breather, with a nose that was flattened onto his moustache—whose name I could not at that instant recall; nor another, behind a closed privy, whose trousers had collapsed round his ankles. Also present: B. Bibelnieks and the plump, humanlike shape of J. Dick's double bass.

"What have we here, friends?" I asked, my teeth all a-chatter. "Canasta club?"

Young Murmelstein hissed a response: "Shhh! Quiet! For heaven's sake, quiet!"

Sheftelowitz added, *sotto voce,* "You'll give us away!"

Salpeter stood in front of his chair. He talked in a whisper. "The time runs short. Let us resume. Mister Pipe, I believe, was speaking."

But Pipe said not a word. It was Printzmettle, with his Chesterfield coat on, who interrupted the pause. "The thing is, how do we know we can speak freely? How do we know this man"—here he turned in my direction—"is not a spy?"

Sheftelowitz: "I thought of that, too. What better place to listen in? People say anything in a comfort station. They don't have inhibitions."

Madam Ellenbogen, the cocktail waitress: "Maybe it's no accident the way he was locked in next door."

"That's right," said her husband. "Tonight of all nights."

Said Printzmettle: "He could hear every word over the partition!"

"That fire! He set it on purpose. A smoke signal! To give the alarm."

You can imagine how my head, already hot with fever, and spinning from the schnapps of the polish reserve, started to ache. "Dear colleagues! Old friends! I am since nineteen forty-three a citizen. Chambers of Judge Solomon Gitlitz. I did this because, like any man, I wanted to get ah-ah-ah—" *Ahead* I had wished to say, but because of the plume, of the sort sold on Pipe's portable dusters, that seemed to be tickling my nose, I declared instead, "Ah-*choo!*"

"Heavens!" cried Madam Ellenbogen. "It's the signal!"

With that, the tobacconist leaped from his seat and with my own muffler tied my arms to the back of the chair.

"I don't approve of this. Gentlemen, this is not right." The speaker was Tartakower, fellow flautist.

"What choice have we got?" responded Murmelstein, the youngest of the Quintet. "Whether he means it or not, the noise will alert them upstairs. If he says another word, we'll have to gag him."

No one, it seemed, was willing to question this logic. The crowd turned toward old Pipe, who now cleared his throat to speak. "Ten cents," said the merchant, whose balding head was covered with spots. "That might not seem like a lot. But add it up. Twice daily, on account of a fruit diet, that's twenty cents a day, one dollar and forty cents each week, and a year costs—what is it? My friend Sheftelowitz is the whiz in math."

"Seventy-three dollars," the fishmonger replied. "And that in my opinion is just the start. I heard he's going to put on a box that takes quarters. That would cost hundreds of dollars!"

"Even worse," Pipe resumed, "what if he charges for number one? What then?"

There was what you would call an ugly murmur. Again Printzmettle rose. Even with my rheum I could smell the Nile-brand pomatum he used on his hair. "There is a rumor I heard about a charge just to get into the restaurant, never mind the sanitation area. Just to come in! After that, the sky is the limit. A dollar to hang up your coat. And then—Jews, the handwriting is on the wall: a non-smoking section!"

Like a schoolboy, Julius Dick raised his hand. "Pardon me. I have a question. The other night I sat down to a goulash. A whole bowlful, almost. But the meat parts tasted peculiar. Like a beetroot. Don't misunderstand me. I'm not criticizing. But was this Hungarian style?"

What a flood of exclamations! One on top of the other. It seemed that all the merchants, the musicians, had something to say.

"The same thing happened to me," Murmelstein declared. "Only not with a goulash, with a meatball instead. And it wasn't a beetroot flavor. It was more like a lima."

Tartakower: "Then I'm not the only one! I thought it was because of my Pall Malls. Whatever I eat, a kidney grill, peppercorn tongue, marrow hash: Everything tastes like zucchinis!"

"Wait," said Doctor Dick, who was one of those Jews you sometimes see at the seashore, in shorts, with muscular calves. "I had another experience. Just the other day Mister Ellenbogen brought me a leftover kreplach, which I cut with a fork. What do you think came out of the middle?"

"On occasion," said Salpeter, "it's a liver puree."

"Or a kind of a fricandel."

Dick: "No, no. Not meat. Something white. Something fluffy. Like cotton."

"Oh, ho!" Mosk exclaimed. "A pirogi!"

"That's what I thought, too. But this stuffing was not made from potato. Oh, no!"

"You must mean a Peking dumpling. That's a fritter they eat over there."

"Veal meat is white. It could be a veal, or a chicken, raviol."

Dick, Ph.D., was, in his excitement, cracking the knuckles of his fingers. Like all double-bassists, he could do tricks with his thumb. "Listen! I took a bite of this kreplach. Not veal! Velveeta!"

"Cheese?" asked Beverly Bibelnieks, in a rhetorical manner. "Of course you are making a joke."

Pipe chimed in: "That's not allowed."

Sheftelowitz: "Correct. Forbidden. Absolutely. If my friend Herb Pipe should eat a cheese kreplach on one side of a table and I should eat a tenderloin on the other, we'd have to put a barrier, like a potted plant, between us. That's how strict the law is."

"It's no joke, alas," said Printzmettle. "Something worse happened to me. Last week I ordered a bowl of schav. Mister Mosk brought it to me, the same way Ellenbogen served the kreplach. I could not believe what was before my eyes. Was it a dream? A fata morgana? Soured cream! From a cow! After which this same gentleman brought me my rump roast!"

There was a gasp, a groan. All heads turned toward Mosk, who pulled at the brim of his Baltimore Orioles cap. "It was only a dollop. Don't make a federal case out of it."

"A federal case? It is worse than a federal case!" Salpeter, when he grew excited, would throw back his head and sniff the air with his powerful nose. "The Steinway Restaurant is the home of the Roumanian broiling!"

Not only that," said Pearl Ellenbogen. "It was the second restaurant in America to serve the pitchai slice."

Old Pipe: "And not, like those Allen Street eateries, boiled from the hoof of a dead horse. M. L. Stutchkoff and Madam Stutchkoff, they'd use only calf's feet—and from the front end, too."

"All right! Sue me! We only carry out what he"—the Lithuanian leveled a finger at the Puerto Rican—"cooks in the kitchen."

Instantly, Martinez broke into tears. *¡No es mi responsabilidad! Señor Schwartz, él me dijo: la leche, la crema, la* dairy."

In the midst of this hubbub, Mister Margolies, the eldest among us, rose to his feet. His arm was crooked before him, as if balancing a stack of dishes. "Nineteen nineteen. Nighttime. The gas lamps are hissing. Softly the Quintet plays *Apple Blossom* selections. F. Kreisler. Hit of the season. What's this? A patron's fork, the meat still on it, waves in the air. The apprentice waiter moves forward. Think of rubberized knees, moustache twitches, unbuttoned spats. 'Young man,' the customer says, 'this is the finest type of Roumanian broiling.' The name of that waiter? Mannish F. Margolies. And the patron? Battling Levinsky. Light Heavyweight Champion of the World."

"Oh, oh," said Miss Bibelnieks. "The poor waiters! What they suffer now!"

"Yes! I am guilty! I knowingly brought in the kreplach!"

Margolies: "Not you alone, Ellenbogen. I too have served false cutlets."

"We're all sinners! All!"

"Meat and milk!"

"It's the same as a cheeseburger!"

"Just wait," said the pessimist, Pipe. "Dairy is nothing. Soy? So what? The real evil is coming. I feel it. I don't have to tell you the kind of establishment I mean. *Jewish style!*"

The employees were clutching their heads. Some literally, some in a manner of speaking, beat their breastbones.

The short man with the flat nose stood now and with his smooth nasal voice calmed the storm. "Listen, everybody. No man is a sinner here, and no woman either. No law has been broken. For this simple reason: The owner of the Steinway Restaurant is not a Jew."

It became then so still you could hear the electricity moving through the rods of the fire. Then the people began simultaneously to ask commonsense questions: "What?" "A non-Jew?" "*Señor Schwartz?*" I dared not utter a word, but I had recognized, from the twang of his adenoids, the speaker.

Rabbi Rymer. A Pepi Pechler acquaintance. Again he held up his plump hands and continued his speech.

"Last April, at Passover, the late owner of the Steinway Restaurant approached me with a problem. He wanted, for strictly artistic reasons, to remain open for business during the holiday. To stage his Jewish Art Theater dramas. I advised him to do what other eateries do to avoid Talmudic restrictions. Why buy a new set of dishes? Boil silver? Engage in yeast hunts and roll on the counters wax paper? A pity to close the bar. Better for a few days to sell the place to a goy. The way the whole state of Israel for this same season is sold to an Arab. I made the contract. Ironclad. Leak-tight. Over Pesach the buyer was forbidden to dispose of the property. On the day after Pesach, he must sell back to the previous owner, *and only to the previous owner,* for the original sum, plus five dollars. But who knew that at the second Seder Pechler would steam-heat a bony fish like a shad?"

Tartakower: "You mean Schwartz bought the restaurant and doesn't have to sell it back?"

"Can't. Not even if he wanted," the rabbi responded.

"Schwartz?" said Margolies. "Doesn't sound like a goy."

"A German. A German name."

"Wait a minute. What about the Widow Stutchkoff-Pechler? Wouldn't she inherit everything owed to her husband?"

"An astute observation, Mister Printzmettle, but one which at this very moment Schwartz himself is attempting to render mute."

"Mute, Rabbi Rymer?"

The rabbi—he whistled in the minor key breathing out, and the major key breathing in—did not reply. Instead, he merely pointed upward, and smiled.

Pipe laid his finger to his lips and gave a largely toothless grin.

Murmelstein, second violin, gave what is sometimes

known lewdly as the sign of the fig. Followed by a wink, a leer, a snort, a snicker.

Sheftelowitz now began to hum. Was I suffering a brain infection? Brain fever? For it seemed to me the fish merchant was reproducing the same five notes, *Da-da-da*-dee-*da*, that I had earlier heard played upon the Rudall & Rose. What could this mean? And what had those pointing fingers, those sniggers and smiles, to do with the blond-headed H. Stutchkoff-Pechler?

"Mister Sheftelowitz, Mister Murmelstein," cautioned Ellenbogen, who in these last years had allowed hair bunches to grow from his ears. "Think of the ladies."

The shame-faced silence that followed was interrupted by Salpeter, the first violinist. "Jews! The night is drawing to a close. We must now discuss the topic which from the point of view of we musicians, and all friends of music, is more momentous even than the mixing of meat and milk. As the whole world knows, it has never been the policy of the Steinway Quintet to heed the passing fad or the clamor of the crowd. Thus, at the height of the Souza craze, or when tango rhythms swept the nation, or when patrons called out now for *The Count of Luxembourg*, now for 'Begin the Beguine,' we went on playing the M. I. Blater tune, 'Katyusha'—even though there is hardly a call nowadays for the lively hymn to that Soviet rocket."

"They don't ask for Ignatz Waghalter the way they used to, either."

"Precisely so, Mister Mosk. Nor for *The Swedish Rhapsody* by the great Helsinki modernist, Moses Pergament—yet the works of both men remain in our repertory, along with our regular Meyerbeer concerts and our evenings of Rumshinsky. With the coming of the Schwartz era, however, all is transformed. First came the decree that all requests must be honored, which led at once to a rash of controversial, even provocative selections: the *Bolero* motif of Ravel, the G. Mahler *Das Lied von der Erde* medley, and the 'Toreador Song' by

Monsieur Bizet—this in spite of the fact that of these three composers, one is a half-Jew, another a convert, and the last hardly a Jew at all."

"Well, well," said Doctor Dick. "The creator of *Carmen* is a Jew on the female side, through the Spanish connection."

Tartakower: "Also, he became the son-in-law of J. Halévy, the *La Juive* composer."

"Nonetheless a questionable case," Salpeter insisted. "But no matter. As a concession to the undoubted musicality of each of these figures, it was decided to perform the requested works. Did that put the question to rest? Not at all. If anything, the screw tightened. You will recall how, toward the end of the fall, a number of patrons, perhaps befuddled by wine, perhaps in the sheer spirit of deviltry, began to call for such ditties as 'Shrimp Boats Are a-Comin' ' and 'Chim Chim Cheree.' "

"I don't remember that," said Pearl Ellenbogen.

"Naturally not. Because, while not denying, exactly, such requests, we instead substituted sounder selections: a lighthearted Yip Harburg lyric, for example, or else 'Smoke Gets in Your Eyes.' "

"J. Kern," said Margolies. "Stuffed cabbage. Raisin-sauce carrots. A derma round."

Salpeter went on. "The response of the management has been entirely out of proportion to these slight evasions. We have been expressly forbidden to continue the time-honored practice of opening our Sunday afternoon recitals with the Mexican national anthem."

"*Es lástima,*" Martinez declared. "*Una obra maestra por Señor Henri Herz.*"

"And so things stood until the crisis of last Thursday night, when one of the diners, the one with the nosebleeds, shouted out, 'How about a waltz?' "

Margolies: "Apt. Real estate. A one-half Jew."

Murmelstein: "Right away the Quintet strikes up a tune by E. Waldtufel, the Waltz King."

Tartakower: "But Apt starts shouting, 'I meant something by Strauss!' "

Salpeter: "We halt. Then, without a word among us, we launch into the *Chocolate Soldier*."

" 'That's the wrong one! Not Oscar! The Strauss with two S's!' "

"One by one," Dick recounted, "we come to a halt."

Salpeter, whose remarkable eyes were set no more than a half inch apart, to either side of his beakish nose, threw back his head. "Here is a fact that you will not hear mentioned in old Vienna. The Strauss family, both Johanns, plus J. Strauss and E. Strauss, possessed also a definite Spanish connection. '*Die Fledermaus*, gentlemen,' I called. But no sooner had we begun than Apt was on his feet. '*R*. Strauss! That's the one! You know: *Merry Pranks*! The theme from *2001*!' Thus, Jews, the crisis. R. Strauss! Of all people! Collaborator with the Beast!"

Ladies and gentlemen, allow me to make here a firm interjection. The policy of the Steinway Restaurant is not the policy of L. Goldkorn. I am a lover of Haydn, Mozart, Schubert, Beethoven, Brahms, also H. Wolf, A. Bruckner, K. D. v. Dittersdorf, and all other members—with the exception of course of such Schönberg disciples as P. A. Pisk—of the Vienna School. A human being is first a human being, and a Jew or a Mason second. R. Strauss, however, is another matter. On various occasions, that gentleman would make a guest appearance before the Orchester der Wiener Staatsoper, as would, in the years 1937–1938, L. Furtwängler, the collaborationist from Berlin. "When Herr Strauss or Herr Furtwängler raises his right hand," so went the witticism among we musicians in the pit, "one cannot be sure it is to conduct." It was with interest, then, that I listened to what the first violinist, whose career stretched back to the Ragstadt era, said next.

"As you all know, we defied the rules. We refused to

render the Apt selection. It is my task now to inform the staff and friends of the Steinway Restaurant that earlier this evening we musicians received our employer's response. R. Strauss will not appear in the repertory. Instead we must play the *Der fliegende Holländer* potpourri."

"*¿Der fliegende Holländer?*"

"In English," said Dick, *"The Flying Netherlander."*

"What? Wagner!" Ellenbogen exclaimed.

"The Hitler favorite! Anti-Semite!"

"You dare not play such a request."

Salpeter: "Not request, Rabbi Rymer. Ultimatum. To wit: Until the Wagner gala is given, the works of the composer of *This Is the Army,* 'White Christmas,' and *Call Me Madam* may not appear on the Quintet music stands."

"Oh, boy," said Mosk. "That's Irving Berlin."

There was the briefest pause, merely a half rest. Then:

"He's gone too far!"

"What does he take us for?"

"Next thing they'll try to ban Gershwin. Like in Germany! In Russia!"

"Does that mean no more *Ziegfeld Follies?*"

"What to do?" moaned Pipe. "What to do?"

That was the question. Some Jews had risen, standing with their chairs fallen behind them. Others sat dazed, stunned, like people at a twelve-tone concert. It was the five-footer, Mosk, who took command.

"What to do? What else can we do? Kill him."

The non-employees, a quartet of Jews, looked at each other. "Pardon?" said Pipe. "Repeat, please."

Murmelstein: "He said we have to hire a killer."

"I still don't understand."

Rabbi Rymer: "A *Kehilla.* A congregation. He thinks we should pray."

Printzmettle: "Gladly. I always said, if God wanted non-smoking sections, he would not have created tobacco."

"We're not talking about prayer," Ellenbogen corrected. "We have something else in mind."

Sheftelowitz: "I get it. These are intolerable conditions. The Steinway workers must go on strike. We, your friends, your neighbors, your patrons, will support you!"

The waiters, the musicians only laughed. From Margolies came a derisive snort. "We are not men in our sixties. Not union members, like the Chicken Pullers, the Kosher Butchers. And this is not an evening in spring."

"In other words," said Ellenbogen, who seemed to have earmuffs, almost, coming out of his ears, "the strikers would freeze in such weather. Or else starve without our leftovers and scraps."

"Why keep beating around the bush? Let's get down to business. Everybody shut up." The stylish Lithuanian—note how the saddle shoes on his feet matched his tri-color headgear—motioned for quiet. Then he pointed toward the closed door of the cabinetto, behind which we could hear some person muttering the opening stanza of "Stormy Weather."

Of course I knew those words, and worsteds. So, apparently, did Herbert Pipe, who went as white as his goose-feather down. "H. H. Levine!" he gasped. "The Dutchman's sidekick!"

Sheftelowitz: "He must have escaped from Sing Sing!"

Printzmettle did up the buttons on his Chesterfield coat. "I will be going."

Rabbi Rymer also backed toward the exit. "This is the hour for morning prayers. The Birkhot Hashahar. I must not be late."

Before either man could reach the portal, the cataract boomed and the jug-eared Levine appeared in the privy door.

"Where are you gentlemen going? I've been invited here by the waiters, the musicians, to do a job."

Miss Bibelnieks nudged Ellenbogen with her elbow. "I don't understand. Who is this man? Who is the Dutchman?"

"The Dutchman? You don't know Dutch Schultz?"

"Schultz?" put in the second violinist. "Do you mean Schwartz?"

Tartakower: "No, no. Schultz. His real name was Flegenheimer."

"*¡Ah! ¡Sí! ¡Comprendo! Der fliegende Holländer.*"

Margolies hastened to explain. "Miss Bibelnieks, Mister Murmelstein, you are too young to remember. This is the notorious hooligan, Happy Levine. He put cement boots on Bo Weinberg. He poured the cement while he was still alive. Then into the East River. Once there was a famous shootout on Allen Street. That was when the D.A. put Levine away for life."

At this a smile came to the lips of Levine: Indeed, is it not possible that his so-called nickname was meant to have an ironical twist, in the way that Americans will call a fat man Tiny, or Slim? "Don't worry, his turn is coming. I'll get him yet."

"Listen," Sheftelowitz interrupted. "Why bother us with ancient history? All this is old hat."

"Because you are loyal Steinway patrons. And successful businessmen, too. Who else will pay?"

"Pay?" echoed Printzmettle.

Levine pulled at his cheek, with its prison pallor. "A hit, sixty dollars. Hit and hide, one hundred and fifty."

"A fortune!" Pipe exclaimed.

"Everything included. I provide the car, a Buick seven-seater. The latest model. Synchromesh. No draft ventilation. Also, I bring the piece."

"Piece?" asked Rabbi Rymer. "Piece of what?"

Instead of answering, the former inmate turned his back, retreating into the depths of the private booth, whose door he shut behind him.

"Uh-oh. Roll-mop salad," said Mosk.

Mistaken assumption. The worsteds did not drop about the bluchers; on the contrary, in a strange, eerie fashion, the newly shined boots rose upward, upward, and vanished. A bodiless voice echoed against the tile. "The D.A.! The Assistant District Attorney. Pasty-face! Pipsqueak! He led the Allen Street raid. Like a Haman! With machine guns! With gas! He caught Dutch's boys—Abe Landau, Lulu Rosenkrantz, Abbadabba Berman: but he couldn't catch me! I knew how to get into the sewer. I knew where to crawl under the street. I came up here, in the same room I'm standing in now!" The large head, the powerful shoulders appeared above the locked door and lurched to the left, following the same course, though in mirror image, of my earlier climb.

"It's true," said Ellenbogen. "I remember the news in the papers."

Margolies said, "I was here. The police came. Also the federal agents. They looked everywhere—under the dining room tables, all through the kitchen, even inside the Stutchkoff apartments. Then they checked the Gentlemen's WC."

Here was the rarest of sights: Levine in laughter, showing his mauve-colored gums. "No one there. Hee, hee, hee. No one in the gents'. I was in the ladies'."

"That's a good one," said Pipe.

"Then the door opened. *That* door," said Levine, pointing at the exit. If you looked closely you could see his lantern jaw, high in the air, slightly a-tremble. "The D.A.! All by himself. With his famous soft hat on! His little moustache! Where's the pay telephone? There was a phone in both comfort stations. There, against the wall. He put in a nickel. He started to have a conversation. He didn't see me. He didn't see my John Roscoe. A thirty-eight. I heard a toot. A toot-toot. Dutch himself! In the seven-seater saloon! A perfect getaway car! All I had to do was pull the trigger. Pull it! Impossible to miss! Only ten feet away! But I held my fire. It must have been the fumes. The tear gas. The gas from the sewer. All of a sudden I started to feel different, dizzy. It was like I was outside, not in; in sunshine instead of electrical light. Strangest of all, instead of being a grown man, a big man, looking down on the D.A., I was a little shaver, looking up at my Da!

"Tsk, tsk," went Printzmettle. "Living in the past."

Asked Tartakower, "Mister Mosk, is this the best possible person?"

Levine was by then visible from the waist upward. Using the elbow of one arm to brace himself against the partition top, he reached with a free hand beneath the water-box lid. "What did I do? I surrendered. Gave up. Turned myself in. You'd think the D.A. would be grateful. You'd think he would thank me for holding fire. No! He gave me life! Life! And if he'd found the piece, I'd have gotten the same as Mendy and Louis and Little Farfel Cohen: the chair! But he didn't find it! Not my John Roscoe! He couldn't, because, because—" As he spoke the gunman continued to grope in the iron tank, like a gigantic cat in a fishbowl. "I stashed it here!"

With a flourish, a spray, Levine swept his arm from the plumbing fixture. In his hand was a weapon. The water, as from a child's toy, a gun for squirts, poured from the barrel. But it was no toy. "Fifty years!" he shouted. "After fifty years!"

Eagerly the little crowd pressed forward, to where Levine held the dripping pistol, green with patina, red with rust, aloft. Moss strands hung from it. The Jews stared upward, open-mouthed, as if the old pirate had plucked a buried treasure from the deep.

"Ahhh," they sighed.

Mosk, standing a little apart, spoke the last word. "Now we're cooking with Crisco!"

It was not the first time I had seen peaceable folk thus transformed by bloodlust. During the Great War, for instance, no work composed by a non–German speaker could be performed at the k.k. Hof-Operntheater; even the composer of *Aïda*, who, you will remember, died in the year 1901, had to have his name on the posters altered from Giuseppe to Josef. Now the staff of the Steinway Restaurant, no less crazed, were shouting, "Kill him! Kill him!"

At these shocking words I found myself on my feet and, heedless of the strict prohibition on speech, shouted out, "No! No! This is madness! Can I have heard you, dear friends, correctly? You want to kill a man simply because he changes the Steinway Restaurant from *flayshedig* to *milchedig*? For this you will deprive him of life?"

The staff members turned toward where I, with the chair on my back, like a peddler, was standing. "That," mumbled Murmelstein, "was the waiters' idea."

"Baloney!" It was Mosk who uttered this interjection. "What about the fiddlers? Didn't they want to shoot him because they couldn't play Irving Berlin?"

Salpeter: "I remind the member of the waiting fraternity that he is speaking of the composer of 'God Bless America.' "

Tartakower now began to wind his orange-and-black scarf around his neck, then did up, on his topcoat, the safety pins that served in lieu of buttons. "The gun. It hypnotized me. It cast a spell. Now I am conscious. No longer dreaming. How could we think of such an action? We should be ashamed."

The tide, it seemed, had turned. "It was mass hysteria," Ellenbogen declared.

"Of course, we neighbors, non–staff members, were not involved."

"You hit the nail on the head, Mister Printzmettle," said Pipe. "We tried to talk them out of it."

Sheftelowitz: "Thank heaven we brought them back to their senses."

Thus did the crisis, in which I shall be immodest enough to claim a timely intervention, pass. Everyone, now, was reaching for his hat, his coat, his mittens or gloves. Only H. H. Levine stood unmoved, the rusted revolver dripping in his hand. "You mean," he asked, "we don't make the hit?"

At that instant there came a roaring sound, an ear-splitting screech, a slam, all from the street above us—a commotion that lasted through the clock of the Warsaw Congregation striking, in three-eighths time, 5 A.M. The Jews stood petrified. Fearful thoughts appeared in our heads. "What is it?" asked Rabbi Rymer. "Pogrom?"

The muscular Doctor Dick leaned his instrument against the wall and, such was the strength of his forearms, pulled himself up to the window ledge. "Mack truck," he announced.

"Uh-oh," said Mosk.

"We've been discovered!"

"Trapped!"

"¡Santa María!"

Salpeter held up his hands. "Shhh," he commanded. "Quiet."

In the fearful hush that followed we heard the sound of the Rivington Street door swinging open and the pounding of feet directly over our heads. Rymer, and most of the others, moved their lips in silent prayer. Even the double-bass, leaning against the tiles, resembled a pious Jew at the Wailing Wall.

The suspense lasted only a moment. The footsteps, the boot thuds, soon ceased. The door banged shut. Then the truck engine roared, and the truck itself drove away. Printzmettle, the first to the Ladies' washroom door, led the rush up the staircase. I trailed the rest, owing to the restraint brought on by the chair seat striking the zone of my hams. By the time I completed the difficult climb, the crowd had gathered at the edge of the dining area. I pushed forward, peering over Pipe's shoulder. Together we stared through the dim light at the blank silhouette of some object, icebox-sized, or more like the squat shape of a stove, which sat squarely in the center of the Steinway Quintet concert platform.

"Psst, Martinez," Mosk hissed. "You order that?"

"*¿Una máquina refrigerante? No, no.*"

Beverly Bibelnieks: "It frightens me. I think we should go."

"Agreed," said Printzmettle. "Let's leave before it's too late."

Tartakower, meanwhile, had begun to move toward the bandstand.

"What are you doing? Come back, Mister Tartakower. That is an order!"

But the flute player, his scarf end trailing nearly to the floor, ignored the summons of the first violinist. Slowly he mounted the platform. With caution he approached the dark shape that rested in the midst of the music stands. The two silhouettes—one tall, thin, with a safety pin here and there shining, the other short, stubby, as in the satirical drawings of the figure Jeff, the figure Mutt—stood only inches apart.

"Oh, this is terrible. I can't look," said Madam Ellenbogen, indeed covering her eyes.

How to describe what happened next? It was as if the world, and all the things in it, were suddenly turned upside down: from utter silence to high-volume noises; from near darkness to blinding light; and, in my own opinion, from one human era, the past, to another, the future, where nonhuman forces hold sway. In brief, at Tartakower's touch the object lit up; orange, green, and purple-hued beams poured from it, like searchlights, while a pattern of reds and blues chased each other over a field of blinking, flashing yellows. It was as if a whole crowd had been somehow compressed into a single box, all of them patriotically waving their colorful flags.

"Oh, ah!" cried the old widower. His arm was outstretched, as if bound to the device by an electrical current, and his face, alternately green and purple, with bulging, shining eyes, was frozen in a contorted mask.

"Curiosity," said Mosk, "killed the cat."

Tartakower's mouth hung wide; but if he spoke we could

not hear him, for the machine, or the compact crowd within it, suddenly burst into song—not the Mexican or American national anthems, but the chorus from *Babes in Toyland*.

"Help! Do something! Save him!" Miss Bibelnieks cried.

Doctor Dick jumped to the platform and pulled at our colleague's topcoat tails. Murmelstein, for some reason holding his hat, as if in a windstorm, also mounted the platform, where an invisible orchestra was now playing selections from *Naughty Marietta*. H. H. Levine circled to the back of the animated machine and with one of his freshly shined bluchers gave it a kick. The lights died, the music ceased. All you could hear was the sucking sound of Tartakower's panting, together with the faint percussion of our hearts.

"*The Red Mill*," at length said Murmelstein, squinting into the dimmed device. "*Sweethearts. The Fortune Teller. Mlle. Modiste*—"

"A music machine!" exclaimed Quintet member Salpeter.

"A jukebox!" said the more up-to-date Rabbi Rymer.

Added Murmelstein, "Filled with the works of Victor Herbert!"

A pause. A silence. Then Salpeter quite calmly said, "Where is the pistol? Hand it to me. I shall kill him myself."

"No," Tartakower, of all people, declared. "Let me be the one. Sixty dollars? One hundred and fifty? Very well. I swear to raise the sum."

There came from our midst an ugly sound, what is sometimes called a growl of assent. But before a further word could be spoken, we all heard the sharp, larklike trill of an English-made flute.

"Here he comes!" someone whispered, and the restaurant staff, with the Steinway patrons, made a dash for the shadows behind the bar. The stone steps of the staircase lead not only down, toward the dual comfort stations, but upward, toward the Stutchkoff apartments, where no nonfamily member, not even Ragstadt, or A. Einstein, or Queen

Wilhelmina, had been known to go. Yet the flautist had certainly been there, for he appeared on the stairway, in shadowy profile, holding his flute. This he put to his lips, and, pianissimo, produced the five familiar notes: *Da-da-da-dee-da!*

"What composition is that?" I said, in hushed tones, to my companions.

"It's what he always plays," Margolies replied.

"You know," said Mosk. " 'The Woodpecker Song.' "

As if in response to the tune, a door opened from above and the light from a candle fell onto the steps. My breath flew from my lungs, from my lips, as Hildegard Stutchkoff-Pechler, in a nightgown you could to some degree see through, joined the seducer on the stairs. Her gold curls, like a vault of coins, glittered, glowed.

"You—you—you," we could hear her say. *You* what? We were not to know. The man, he was dressed in a coat with a herringbone pattern, gripped her in his arms. Her white powdery thigh area trembled against his flanneled leg. Then, quick as a sylph, in spite of her full figure, she pulled back, turned, so that one bosom swung against the other, lazily, the way one weary traveler might jostle another when hanging from a strap upon the IND. Then she moved, holding her burning candle, up the stairs. The ravisher remained for a moment in the fall of light. I could make out the view of his face—the dyed black curls of his close-cropped hair, the wisp of a black moustache, dimpled chin, a gap between the two front teeth. I knew him! I could not forget him! The Graduate! The Gauleiter! A member of the Austrian Nazi party!

"H. Maltz," I said aloud.

H. H. Levine knew him as well. He leaned forward, as if he meant to vault the bar top. He trembled, causing the glassware, the crystal, to shake. His eyes narrowed. His lips curled back. Then he said, in a snarl, "Thomas E. Dewey!"

II

TIME: *4:10 AM*
DATE: *1/10*
TEMP: *50 F—10 C*

Have you noticed how, no matter where you happen to be—
the city of Lisbon, perhaps, or the Pomeranian Bay, or even
Nova Scotia—the natives will claim their balmy clime is the
result of the Gulf Stream? Jump in the water! Wear sleeve-
less shirts! Rub into your scalp Wildroot Cream Oil! No sign
of that boon to tourism in the icebound Isle of Manhattan.
True, the temperature, in the opinion of the company Coca-
Cola, has continued to rise. But this is surely an error. My
fingers in the moon rays are a definite blue. How to continue? Soon, like Hans the clever horse, I must grip the pencil point in my teeth. What is that noise? From far off? Far

below? The crack of a hammer upon the head of a nail. Erection, then, of the gallows! Very well. I have lived, since 1901, long enough. Did I think to live to the year 2000? Two thousand and one?

The sound, the *crack-crack-crack* of the hammer, has wakened the sleepers. It is, they know, the crack of doom. How quickly, with its penalty of death, approaches the dreadful dawn. One by one the victims drop their shark-skins, their denims, and respond, upon the potty, to nature's unceasing call. *Rap-rap. Crack-crack.* The horrible hammer continues to fall.

Question: Which will first be depleted, the sheets of tissue, the sands of time? Even now a dark-favored youth, Nike-brand footwear, mauve-colored twill, pulls recklessly upon the dwindling spool. *Young man,* this is how I should like to address him. *Conservation of natural resources, our great redwood and fir-tree forests, is the duty of every citizen.* A useful homily that shall go undelivered—not for fear of a lively riposte, since it is hardly likely that, in 1963, the year of the flute theft, this Harlemite was yet born, but because that very slogan, "Conservation of energy, Mister Goldkorn; let's all chip in!" is what F. Fingerhut tells me when I beg him on knees to send to fourth-floor reaches more currents of warmth.

Fingerhut! He thinks I am unaware that he brings to the former Clara Litwack bon-bon treats. In hopes of inducing that abandon of morals that accompanies a blood-sugar attack. Or worse: to free himself of the burden of a rent-controlled tenant. It is he who releases into the hallways the fierce, fanged canine who lunges at gabardine cuffs. *Boxer rebellion,* ha! ha! A frosted glass in one hand; at the other, a cuticle expert in rayon bathing costume plies her trade. Lazily, with sand cones heaped on his belly, the landlord watches the playful porpoise leap from the blue sea into the blue air, the blue sky. Miami Beach! Practically the center of the Gulf Stream zone.

Mama! Mama! Even in sleep the dusky Negro hears the

painful pounding at the gallows. They say at the moment of death a man sees the whole of his life pass at a quickened pace before him—like the figures in a news Pathé: the funeral parade of His Imperial Majesty, perhaps, or the brave German soldiers who leap from the trenches at the Marne. What then does this doomed darky dream of? The mud huts of his youth? The water horses who sport in the Congo? The shimmy skirts made from grass?

No matter: The Austro-American's thoughts return as well to scenes of childhood, to his own tawny river. Of course the musical steamship, the paddle-wheeler, could only ply the Iglawa during the summer season; in winter, during the freeze, the band was quartered at the former monastery, with the regiment of uhlans. The player of the Swiss fife was a pale, mole-covered Jew, who often, in the downstairs parlor, performed for his favorite, Minkche, lively marches. Or half-marches, since Yakhne, our thin elder sibling—wire glasses, a white scalp showing through hair bristles, as the lost hen's egg will peep through a nest of straw—would burst through the bead-glass curtain and wave, on principle, as an adherent of feminism, her Trabucco-brand cigar: *Seh mal, Liebespaar: hier ist meine Freiheitsfackel!* A torch of freedom, that's what she called the cheroot. That cigar was a product of the local Imperial and Royal Tobacco Monopoly, where the majority of our citizens, German-speakers and others, were employed. In Humpletz, in Budwitz even, you could smell the licorice-scented fumes; or, with a west wind, in the far-off town of Tabor. All the leaves, the tree leaves, along the riverbank, like the river itself, were yellow by the month of June.

Also June: L. Goldkorn, age eight, attempts to smoke his first black-tobacco cigar. A Trabucco D.D., or *Doppeldezimeter,* eight American inches, capable of being lit by phosphorus matches at either the large or small end. This I accomplished with careful precautions: to wit, at night, within the silver-mine shaft, at a level of fifteen meters. After a moment, the entire cavern filled with a fog, a fermented honey-licorice, out of which I, in my Bermuda kneepants, came running, with the crazed loops of a bat. Still puffing, hollow of cheek, I emerged from the cave mouth and wandered blindly until I came to the clearing by the Ferdinand Column. There I sat, with the smoke still pouring from my head, like the thick, black clouds from the funnel of the *Leopold II.*

What was that? *Musik? Musik um Mitternacht?* Was I drunk, as well as dizzy? No. Someone, somewhere, was playing a woodwind in the upper register. No melody. A simple scale. One note. A rest. Another. In the pauses, voices, laughter. I rose—no easy task—to my feet. Strange: There seemed to be two granite columns, celebrating, perhaps, two Ferdinands, two Pledges of 1527. I looked up. A pair of half moons hung in the sky. Trailing dark fumes, I stumbled toward the nearby hedgerow and pushed my pulsing head through the briars. There, in the bower, were Miss M. Goldkorn and Rudi, the naval fifer—that is to say, a quartet of Minkches and Rudis, *Fräulein und Herren,* not one of whom was wearing a stitch of clothes. Sunbathing? Not possible. But could a person, or persons, receive a healthful tanning from a moon, or moons? I took a deep, fume-filled inhalation, and looked again. The musician, or musicians—it seemed to be a case of Siamese twinning—was lying on his back, with his *Schweizerpfeife* to his lips. Minkche, also doubled, had an instrument in her mouth as well. Impossible with certainty to say who at that moment was playing what. Miss, or Misses, Goldkorn, her hair down, her breasts depending in the manner of breadfruit, seemed to blow into what looked like an ivory pan pipe. But the note came from her partner's fife.

"There's a D-sharp!" said Rudi, a diminutive of Rudolph, taking in a sudden breath. "Now let us have an E."

Minkche lowered her head and puffed up her cheeks, as would any novice woodwinder, and blew on her flageolet. The note, full of vibrato, came once more from above.

"*Oh, E-eee!*" exclaimed Rudi, on whose pale body there seemed as many moles as there were bright stars in the sky:

but instead of asking for an F-flat or some other note, he raised his head from its prone position and said, "Do you smell a cigar?"

At that instant precisely a half liter of barley bean soup, *mit Champignon, mit Karotten, mit Kalbsfette*—my dinner, in short—shot with such force from my mouth that in one large arc it cleared the bower and threw me, in a kind of recoil, into the thorn hedge, which held me fast. The duet jumped up and rushed here and there, putting their limbs into the sleeves and sockets of their clothes. A wave of weariness overcame me. *"Das Konzert ist kaputt?"* I asked, unable to stifle a mighty yawn. "No more scales?"

To my amazement the musical partners approached me on their knees. Minkche—her face had many dimples: in her cheeks, by her temples, her throat zone, and at her chin— began to squeeze and kiss and rub my hands. The member of the *k. & k.* naval forces started to whine. He pleaded. "Anything. I give you anything. Tell me what you want. Name any object. What I possess is yours!"

My eyes drooped down. The cheroot end fell extinguished from my fingers. Before sleep overcame me I managed a single article, with noun:

"Der Schweizerpfeife."

I see for the moment the tissue roll is non-occupied. Time now, in my small, neat, Palmer-style hand, to resume. A last word of explanation. That instrument I kept with me, a replacement for my childhood pan pipe, until the day, a half decade later, I passed through the doors of the Akademie für Musik, Philosophie, und darstellende Kunst. Peace, brother. No need to cry out for your mother. Peace, good Afrikaner. What a long journey we have taken, you from your river, I from mine. Only to end together, in a new world, on the banks of the frozen Hudson.

2

That river is named, of course, for H. Hudson, the famed explorer. The *Half-Moon* captain, having been duped by the saltiness of the tide into thinking he had arrived at the passage to the Pacific, sailed upward and upward, to the site of the present city of Albany, capital of the Empire State. Hence, the influence of the sturdy, industrious Dutch: My own home, for instance, is located between the Columbus Avenue and that called Amsterdam. Note, also, the Harlem quarter, and the nearby village of Flushing. On Friday, at dawn, the Columbus speedway was deserted. No vehicles. No person. The world, save for the all-night Shamrock, was sleeping.

There, near the corner, upon 80th Street, the tenement stood. I entered, wearily treading the innumerable stairs. Why this foreboding? The feeling of catastrophe pressing near? Was not all still? There lay the boxer, devotee of Wagner,

smacking together in sleep his loose, black lips. No need for
Tannhäuser improvisations. And was not his owner, Fingerhut, with his cherry-filled bon-bons, flower bouquets, his
midnight kippers, far away? Old salts, however, fear most the
calm sea. Witness H. Hudson, who, for all his fortune, the
great bays and rivers to which he has given his name, was set
by mutinous sailors adrift in a rowboat and never again seen.

"Sweetheart!" I called, stepping across the threshold. "I
have purchased beer nuts!" Yes, and for protein, a beef stick,
also a Shamrock item. For myself, against the effects of catarrh, a half-pint bottle of menthol schnapps. Only the odd
coin remained: for a single telephone call, and one-way fare,
IRT/IND, senior citizen rate. "Greetings, Clara! A jerky to
suck on!" No answer. I paused, sniffing, in spite of lingering
rheum, the air. At once I made out the smell—so reminiscent of the glass-domed monkey house at the Prater—of natural gas. I darted across the foyer to the kitchen arch. The
room was filled with the deadly fumes! The wind, gusting
through the window, must have extinguished the flames. And
the former Clara Litwack? Still breathing, I saw, though slowly:
between one bosom expansion and another, as between following waves on the landlocked Sea of Azov, a whole moment went by. And, like that body of water, her skin was tinted
blue.

Everyone knows what must be done in such cases.
Crossing rapidly to the window, gripping the tightly closed
sash, I prepared to do it. *Tightly closed?* Then the flames could
not have been snuffed by the wind. This called for deliber-
ation. What if, as now seemed likely, Madam Goldkorn had
turned on the gas herself? A purposeful act of volition? Had
I the right to turn it off? I looked at the sleeper once more.
Upon her mouth, lacking dentures—these sat in a nearby half-
glass of water, like a mollusk which waits for floating mor-
sels—there played a smile. Dreaming, darling? Perhaps this
was the happy phantasm that came often to me: a dream of
our daughter, Martha, in a pink dress, with wobbly knees,

dancing, leaping, flying, the little ballerina, even though, had she thrived, she would now be the same age as Miss Bibelnieks, with a bust of her own. Dare I disturb such a vision? Fortunate Clara! To end her life in such bliss!

Just then my spouse opened her mouth and began to speak in her native tongue. *"Frankie! Frankele! Derlang mir ai baba-rhum! Vo bisty, Frank? Kum zurick fun Florida!"*

Where, now, was the he-man matchbook? Tartakower's match? That was the solution: one spark, a single flash, an ember. Then the former family Goldkorn—the stout-armed Clara, the fortyish flautist, and Martha, twinkle-toed—would be reunited, and could begin their life once again. There was no match, alas. Thus while the Admiral TV made a poppyseed pattern, and sounded a disparaging hiss, I threw up the sash, turned to the off position each of the oven handles, and retrieved from the Frigidaire crisper the syringe, whose expensive fluid I injected beneath my sweet wife's vein-filled skin. She gasped, she groaned, and—I saw how her nightcap made her head arrive at a point—woke at once.

"What's this?" she asked.

"Slim Jim," I replied, placing the delicacy into her hand.

"It has been previously chewed, Mister Goldkorn."

Already by the bedroom door, I turned. "Only, my dear, to make it softer for you."

One minute later I lay flat on the spring box of the fourposter, with my eyes closed, my hands on my chest, in a simulation of sleep. But sleep would not come. First the events of the evening were forced to march once again through my brain; then my lips began to form and reform the cryptic code, Stuyvesant 9-2974. The Bell telephone number of the Steinway Restaurant. Woe unto L. Goldkorn should he forget it. The entire plan rested upon placing that call within seconds after observing the so-called Schwartz pass through the eatery door. The instant he picked up the receiver I was to wave from the door of the Rivington telephone kiosk a white handkerchief, which would in turn cause Rabbi Rymer, parked at the curbstone, to turn on the lights of the Buick seven-seater, and sound its mellow horn. *Hello! Hello!* I would say. *Hello!* the former H. Maltz would undoubtedly answer. Then what? I must engage in innocent conversation, light badinage, until H. H. Levine, in the beams of those headlamps, shot him dead with his Roscoe-brand gun. *"Well, Mister Schwartz! And what are we doing in America? Hans across the sea? Ha! Ha! A little jest."*

One question above all others must be on your lips, friends, as earlier that evening it had been upon mine. What about the Widow Stutchkoff-Pechler? How to prevent her from responding to what was after all the ring of her own telephone? She would then be in danger! In the line of fire! "Ah," Mosk had said. "That's the beauty part!" Let me briefly describe that portion of the ingenious plan. This was now Friday morn. It was our employer's custom upon Sabbath evenings, when of course the Steinway Restaurant was not open for business, to steam himself at the Beaux Arts Baths, formerly the Stamboul Geyser, after which he would stroll through the street to his assignation.

"Arrival," Salpeter had confirmed, "at half past seven." At precisely seven P.M., then, by the bells of the Warsaw Congregation, Tartakower would appear at the Rivington Street door and warble a simulation on his own instrument of the five notes in the key of G major. D. G. B. D. B. In short, the W. Woodpecker Song. When the cash-register expert opened the door, the three strongest among us—beneath our masks, young Murmelstein, Mister Martinez, and of course Doctor Julius Dick—would seize her and quite gently but firmly lead her from harm's way.

Who is this? Who is speaking? What do you mean, doing in America? Here, clearly, was the weak link in the plan. How was I to hold him? Pique his fancy? Or, as mechanically minded Americans say, rivet him at the spot? Everybody, it is true, likes to talk about the weather.

What a cold winter. Not like those warm mists that rise from the Danube. Of course, sometimes we receive a sudden snowstorm. Right from a clear sky. Do you remember March? March 1938? Immediately after the Anschluss? Snow on the Ringstrasse. Snow on the horses of the State Opera Theater. And inside, a smell like manure! What were your words, Mister? "Ladies and gentlemen: I believe we have a non-Aryan here." Hello, hello! Stuyvesant 9-2974? 9-2974, 9-29— . . .

At last the curtain of sleep descended, while that of dreams—brightly painted, like the Asbestos at the Opera, with scenes of Hades, of Hell—slowly rose. Spread before me was the *Die Zauberflöte* panorama, Act One finale, a grove with three temples—Tempel der Weisheit, Tempel der Vernunft, Tempel der Natur. How beautiful the green willows! The singing larks! The call of the lambkins! Rainbows sparkled in the fountain spray. In the midst of all this stood a tenor, playing upon a flute. A deer, a bear, a lion, little scampering squirrels: All poked forward their heads, summoned—look, *eine Schlange, eine Pythonschlange!*—by the music of Mozart. Dream tricks? Not in the least. Everything, from the windup rabbits to the rubberized neck of *die Giraffe,* were well within the technical means of the k.k. Hof-Operntheater, though this particular performance was in fact staged two full decades after that day in November 1918 when the k.k., the Hof, and the Double-Headed Eagle all disappeared, together with His Apostolischen Majestät himself, from the new Republic.

The tenor, Tamino, laid down his flute; at the same instant, within the pit, H. Maltz removed a similar instrument from his moustachioed lips. Yes, the poor sport, the Akademie runner-up. And the prize winner? Graduate Goldkorn? He took up a box, a sort of glockenspiel, filled with little bells. Time to play the Papageno dance:

> *Das klinget so herrlich,*
> *das klinget so schön!*
> *Tra-la, la-la-la, tra-la-la-la-la!*

In America we say, for general factotum, an all-trades Jack. My role at the State Opera was the same as it had been at the Imperial and Royal: to play just those instruments—the title woodwind in *Schwanda der Dudelsackpfeifer,* for instance, or a type of mideastern ram's horn in *Der Barbier von Bagdad*—that no one else was trained to perform.

With a hard-rubber mallet, I thus struck the chimes. On the stage, however, the bird-man, befeathered Papageno, let his mock instrument droop. Black Monostatos, the Moor, with a gang of slaves, was supposed to be driven into a dance by the power and sweetness of my bells—just as, in the J. Weinberger opera, the wail of Schwanda's bagpipe sends even the devil into a jig. But what was this? *Was ist Das?* The whole crew stood about with hands on hips. Had I missed my cue? I played the first measure again. The chimes rang out, faded away. I looked toward the string section, upon whom the composer specifically calls for a pizzicato, to accompany the Papageno-Goldkorn tune. The violinists, the viola players sat with their instruments on their laps, their horsehair bows on their knees. Sweat drops now formed on the skin of my late thirtyish scalp. This was not one of those dreams in which the dreamer attempts to flee but is unable to move, play his instrument but no note comes out. No. In this real-life adventure, only I seemed to be living, breathing, making the music, while the rest of the world was turned to stone.

A third time I struck the box of bells. Even the animals, the beavers, the bullfrogs, and the rest of the forest folk stared toward my pit position with their hard, unblinking eyes. On the podium, the fiendish Furtwängler remained with his arms folded, hands trapped in his armpits, sucking with his powerful muscles at his hollowed cheeks. Above me, behind me, like wind through a wheatfield, I heard whispers and the rustle of programs. It was at this moment that my classmate, the runner-up flautist, rose from his desk in the woodwinds.

"*Damen und Herren:* I believe we have a non-Aryan here."

During the terrible silence that followed, I had time for

two separate thoughts: first, how smart Hans Maltz looked, with his pomaded hair, his waxed moustache, his pressed brown uniform with armband in red and black; second, what did he mean, non-Aryan? To whom was he referring? Then I noticed that the broad-shouldered triangle player and the elderly, bent-backed kettledrummer, together with the rest of the percussion section, had shrunk back from the glockenspiel player, leaving him entirely alone.

From far off, kilometers distant, it seemed, a voice floated down from the standees: "Where is he? Which one?"

Closer by, from the private boxes: "I thought we'd given those types real work to do—scrubbing the pavements, the streets!"

Still nearer, an aisle seat in the orchestra section: "Have we not disinfected the Staatsoper of lice?"

Here Herr Maltz, already a sub-Gauleiter, an old party member, raised his hands for silence.

"The issue is, are we to allow a work that draws from the deep wells of our popular drama, from the myths of our people, the race fantasies, the fairy tales of the Germanic folk, to be performed by—let us not mince our words—a Jew?"

For the answer to that question, my pit colleagues, the members of the Orchester der Wiener Staatsoper, turned toward the back of the theater; so, too, did Herr Furtwängler and the men and women in the orchestra section—all lifted their gaze upward and back, to the flag-draped box, first tier center, where in the fall of 1916 I often saw the Emperor Franz Josef, seated next to my beauty-marked sibling. Now, looming from the shadows, the plumpish, whisker-free face of Field Marshal Göring nodded and grinned. Slowly, slowly, he raised a single finger, and the next thing you knew, from out of the semidarkness, a round object flew through the air, trailing a plume of smoke. The band of indolent slaves scattered right and left, to either side of the affair that, sputtering, spinning, emitting a yellow smoke cloud, had landed in their midst.

"Ein Stinkbombe!" the kettledrummer declared.

What a smell! Like the odor of one of our white-striped forest *Skunken*. A cry went up from the ladies as, from the left loges, from the right, two more of these devices came hurtling down among the grove of temples and trees.

Panic, then. A rush toward the crowd-filled exits. The fire curtain descending partway, and halting. Female music lovers swooning across the backs of their chairs. A moment, in short, of the most extreme danger. What would happen next? I strained forward, squinting through the sulfurous clouds, to see. There was L. Goldkorn, our central figure, his head shining and damp. He had with him—a nice, realistic touch—his Rudall & Rose–model flute. What then? He stood on his cane-bottomed seat and pursed, in the manner of a man about to kiss a woman, his lips. Thus there went through the riotous air the tones of a W. A. Mozart melody: the song that Tamino plays to quench the flames in the cave of fire, to calm the waters in the cave of the flood:

> *Wir wandeln durch des Tones Macht,*
> *Froh durch des Todes düstre Nacht!*

At this golden or, more precisely, silvery sound, the smoke cleared from the stage, as if blown by a giant, invisible fan. The audience of my countrymen and countrywomen remained motionless, stunned. All about me, on the stage, in the orchestra pit, colleagues stood with beams of light and joy upon their faces. Far off, in the flag-draped box, the face of the field marshal suddenly paled. Was it too much to hope that the power of music, yes, *des Tones Macht,* might not strike also into the heart of the Reich representative, so that we Austrians and Germans, Masons and non-Masons, Gentiles and Jews, might live together in friendship, in harmony?

> *Nur der Freundschaft Harmonie*
> *Mildert die Beschwerden;*
> *Ohne diese Sympathie*
> *Ist kein Glück auf Erden!*

I played with my magic flute the notes that accompanied this call for peace on earth. Behind me, the forest folk, the fur-covered and scale-covered creatures, crept forward. Before me, a field of dewdrops, a meadow of diamonds, sparkled in a thousand pairs of eyes. And the Reichsmarschall? Yes! He, too, was weeping! Even he! "My friends!" I called, spreading wide my shortish arms. "Let us learn from the example of these simple beasts, the larks, the milch cows, who do no harm to each other, who are not separated by language, by religion, and who from the beginning of time have communicated with every other member of their species, across all national boundaries, like speakers in the L. L. Zammenhof system. Forward! Together! To the Temple of Wisdom! The Temple of Reason! The Temple of Nature!"

Before this plea had died on my lips, the tears began to roll from my eyes, over my cheeks, onto the four-poster bed. What beauty about me! How splendidly I had played! What a wonderful thing to be living! Then, even as, from the tension of the coiled-up box springs, my body shook and trembled, I recalled a series of sharp, angry cries:

"There he is! And he's not even wearing a star!"

"We'll show him!"

"After him! Seize him!"

The triangle expert—odd to find such a big man master such a small instrument—gripped L. Goldkorn beneath the armpits and lifted him over the front edge of the pit, into the orchestra section. Bowed, bewildered, this bald Austrian citizen was forced to walk up the central aisle, as though through a gauntlet, while the people of Vienna, lovers of sausage, lovers of sweets, either screamed painful insults or turned their backs. At the main entrance an usher, also in brown, propelled me with a single kick to the swallowtail zone through the great arches, into the Ringstrasse, and onto a bank of sudden spring snow.

All dreams, said S. Freud, fellow Viennese, are the fulfillment of a childhood wish. True! Too true! Only a child, an infant, an ignoramus could think men might live as brothers. In harmony. In friendship. It was from no dream, then, that I finally woke to find—where was the light? The daylight? Had I slept from dawn to dusk?—that I was late for my fatal, fateful appointment.

3

Late, indeed! Before I, with my Gladstone, had climbed the last step of the Delancey Street IND, I heard, drifting upon the ether, the strains of the "Tritsch-Tratsch Polka." Seven o'clock, then! Seven P.M.! I reached Rivington Street and turned leftward just as the last of these chords faded away. There, huddled before the First Warsaw Congregation, were—let us, following the example of our intended victim, not mince words—the assassins. Stamping their boots. Giving self bear hugs. Jetting cold breath from their mouths. But why was Tartakower, in his rainwear, his lengthy P.U. scarf, among them? He ought at that moment to be standing with his woodwind at the Steinway Restaurant door. Why, for that matter, was Murmelstein unmasked? Ditto Martinez and Julius Dick? That trio also belonged on the far side of the street, so as to be ready to seize the widow.

"Snafu," said Mosk, who had emerged as the leading force within the waiters' contingent.

Ellenbogen supplied the details. "It's Tartakower. He doesn't have his flute."

"What? No flute! How could this be?"

"I sold it!" the Powell-model player exclaimed. "I had to. To raise the money. It was the only way."

At the back, H. H. Levine loomed over the others. "One hundred and fifty dollars. For that money I dispose of the corpse. The same as Bo Weinberg. Cement boots included. They're still searching for him. Even Hoover can't find him. Not the head of the Bureau of Investigation."

Inside of my lumberman's plaid I broke into a sweat. "But what about Madam Stutchkoff?"

The giant Jew rubbed with one hand his blue-colored jaw. In the other I saw his trusted, rusted, pistol. If I had enjoyed the possession of head hair, it would at his next words have stood upright in horror, or turned white from shock: "Okay. You drive a hard bargain. We dispose of her body with the D.A.'s."

Salpeter leaned forward. In the dim light his eyes drew even closer together, like a cyclop's single orb. "What else can we do, Mister, ah—"

"Goldkorns. Señor Goldkorns—"

"We can't break down the door."

"Wait!" I cried, through a throat, an entire esophagus, suddenly cracking and dry. "I know where a flute is! A wonderful flute! At the Beaux Arts Baths!"

Then I whirled round, running off at a trot. Behind my back I heard a remark, in the Lithuanian's lisp:

"The Beaux Arts Baths? Oh, boy. That place is full of fruits."

Many men, starting, as Professor Pergam once taught us, with the Greeks, the Hindoos of old, believe that their souls return to earth and that they live their lives—perhaps in the form of a dustbin custodian or water carrier, or even a grasshopper or cow—again and again. On one occasion, our plumpish professor delivered a lecture upon the theory of F. W. Nietzsche, the non-Wagnerian, who had himself died only fifteen brief years before: "The number of molecules that make up matter, ceaselessly shuffling, combining, recombining, is finite; but time is infinite. Ergo, every physical body, including, dear children, your own, will be reformed, and each moment of our lives must be repeated forever."

"But this is *Eine ausgezeichnete Idee!*" exclaimed none other than the black-haired Hans. How his eyes, full of philosophy, were shining. "This cannot be refuted!"

These memories passed through my mind as, Gladstone in hand, I moved hurriedly toward the very bathhouse where, a new citizen, I had been employed some forty years before. The building was located on a street named—was this the explanation for Mister Mosk's cryptic statement?—Orchard, and looked from the outside just as it had when it was known to Jews and others as the Stamboul Geyser: There, in the lamplight, were the green-tiled arches; the painted, glazed windows; the pattern, in brickwork, of curved crescents and swords. The familiar steam wisp rose from the dome top, hanging in the night sky like a towel about the loins of a black-skinned bather. My knees, as I stood gazing at the facade, the ersatz Islamic, began to tremble, to ache—less from fear at meeting again my old tormentor as from a shiver of awe, an organic reliving in the Nietzschean manner of the days, June 1945–March 1947, when the international flautist was required to sit cross-legged at the pool of the Geyser, with a conical hat on, and baggy trousers, playing over and over upon the Rudall & Rose such tunes as the "Salaam Aleikum" chorus from *Der Barbier von Bagdad* or selections from *Scheherazade*.

Experience had shown that for wind players the Turkish-type bath is superior to either the Finnish or Russian. So it was that on a fine cloud-free morning, spring 1947, a visitor to the Stamboul might have seen the NBC woodwinds at the very top of the spiral, thereby drawing the hottest vapors into their high-capacity lungs. Below them, at various levels of the snail-shell structure, lounged or lay other musicians; while at the bottom, in the blue pool waters, paddled the Maestro himself, only a playful splash away from where the thick-lipped Persian, the pasha, his knee joints aching, was playing *Die Ägyptische Helena*. Of course I recognized the four-time Staatsoper guest conductor: Milan Scala, 1929; New York

Philharmonic, 1930; Dollfuss memorial, 1934; and, in 1936, *Fidelio,* with L. Lehmann in the leading part. The question was, would the Maestro remember the Magyar? Wearing, as it happened, a Shriner-type fez? Before the answer could be determined, a cry echoed downward from the upper reaches.

"Help! Help! It's Wormes! He's having a steam fit! Heatstroke! He swallowed his tongue!"

This was not, at the Stamboul Geyser, an unusual event, owing to the fact the temperature under the dome top exceeded Fahrenheit one hundred and twenty. S. Philo, the famed masseur, assured the assembled instrumentalists that their colleague, who had been quickly brought down to the cooling geyser, would be himself again within twenty-four hours.

"*Ventiquattro ore! Non è possibile! Non è possibile! Enrico! Enrico Wormes!* Waked-up! Waked-up!"

So saying, the Maestro, himself still waist-high in the water, began to slap the floating face of his number one woodwind. The other musicians, male members only, wrung their hands.

"What will we do?"

"We're due in Studio A in an hour!"

"How can we record without Henry? He has a solo!"

"We'll never find another flautist in time!"

Between a life rich in rewards, and one filled with bitter gall, lie just such moments, which a man either neglects or boldly seizes. At once I jumped to my feet and faced the pink-chested conductor, whose wet locks clung to his noble brow. "Maestro," I said, clicking the soft heels of my curly-toed, jester-type shoes. "Here is L. Goldkorn. Flute graduate, Akademie für Musik, Philosophie, und darstellende Kunst; auxilliary instrumentalist by appointment of the Emperor, the k.k. Hof-Operntheater Orchester 1916–1918; and 1919–1938, Orchester der Wiener Staatsoper. From nineteen forty-three, a citizen of America. Home delivery subscriber, New York *Herald Tribune.*"

A. Toscanini looked up from where Wormes was thrashing in the bubbles of the Geyser. "*Sì? È vero? Un musicista? Flauto? Bravo! Signor Goldkorns, un disco grammofonico!*"

Which is how, ladies, gentlemen, L. Goldkorn became, for the space of a single afternoon, a member of the National Broadcasting Company Orchestra. Single afternoon? Only in the most crude, most literal sense. Our transcription, "Beloved Opera Bouffe Overtures," upon which, as you know, I perform in *The Secret of Susanna* a solo cadenza, will last for all afternoons to come.

"*Imbecille! Cretino! Assassino!*" the Maestro cried, breaking his baton stick over his knee, chewing one piece in his powerful molars, and throwing the other at my unhatted, hairless head. How different this great musician in rehearsal, when making reproducible disks, from the conductor at Salzburg, at Vienna.

"*Madre di Dio! È suono come un gatto! Un gatto in calore!*" With these words, the Maestro took off his wrist chronometer and stamped upon it so forcefully that the springs flew out. Then he took a second timepiece and, with both feet, repeated his leap. What a fit, a frenzy, came next! He tore open his jacket, ripped apart his shirtfront, and raked with his nails his bare breast. A foam, like a toilet lather, appeared at his mouth. His blue eyes fixed full upon me. For what seemed the hundredth time I picked up my Rudall & Rose. The cadenza. The solo. What was this? No cries? No curses? No airborne missiles? The light witty trills, the arpeggios, flew upward toward the microphone cluster, and then all was still. We had, with our struggle, come through! The Maestro stood, with his index finger pointing straight at the side of his temple, as if to say, *At last I have found a man who has reproduced what I hear in here!*

Friends, there remains some hope you may attend these sounds yourself, at an afternoon or early evening concert, WQXR. The actual recording was such a timely success that it is now almost impossible to find, even in the rare-disk bins. To spare you that trouble I will share with you now Susanna's secret. She, like Yakhne, was a smoker. Cigars! Cigarettes! Cigarillos! Imagine the stage filled with smoke! *Opera Bouffe!* My poor, dear sister! Possibly it was nicotine that caused her hair to fall out. Revenge at last! The time had come to plunge though the Moorish-style doors and hunt down the man who had killed her.

At first the interior of the baths seemed as little altered as the brick facade. One passed through the turnstile, where the fee was collected upon departure. The dressing area still began at the right, and curved around the outside of the building in one, unbroken chamber, until one reached the quarters, open on alternate weekdays, of the opposite sex. Here was a change, indeed: I moved through the tunnel, encountering various gentlemen in their pastel briefs, and came clear round to the entrance foyer. An all-male establishment, then. No ladies allowed. My plan—in truth, it was nothing more than an impulse, a vague intention—had been to walk through the dressing area, in the hope that Schwartz, so-called, had left his instrument on the open shelves with his clothes. But what met my eye? A second innovation. Row upon row of stainless steel cabinets, each with its stout iron lock. Nothing to do but strip off my clothing, my outsized gabardines, and with toe thongs and towel pass through the glass-windowed portal, into the steam bath itself.

What had Pergam—how smartly he would tweak our ears at an incorrect answer, how lovingly, at a proper response, pat our buttock and hip zones—remarked? That the molecules of matter combine, recombine? Perhaps that might account for the many transformations taking place about me: the Steinway Restaurant, origin 1901, changing from meat to milk, from Halévy to Herbert; and the old Stamboul Geyser, turn-of-the-century too, which had undergone a metamorphosis from a Turkish to a Finnish-type bath. How else to interpret the sights, the sounds I encountered beneath the great dome? From hidden, heated stones, clouds of vapor rose through the air, so thick, so heavy with water droplets, that the topmost ranks of the spiral were completely obscured. Through that high haze, however, the voices of the sauna-ists rang out in strong ejaculations: *Oh!* they cried, or *Ah!*, as the sharp birch twigs fell upon their shoulders, upon their backs. Closer to hand, at poolside, naked men had paired off in a game of leap-the-frog, with one partner on all fours and the other standing behind him; while in the geyser itself, and upon the various spiral ramps, groups of health enthusiasts were performing en masse their physical jerks. Off to one side, on the floor tiles, a tanned, wrinkled fellow, wearing only an earring in the lobe of his ear, was giving a client an oil massage. Suddenly an involuntary exclamation rose to my lips.

"Mister Philo! Is that you?"

The old masseur looked around: What a shock to see the red paint on his cheeks, his lips. From his eyes the black cosmetic shadow came dripping. He grinned. "I know that sweet face. I know it from somewhere. Haven't you been here before? In bloomers, am I correct? With Persian sandals?"

"No, no," I stammered, backing toward the vacuum-sealed doorway. "First visit. Newcomer. Perhaps you can tell me: Where are the fruits?"

"Yoo, hoo!"

"Hello, there!"

"This way!"

From all directions warm, welcoming voices cried out, beckoning in a friendly manner. The massage recipient raised his head. For some reason his eye was winking. He said, "I admire your boxer shorts."

"Ha! Ha!" I laughed, while placing my Gladstone before the western motif: red stallions, Texas-type steers, daring buckaroos. "From the now-defunct Klein's."

Now Philo himself approached me and, in the French manner, put his lips to my ear. Then he whispered a request that created in me—as it would in any of the long list of Mosaic musicians, from pious Alcorn to E. Zimbalist—a state of the most profound shock. For a moment everything before me went blank, without color or form. It was as if the steam, the vapors, arose not from the hidden stones but from the boiling blood passing over the hot, feverish rock of my brain. Then, beyond this realm, seemingly in another world, an object in motion caught my eye. A fedora! I rushed to the door. On the far side of the glass porthole a lone figure, fully dressed, was walking through the dressing chamber. Flannel trousers. Herringbone topcoat. And in his hand, like a rod of light, a scroll of silver, the Rudall & Rose. Schwartz! The seducer!

In two seconds I had pushed through the sealed exit and was after my quarry. "Stop! Stop!" I cried, slapping down the tunnel upon my thongs. "Stop!"

To my amazement, the foe, halting only five yards within the turnstile, obeyed my command. Now what? I approached, panting. I did not think. I did not plan. It was as if some other, more cunning person spoke from within my heaving chest.

"Shine, mister?"

Within one quarter hour, still in sauna attire, I found myself again upon Rivington Street, surrounded by Steinway Restaurant co-workers and patrons. There, I drew apart the Gladstone's double hinges and revealed, nestled within its cushioned depths—Found! Found! The silver needle in the fabled haystack!—an instrument of London manufacture.

"A flute!" exclaimed Miss Bibelnieks, clapping together both her gloved hands.

Murmelstein, the still-promising second violin: "How did you do it?"

An excellent question. Even at this moment, in the relative calm of my prison aerie, I can feel a liver sensation at the memory of that tension-filled scene. "Shoeshine?" echoed the dapper Don Juan, in well-mannered tones, like those of the old BBC wireless broadcasts. Hardly an Austrian accent at all. Then he sat on a wooden bench, the Rudall & Rose across his kneecaps, and extended his wingtip shoes. "Very well. I have a moment."

I approached, crouching, kneeling, and at once lowered my head to within inches of the expensive footwear, lest in spite of the passage of years, the hairlessness of my cranium, I be recognized. Carefully I spread my pastes, my brushes and rags. Then I ventured to speak—in a low register, a mumble, so as to cover my Bohemian-Moravian twang.

"What cold weather! Is that not so, mister? Unlike the mists of Vienna."

"I cannot say, really. It has been a good many years since I was last in that city."

A battle of wits, then. Cat and mouse. Round and round went my soft cotton cloth, spreading the Kiwi-tint upon the cinnamon-colored leather. "Tell me, mister: What is your opinion of the Jewish Question?"

Was it my imagination? Did this number nine size make a nervous jump? I risked a glance upward, at the foreshortened chin, the neatly trimmed moustache, the saucerlike fedora brim. Were those beads of perspiration upon his brow? "What man does not regret the fate that has befallen that people? The most painful part, if I am not mistaken, is that the tragedy might have been avoided. Why did the leaders of that doomed tribe not urge them to depart for Palestine? Or for the Isle of Madagascar? What a paradise they could have had there! With cocoa trees. And pepper plants. Like a botanical garden!"

Now it was my turn to quiver. My whole throat, as if fingers had closed upon it, grew taut. No words would come out. Not one! But other words, old words, echoed, re-echoed. April 1938. The Türkenshanzplatz, the very block of the Akademie. On my knees I polished the curbstone, the sidewalk, even the rails of the electrified trams. Using the same toothbrush with which that morning I had cleaned my teeth! What a good joke for my fellow Viennese. They looked down on the bent backs, the black coats of the laboring Jews: "Like a pack of armadillos," said one. In my own tongue, *das Armadill.*

Another: "What a snout on that one! An anteater!" *Ein Ameisenfresser.*

"They should put them all in a zoological garden!"

"With all the other bent-noses!"

"A forest of elks!"

The last speaker wore a pair of black cavalry-type boots. I had already recognized his voice: Maltz, the sub-Gauleiter. Now in charge of all musical matters. Slowly I rose. I drew near him. Forbidden for Jews to say *Heil, Hitler!* "Hans," I said, instead. "There are five of us. My sisters. My parents. Myself. Give us an exit permit. For Paris. For Hungary. For Prague. In return, I am prepared—that is, I am willing—I will give you, part with—"

"What?" said the gentleman in the Beaux Arts Baths. "I cannot make out what you said."

I dared not look up. I forced the words through my lips. "You are mistaken, mister. Misinformed. Not all Jews refused to leave Vienna."

The customer's voice floated down, as if from a lofty height. "Undoubtedly you know more on this subject than I."

"Not to the desert, to Palestine; not to an exotic isle. Only to the east or west border. To Czechoslovakia. To Switzerland."

"I stand corrected. Please, no more polish. I must now be on my way."

"Even after the Anschluss, the spring of nineteen thirty-eight, Jews kept escaping. Everyone knows the case of the nerve doctor, S. Freud. But even less famous folk, the small fried potatoes, as Americans say, the mere members of the chorus, or other musicians, musical figures of every sort, could in certain circumstances, for a certain sum, arrange for departure."

Here the former little Hans—with every passing moment I grew more certain that this Dewey double was in fact he—planted both feet, preparing to stand. I lifted the mechanical buffer, as if to say, Only a moment more! Soon done!, and hurried on with my speech.

"Perhaps you have heard of the ship *Kalliope?* Not a ship. That is an exaggeration. What is the word? Dinghy? Skiff? No! No! Barge! You know, mister. The self-propelled vessels which ply the Danube, filled with black mountains of coal."

Ha! Now I had him! Like the King in the drama of Hamlet, Schlegel translation, his conscience stood revealed by this scene from the past. And not only his conscience. What of my own? I hardly noticed the dollar bill my client thrust toward me, or the way his feet, guilty things, squirmed beneath my twin rotors. It was the craft itself, listing, rusted, filled not with coal but with people, which hove up before me, out of the mist, out of the night. "Excellent name. Kalliope! Mother of Orpheus. Expert on all instruments. Oft pictured with wind trumpet in hand. Remember, mister, the lecture of Professor Pergam? *Über die Musen.* On what better vehicle might these musical passengers—woodwinders, string players, music critics, historians of music—drift down the Danube? In darkness. In night. Only forty-five kilometers to the Czech border. As flies the crow. Only seventy by the meandering river. And why stop at Pressburg? The weather is fine. It is springtime. Why not sail on to Komärno? To Eszterhom? To Budapest?"

Such, indeed, was the plan of the family Goldkorn, which had packed many cucumbers and tins of liver pâté. We stood together at the stern: mother and father; Minkche, her beauty mark pasted for this occasion on the middle of her forehead, like a jewel in the Buddha's brow; the semi-bald Yakhne, in gentleman's trousers, puffing upon her Trabucco cheroot. Behind us, all around us, the anxious faces of Viennese musicians, somewhat Jewish, each of whom had made an arrangement similar to my own with the sub-Gauleiter. That Akademie graduate stood just below, upon the floating dock. We watched as he turned his back, raising his arms in the air. At once a small Gentile orchestra piped up, upon the unfamiliar instruments that had belonged to the departing Jews. It was the waltz, "Der Blaue Donau."

At that signal, the sailors on the quay began to cast off woven ropes. From the small cabin a whistle sounded. The little wavelets sent up a spray. Then the Strauss melody ended, and H. Maltz turned once again, his hand raised toward the barge. Wordlessly, I leaned over the railing and extended, head section foremost, my Rudall & Rose. At that precise moment a wind gust—for how else may we explain the strange thing that happened?—blew over the exposed embouchure, and the flute, with no human playing upon it, uttered a low, heart-rending moan. Aghast, I loosed my grip: The silver tube flew end over end into the Danube.

Do we not have the saying "Quick as J. Robinson"? And by invoking the name of the Negro-American sportsman, do we not mean to express lightning speed? That, friends, was the velocity with which I vaulted the rusted gunwale, threw myself upon the pontoon-style jetty, and plunged my arm into the frothy deep. Herr H. Maltz, however, was even quicker. Dripping, streaming, he leaped upward from his prone position with the flute in his grip. He grinned—see how the triumphant plumber finds the leaky pipe—his gap-toothed smile. I turned and saw—oh, horror! The *Kalliope* had moved from dockside and was slipping into the central channel.

"Leib! Liebchen! *Leibchen!*" The words floated above the dark, the black, the never-blue Danube. A mother's cry!

"Stop! Attention, captain! Man overboard!" My own call was lost in the sudden eruption of the engine, the thrashing of the propeller blades against the waves. Off on their journey! To safety! To gay Budapest! And I, fluteless, familyless, left behind.

Dear American friends: You will surely shake with disbelief your heads when I tell you, as now I must, that, painful as that moment was, the one which followed was worse by far. It took no more than a few ticks of the clock for me to realize that the barge was not flowing eastward with the current but instead, with huffing and puffing, was forcing its way upstream against it. Westward! *Mein Gott!* Toward the Third German Reich!

I gripped by his shirtfront the man in charge: "Hans! Hans! Gauleiter Maltz! What is happening? That is not the way to Hungary! What does this mean? Where are they going?"

My old classmate replied as he once had to our long-ago geography quiz: "The Donau joins with the Isar. The Isar becomes the Amper. The Amper flows through Dachau, a pleasant town. Here the passengers will receive special treatment."

Suddenly, all was clear. My flute, in its leap from my hands, had saved me. But the others, the boatful of Jewish musical figures, the family Goldkorn—was that they, huddled in the vanishing stern? I could see a shine of spectacles, my father's; my mother's handkerchief; and the tiny spark, so much smaller than the fireworks that shot from the smokestack, of my sister's cigar: All these were sailing westward, into the open jaws of the Beast!

"You have tricked them! Betrayed them! You have sent them to their deaths!"

"Why are you shouting? This steam bath is a public area. What are you talking about?"

"You know! You remember! Don't pretend you don't understand."

My antagonist got to his feet. His true colors showed now. "Don't talk to me about Jews. I have enough trouble with that crowd already. A fuss over cream in coffee. In my own restaurant. The musicians won't play *The Grand Canyon Suite* or anything by Cole Porter. Stiff-necked people! But you'll see! I'll show them yet!"

I, too, jumped up, to confront the man face to face. "This was not our bargain! I want my flute back! Give me my prize!" Without further ado I plucked the silver instrument from the ex-Nazi's hands, just as I had upon the quay, and placed it within my Gladstone. Nor was that all. I took the hat off his head and calmly put it on my own. Then, not rushing, with no unseemly haste, I paid the fee at the turnstile and walked through the bathhouse door.

But no. Come, come, you say, and begin to put a thousand questions. Did the Steinway Restaurant owner not protest? Seize me? Run after? I will respond, if I may, by repeating here the few words with which I answered Mister Murmelstein's similar query, as the Steinwayites clustered about me on the steps of the First Warsaw Congregation.

"How did I do it? you ask. As our colleague, Mister Mosk, might put it: no problem. While I was shining our employer's shoes, I recalled a trick from boyhood, from the gay years, so full of games and japes, at the Akademie: I tied the laces together! He lunged. He grasped. And fell face downward. We have five moments in which to save Madam Stutchkoff. Perhaps even ten. Mister Tartakower: Here is a twenty-five-cent coin. You take my place in the telephone kiosk. I, with my flute, shall rouse the widow. Do not worry. The knot is a firm one. A double diamond. As demonstrated to we youths of Vienna by none other than the founder of the scouting movement, Sir R. Baden-Powell."

4

Difficult to believe, on that cloudless night, the thesis that matter is finite in nature. The leaves on the trees might be counted. Also, upon beaches, grains of sand. But let us look up: The shiny stars stretch numberless beyond the reach of the naked eye, of the most powerful telescope, through the nighttime sky. Not only that: Each of these fiery lights is a sun, much like our own, surrounded by planets, by moons. Was it not certain that on at least one of these heavenly bodies a figure, human in form, and with a towel over his shoulder, in Roman fashion, was also opening a Gladstone and reaching inside? Surely, in the whole of the mighty universe, I was not the sole creature to feel such joy.

"What are you waiting for?"

"*¡Hace frío, Señor!*"

"This is no time for daydreams!"

The speakers, I knew, were the youthful Murmelstein, Martinez, and the muscular Doctor Dick—but which voice belonged to which man could not be determined, since the nylon-type stocking each wore on his head transformed his features into what looked like a kneecap. Again I groped in the Gladstone, this time grasping, removing—how it glittered, quivered, like a living object: an electrical eel fish, the happy tail of a pup—the genuine Rudall & Rose.

Once more the voices of my faceless friends:

"Hurry up! He'll be here any moment!"

"Haga la música con la flauta."

"Play! Go on, play!"

But how could I play? My fingers were frozen, my lips covered with ice, and my nose—that tool for inhalation—blocked by a catarrh. No sooner did that doubt cross my mind, however, than I began to feel a warmth, a glow, spreading from my hands, through my arms, and into my chest, which in turn swelled with the pride of an Aaron about to wield his rod. Up, up rose the instrument, floating on its own like a Yogi's rope; then, before it reached my lips, before my breath fell upon it, the notes, the call, the birdsong, rang in the air: a D, a G, a B, a D, a B.

All was still. Above me, the stars shimmered, shook, hanging like drops of water about to fall. My companions crouched, waiting for the door to open. "Come in," said a female voice from the other side.

The three hooded figures looked at each other, then turned their smooth, blank faces toward me. I inhaled: but again, before the exhalation, the clear laughing tones, *Da-da-da-dee-da!*, wafted out of the silvery flute. From the interior of the Steinway Restaurant came the familiar voice of the Widow Stutchkoff-Pechler: "Door's open, dear!"

Fellow Americans! In a kind of dream I stretched out my hand to the knob and thrust the portal aside. The abductors fell back as I stepped across the threshold into the pitch-black room. For a moment I stood, blinking, staring into the dark. Then, blindly, like a somnambulism sufferer, I started forward. In the opera *Macbeth*, by G. Verdi, a dagger lights up to guide the baritone upon the stairs. So now I found myself at the Steinway Restaurant staircase and, led not by my own volition but by the rays of light that danced along the shining cylinder of my Rudall & Rose, climbed upon it. Onward I went, upward, placing one thong above the other, until I saw on the landing above me a movement, a shadow, and then the golden curls, like gilded corkscrews, of Madam Stutchkoff's candlelit hair.

Still I continued, like an insect, a member of the moth family, drawing nearer and nearer the flaming taper whose beams were bound to expose me. Just above, upon the landing, H. Stutchkoff-Pechler leaned forward, so that both bosoms tumbled like acrobats over the negligee top. "Ah!" I exclaimed, halting at last in wonder: "*Choo!*" The flame in this blast went out. In the utter darkness, the soft form of the widow pressed close, against the cotton of my S. Klein's drawers. A warm breath, with a hint of a caraway scent, wafted by me.

"Hello, cowboy," whispered the widow into my ear.

Bloch, Berg, Bruch, the famous Three B's: also Zemlinsky, Schönberg himself, with his disciples K. List and Pisk—these are the modernists, the twelve-toners, whose obsession with freedom, with newness, has led to the animal sounds, the machine-shop rhythms, and scarcity of tune content so often heard on the WQXR midafternoon concerts. Art, in my opinion, requires inhibition: a limited palette, a restricted scale, the moderate censorship of the Czar. Witness, as proof of this statement, the moment in *Die Zauberflöte* when Papageno sings an entire aria, *hm! hm! hm! hm!*, with a padlock on his mouth; or stands in stupefaction before his paramour, *Pa-Pa-Pa-Pa-Pa-Pa-Papagena!* Thus mute, in the blackness of night, I stumbled after the footfalls of the cash-register expert into the Stutchkoff apartments. A single word, I knew, would undo me: and worse, put the darling, the dowager—my enlarged pupils made out where she stood, pulling her nightgown, the size, the shape, of a scout movement pup tent, over her torso zone—in terrible danger. Yet how much I yearned to say! First, to warn her that Schwartz, the man she took me to be, was a scoundrel, war criminal, the enemy of the Jews. And then, even more urgent, to speak in my own behalf: *Hilda! Pardon, sweetheart! To speak frankly, I love you!* No! Impossible to resist such a deep, heartfelt impulse: "H-H-H—" I burst out, in the Mozart manner, only to swerve at the last moment into the first notes of a popular *Lied: "Heidi!"*

Husky, her voice: "Harry! Honey! Is not sensible to be at this time singing. Here! Hurry! Come!"

To my dismay she ignited a Bic-brand lighter and held it to the candlewick. Two problems concerned me: the hairiness of my shoulders, the hairlessness of my head. The towel, draped lengthwise, concealed the former blemish; and the hat, named for Fédora, heroine of Sardou, covered the latter, just as its turned-down brim veiled my facial features. Note, however: Madam Stutchkoff's painted eyes were directed at none of these places but instead were cast down, toward the spot where my Jewish-style member had burst, like one of the Texas bulls from its corral, through the cleft in my western drawers.

A brief pause before she, smiling, snuffed the little flame: time enough, however, for L. Goldkorn to be discovered, and to discover: For there before me were the flesh folds, the belly-zone creases, thigh dimples, the sag of the leftmost bosom, the droop of the right—in short, the whole dear body melting, dripping, falling, like the soft white wax of the taper, now extinguished.

"Halt! Halt! A Jew!"

Do not think this command was issued by the spouse of the deceased Vivian Stutchkoff, helpmeet of the late Pepi Pechler. No. The truth is, in the torchlights, the ice glare, it was not possible to determine whether the speaker was a Death's-Header from Deutschland, one of our Austrian Nazis, or a member of the no-less-dreaded Swiss Guard: That latitude of the Bodensee, frozen, without landmarks, might have belonged to any one of the three nations. All I could see were four armed figures, standing at each compass point. Thus what was to become a long, adventure-filled odyssey, originating in the border town of Bregenz and terminating in the harbor of New York City, New York State—via Switzerland, Marseille, the Pyrenees goat track, Córdoba, Lisbon: The whole of this journey seemed to be over before it had begun.

"*Ein Jude?*" I said, stammering slightly. "Do you mean me?"

"Your papers!" the same officer said.

"*Ja! Ja!*" I had only my old identity card, without the red letter *J*—the requirement for which, in fact, had made me decide to risk this midnight dash across the barren Lake of Constance. I handed it over. The other patrol members drew near, shining their electrical torch beams onto the outdated sheet.

"*G O L D K—*" Under his helmet, the soldier sounded the letters.

"Goldkorn!" said a smarter second.

"Isn't that a Jewish name?" said the quick-thinking third.

"Ha! Ha!" I laughed, making light of the moment. "Everybody makes that mistake."

"Don't try to trick us. The middle of the night, the middle of the Bodensee, a name like Goldkorn: What are you if not a stinking Jew?"

Here, as if stored in my mind against just such a moment, the sudden opening of this very crevasse, all my childhood memories, the accounts of Amundsen, the journals of R. F. Scott, rose to consciousness: "*Ein Fischermann!*"

My countrymen, for such I now saw them to be, broke into laughter. "A fisherman! Ha! Ha! Ha! Upon a frozen lake?"

The time had come, as it had for the famous Perry, to

make the final dash. In one quick motion I snatched the weapon of the nearest soldier and, instead of aiming the point at the others, I smashed the bayonet into the ground. "Ice fishing!" I shouted, breaking through the solid crust. "Like the Eskimos! This is how to catch *das Schnurrbartfisch*"—in English you say a crappie, a sort of whiskered trout.

The patrol stepped back, their rifles at the ready. The fourth soldier held up his arm. "Enough. We are wasting time at these games. There is a simple way to tell who is and who is not a Jew. You. Herr Goldkorn. Take down your pants!"

All hope lost. The three others moved forward, gripping my trousers, pulling from my shoulders my suspender straps. Condemned by the covenant! Forsaken by foreskin! Yet one last chance remained: Down fell my trousers, up went my flute. Tamino's melody—from the grove with the temples, the larks and lambs, the rainbow in the fountain—rose over the windswept wastes. Alas, my woolies dropped to my ankles. A chill gripped my groin zone. A beam from a torchlight played over my parts. Then, while the fourth soldier squatted before me, one of his fellows raised the cry:

"Look at that!"

From another: *"Mein Gott!"*

The third: *"Ein Phänomen der Natur!"*

The entire quartet stared then toward the air hole, where a school of crappies swayed to the melody, the Mozart, bumping their rosy, moustachioed faces in rhythm against the crystalline ice. Hastily, I drew up my clothing, and while the soldiers stood struck with wonder—thus does music appeal to the senses of even non-mammals, an important phenomenon whose commercial aspects are only now being explored by henhouse managers and the owners of oyster beds—I slipped away toward the distant lights of what turned out to be the little town of Egnach, canton of Thurgau, in the land of the neutral Swiss.

* * *

How, since I have only just issued a call for artistic restraint, can I describe what in the private bedstead happened next? We are, are we not, mature adults? Men of the twentieth century all? No need to tell you the act I refer to is common enough in the world; indeed, there is little room for doubt it occurred several times between Madam and V. V. Stutchkoff, and has definitely taken place on at least one occasion—the Victrola was playing, her hair, all unloosened, hung to her grippable waist—between the present speaker and his wife.

Upon Rivington Street the task was made more difficult by the need to cling with one hand to my hat and the other to my Rudall & Rose. Once upon the Sealy-brand mattress together, this darling nipped at my body with her playful molars; with sly pinches she pulled at my eartabs and sent, with the nails of her fingers, the blood racing about the surface of my skin. What tumultuous doings! Elbows, ankles drummed upon me. Her abdomen thrust me skyward, as if upon a heaving wave. Gasping, blinking, I raised my head from her double bosom and then, as one upon All Saints' Day customarily bobs at apples, lowered it again. And so it came time—the breath roared in my nostrils; a warmth like that of a toddy spread in my loins—to attempt in my humble way a penetration.

Alas! No sooner had I raised myself to my knees, spreading my arms in a propeller motion, than I heard the clangorous sound of the Steinway Restaurant pay telephone.

"Never mind," said Hilda. "Not to give attention."

But the instrument rang once more, its clapper seeming to beat against the insides of my hatted head.

"Don't stop! Mister, um; Mister, er; Mister, ah—continue!"

But how continue? Within seconds we heard a more terror-filled sound even than the ringing of the phone. Its failure to ring! Complete silence! That meant the Steinway

Restaurant owner was directly below us! He had answered Tartakower's call!

The ensuing events flashed by in less than a single moment. First, suddenly, the headlamps of the parked seven-seater came on, illuminating the tableau of mistress and man: she, upon her back, crossing her Flemish-style arms over her breasts, which seemed to dive like white-suited sailors over opposite sides of her bust; and myself, whose organ still retained—was this any less a miracle, a defiance of the laws of gravity, of time, than that of the floating flute?—elastic properties. Then the horn of the Buick saloon gave a toylike toot. Then tooted again.

Printzmettle, according to prearranged plan, was meant to turn on the music machine, in order to mask with its noise the fatal explosion. Before the first measure of the *Mlle. Modiste* medley had finished sounding, I had leaped from the bedstead and was at the door of the Stutchkoff apartments. In another bound I gained the landing, which overlooked the whole of the dining room floor. I took in the scene, brightly lit in the flashing colors of the tune box, at a glance. By the far wall our victim stood, openmouthed, white-faced, and of course bareheaded: The Bell Company receiver was in one hand and his wingtips, still securely bound together, were in the other. Opposite him, just below me, with his arm fully extended, stood the jug-eared H. H. Levine. The three masked abductors crouched inside the doorway. Madam Ellenbogen and Miss Beverly Bibelnieks, the first in a cloth coat, the other in a garment sewn from raccoons, were hugging each other behind the bar. Here, there, under a table, in the kitchen doorway, or, in the case of Sheftelowitz, simply standing with an index finger in either ear, the rest of the conspirators had gathered. What was that in Happy's hand? The J. Roscoe! The gun!

"Don't shoot!" I cried, waving my flute in the air. "Hold your fire. Let us forgive him!"

Too late. Levine's head jerked around, his arm flew up,

and a tongue of flame shot from the end of the weapon, together with a deafening report. What happened was that, first, every pane of the Steinway Restaurant window cracked and shattered, and then, through that sudden gap, the stocking feet of the former target went flying, with the rest of his body attached.

"Missed," said Mosk.

Behind the bar top, the scene of so many pleasant gin fizzes, Madam Ellenbogen began winking, blinking, and chewing her lips. Each person in the room, including, above me, the berobed Hildegard Stutchkoff, followed her gaze, and her pointing finger, through the sulfurous clouds, the yellow gunsmoke, to where Mister Tartakower, with a fresh boutonniere at his breast, stood in the open door.

"Look," he said, with an odd, pale-lipped smile. "I got the quarter back." Then he took a single step forward, spun around, so that we could see the spot at the back of his topcoat where the bullet had made its exit, and fell at Salpeter's feet.

"Quick," said Mister Pipe. "A soda water."

But the first violinist, kneeling over the still form of the Quintet member, shook his head. "Mister Monroe Tartakower," he announced, and there were tears in his narrow-set eyes, "has given up the ghost."

III

TIME: *6:25 AM*
DATE: *1/10*
TEMP: *57 F—14 C*

The glowing script, *Coca-Cola,* is not now legible against the pale, pink sky. The many prisoners yawn, stretch, and turn dark faces toward the dreaded light. The hammer blows! A thousand cruel carpenters at their unending work. It sounds as if the sky itself, the firm earth below, were cracking. *"Mama!"* cries the Afrikaner, and wakes at last. Look with what wild eyes he stares about him. His life, too, must be measured in moments. How much I once thought I might accomplish! How high I would build the tower of song! Think of E. Rubbra, of W. Egk, both born, like myself, in 1901. The man in the street now knows little more than their names. Yet each was in his prime—think of the former's *Ballad of Tristram*, the latter's 1936 Olympic Games theme—a world-famed composer. Even the work of Karl Ditters von Dittersdorf, fellow Scorpio, rarely appears in the repertory. Now nothing is left me but this single tissue square on which to etch my tale. To the task! Thus medieval monks labored to transcribe the lives of saints onto a pinhead.

Hark! What is that sound? The breath catches in our throats. The condemned men cower. A shudder passes through the room. Footsteps! Unmistakable footsteps! Ringing down the row of death! It begins. It commences. Closer. Yet closer. And what of these poor Negro-Americans? For them no sign of comfort. No hint of cheer. How much more fortunate I, who have come to this land of my own accord, willingly, and am not the descendant of those chained to the hold of a slave ship. What might I do to help them? Could I not yet offer some encouraging motto, some word of hope?

"Friends! Brothers!" Their bowed heads lifted, looking toward where I stood, my hands held high. My words came quickly, since the fatal footfalls now echoed just beyond our barred door:

> *"There is a Reaper whose name is Death,*
> *And, with his sickle keen,*
> *He reaps the bearded grain at a breath,*
> *And the flowers that grow between."*

"Jackson!" called the Reaper himself, in the guise of a prison guard. "You're first. Let's go." An ebony youth who possessed a mere half my years stepped toward the narrow gate in our cage. His shoulders sagged. His neck bent low. To my eyes sprang tears of pity.

"Do not despair, lad!" Thus I addressed him. "Remember the lines of our great national bard:

'The grave itself is but a covered bridge
leading from light to light, through a brief darkness.'"

The door clanged shut. The doomed black youth shuffled from view. Immediately the brave words, the H. W. Longfellow sentiments, turned to ashes in my mouth. Plato was correct to banish the poets. Liars! Deceivers! The truth is the reverse! The opposite! Even a child knows that bitter lesson.

A child, to be precise, at the age of seven. That was when, grasping the hands of my two older sisters, I climbed half the day into the Bohemian-Moravian Heights, the plateau east of Iglau. The whole town, it seemed, together with the populations of Polna and Teltsch, had already gathered upon the surrounding hilltops. The k. und k. Kriegsmarine band sat upon portable seats, wearing their blue pants, the crimson tunics, with instruments in their laps. There was Rudi, who had at that time only begun his parlor visits, sitting among the woodwinds. A detachment of uhlans, with feathered shakos, stood with rifles raised. Everyone seemed to be carrying silver cigars, which in fact were our local Trabuccos, especially wrapped in foil for the occasion. An hour, two hours, passed. A fine rain fell. The clouds drew lower, darker, thicker. The mayor of Iglau made a speech, followed by the mayor of Teltsch. A herd of goats moved through the valley, with bells about their necks. Nearby a man was snoring. A baby cried. Then the manager of the tobacco monopoly, his beard damp with dewdrops, stood on a sort of extendable ladder. "Listen," he said.

From well off, southward, came a drone, a growl, a rumble. The next thing I knew, my father had swept me upward, onto his shoulders, so that the top of my head seemed to graze the iron lid of the clouds. From this great height I looked down upon my countrymen, all of whom seemed stirred to sudden action. The bandmaster waved his baton, and the band broke into brisk marches. The uhlans, at attention, aimed their gun muzzles high. The whole crowd was standing, staring upward, and waving their silver cigars. Above this tumult, the sound—now it seemed to come from everywhere, from all directions—grew and grew. The very ground was shaking, vibrating through Papa's shoes, his shoulders. Yakhne stood frowning, her arms crossed upon her nonconvex chest; Minkche, however, raised her arms and lifted her face, as if to catch the rain needles in her mouth. Behind me, a tremendous detonation: The soldiers had fired a salute.

Then, from out of the black clouds, the silver cylinder of the *Zeppelin IV* came into view. There was no sun, yet the great craft, along the whole of its one hundred and forty meters, was shining, brilliant, illuminated. Lower it dropped, heading toward us, until we could see the figures in the gondola below: Count Zeppelin himself; the Archduke Ferdinand, with Sophie, Duchess of Hohenberg; Aehrenthal, the Foreign Minister; L. J. Lumière, at his cinematograph apparatus; the Emperor of Abyssinia, too. All these swept overhead, trailing royal bunting. The populace, whose towns lay directly in the path of the flight, Graz–Görlitz, held in honor of His k. und k. Apostolischen Majestät's Diamond Jubilee, threw up their hats, waved their cigars, and shouted "Huzza!" The band played wildly. The black and chestnut mounts of the uhlans reared and snorted and neighed. I heard none of this, however. In my ears there was only a kind of humming, as if the flammable air within the floating column were being blown through a vast musical horn: wind instrument par excellence! Then, as suddenly as it had dropped from them, the shining airship disappeared into the thick coils of the clouds.

The Bohemian-Moravians fell hushed, still staring upward. They, too, seemed to know that what they had seen— shining, buoyant, suspended for an instant between blank, meaningless mists—was the image of life itself. But for one in that crowd it was something more, a sign, an omen, an aluminum rainbow set in the heavens: the promise of the flute he was to possess, the flute player he was to be.

Alas. The *Zeppelin IV* was wrecked that same year in a storm. The Archdukes and Emperors, even Franz Josef himself, whose long life and reign made us believe that the laws of time might after all be overcome—all these have been swept back into the darkness, the shadows. And the sign that was shown me? The promise made? I took a breath. I looked about me. The bitter taste, the gall, remained in my mouth.

"You! Thieves! Schwartzers! Which of you has stolen my instrument? Who, on the Avenue Amsterdam, robbed me of my silver flute?"

Again the steel door clanged. The next man against whose name—again I use the words of our laureate—the fatal asterisk of death was set, was being led away. It was the Afrikaner. The man who had called for his mother throughout the night. He stopped. He turned. He pressed his face to the bars. "I know that instrument. Got a curse to it. Hexed. Like voodoo. Ain't nothing good happened to me since the day I took it."

2

Sardines. It is to these youthful herring, packed head to tail, that Americans refer when they wish to speak of high density populations. Perhaps you have seen in the daily newspaper a photo of the Tokyo underground tram. In 1936, at the Kruger-Kino, I witnessed the film *Eine Nacht zum Opera*, in which C., H., G., and Z. Marx, shared, with numerous other Jews, the same stateroom cabin. In America, in the gay Fifties, it became the campus fashion for many scholars to squeeze themselves into telephone kiosks, and then place their call. I mention such examples of crowded conditions only to dismiss them. None could compare with the hellish struggle for existence that took place when the entire staff of the Steinway Restaurant, together with the Steinway Restaurant patrons, the corpse of Tartakower, and a full-size bass viol, forced their way into the Buick seven-seater saloon.

On Rivington Street lights were now blazing. The heads of men and women were thrust from apartment windows. Worse, from Houston Street, and rapidly drawing nearer, came the wail, the whoop, of a motorized siren. From his spot on the footboard, H. H. Levine issued commands. "Step on it, Jack!" said he, and threw the still-smoking revolver over his shoulder, onto the shards of the window glass.

The rabbi's breath sang in his moustache. He pulled knobs. He twisted levers. The Buick, all on its own, leaped forward, over the curbstone, and halted. The rain wipers, like inverted metronomes, came on. Because some person's elbow was pressed upon it, the Klaxon rang out.

"Ha-ha," laughed J. Rymer. "Non-driver."

Pearl Ellenbogen, who shared her husband's lap zone with Mister Martinez, manipulated the stick of the gear box. The limousine responded by lurching backward and describing a semicircle. "He's getting the hang of it," Murmelstein shouted, just as the black-and-white sedan of the police forces, with its blue, flashing lights, hurtled around the corner, into our path.

"The throttle!" screamed Printzmettle, the last of the front cushion occupants. "You have to push it with your foot!"

There was a roar, a screech, as the balloon tires spun against the macadam: Then the entire vehicle, with animate and inanimate contents, shot like a howitzer missile past the officers of the law. Levine, whose arm was hooked from the outside around the window post, thrust his low-browed head into the driving compartment: "Turn the wheel. Turn it left! Now right! To Brooklyn! We've got to get rid of the body!"

The scene in the rear of the Buick resembled that in which the sons of Laocoön struggle in the grip of the serpent. From the carpet, clutching my Gladstone, I clawed my way upward, through the mass of humanity, to gulp a fresh breath of air. On the seat the surviving Quintet members were bent together into a Yoga-type position, while on one of the jumpers sat Mister Margolies, massaging a bend in his neck. The headlamps of approaching vehicles, unused to the British custom of left-lane driving, parted on either side of our path.

"Get a horse!" cried Mister Mosk, from his perch on the second jumper, to a Checker cab driver who was compelled to steer his vehicle onto the steps of the Essex Street IND/BMT. And then, of a sudden, the lights of other autos, the sounds of their engines, together with all the varied motions of the life-filled city, disappeared beneath us, as our wheels lifted from the roadway and we soared into the air, into the nighttime sky, into the firmament.

Said H. Pipe, "Williamsburg Bridge."

The needle of the velocimeter trembled dangerously near the red zone. The chassis shook. The wind whistled by. Below, the ice-choked river reeled. Unluckily, the blue lights, the wailing siren, were still behind us, and rapidly closing the gap. "Slow down!" cried Hyman "Happy" Levine, much to our amazement. "Move all the way to the right!"

In addition to one foot, which remained on the throttle, Rabbi Rymer now applied the other to the brake. The back of the car made a zigzag motion and the vehicle drifted toward the extreme verge of the bridge. "Ah! Ah!" the passengers exclaimed, aware of the sudden peril. Just then the door to the rear compartment was flung open and the gunman groped inside, toward where the former flautist was hanging on the suit hook by his collar.

"What is this?" Salpeter demanded. "What are you doing to the Quintet member?"

"He's evidence! Evidence! We've got to get rid of him! Now!"

With both hands, recklessly, Levine commenced tugging. Salpeter loyally pulled back. Caught in the middle, the backseat occupants shifted position. Feet and elbows appeared and disappeared. Torsos heaved about. Then, with a slight sound of suction, one of our number became disentangled and pitched from the doorway. There was a bloodcurdling scream—may I not live to hear another like it—and the dark form flew over the railing and fell in a spiral toward the distant river.

"No! No! Nooooo!" echoed the scream, from the throat of Dr. Julius Dick. "My instrument! My double bass!" He half rose, arms before him, as if he intended to follow the flight of his fiddle to where, with an audible percussion, it exploded on the ice below.

His quick colleagues restrained him, however, and some soul slammed shut the door. Twisting about, squinting through the steamed rear window, we noted how the pursuing policemen had come to a sudden halt. They jumped from their platoon car and peered over the railing of the mighty bridge. Safe, then! For a moment nothing further was heard but the hum of the engine, the hiss of the vulcanized tires, the soft sobs of Julius Dick. Poor fellow! Impossible not to feel a spasm of the most profound pity. Reflexively I clutched to my chest my Gladstone, so as to make certain, through the hide of ersatz alligator, of the presence of the beloved Rudall & Rose.

At last Mister Pipe said, "Now what are we going to do?"

Mosk, after a thought-filled pause: "There's the Queensboro Bridge. Also the George Washington; that's a double-decker."

Sheftelowitz: "We could go back to the river. Wasn't that the original plan? Like with Bo Weinberg, the boots of cement?"

Once more Levine ducked his head into the window. "What river? You saw it. Nothing but ice."

Smoothly, the seven-seater rolled down the exit ramp, into the Borough of Brooklyn. The next person to speak was the second violinist. "Once I heard of a case where a body was cut into pieces and put inside a suitcase, and the suitcase was mailed to Elmira."

"Ah, Mister Murmelstein," exclaimed the bushy-eared Ellenbogen. "You too are a reader of the New York *Post*. In that journal I saw where a murder victim was cleverly fed to a lion at the zoo."

"Another time a man gave his wife an injection, and the doctor said it was a heart attack. Maybe Botnik, M.D., or Goloshes, could do us a similar favor."

"And how," said Salpeter, in his most sarcastic tone, "are we to explain the holes where the bullet passed through?"

"Moths, maybe?" said Pipe.

Printzmettle: "Think a minute, everybody. The reason you know about these cases is they didn't work. The successful ones you don't read in the paper."

Rabbi Rymer now felt enough confidence simultaneously to speak and drive. "Why, may I ask, are we discussing the idea of sending the deceased through the air? Or sinking him under water? Not to mention the rest. A Jew when he dies ought to be buried in the ground."

"Yes! This is correct!" said M. F. Margolies, who, because of his neck twist, had to make the exclamation over his shoulder. "Turn at Myrtle Avenue. We'll go to Queens! The cemetery of Hachilah Hill!"

At this there was a rush of enthusiasm. The black Buick actually swerved leftward, as directed, toward the Kew Gardens section. But Printzmettle, the pessimist, spoke up again. "How can we bury him? In what burial plot? We have no tools. No shovels. There's nothing to dig with."

Murmelstein: "Not only that. The ground is frozen. It's hard as a rock. We'd need a pickax. A pneumatic drill."

A moan, a general groaning, filled the sedan. "What will become of us?" Madam Ellenbogen cried. "We'll have to drive around forever!" Then silence, as a terrible vision passed before all our eyes: a doomed chariot, ceaselessly moving, never stopping, from borough to borough, carrying the skeletons, the souls, of the damned. *Der fliegende Holländer!*

"No!" cried Margolies, pointing, in spite of his painful skewed shoulders, directly ahead. "Mister Tartakower was a longtime Steinway Restaurant employee. Entitled to a pension. Thus we are going to Hachilah Hill. But not to dig in the ground. No! No! Onward! Onward"—and here the 1933 model, like a steed responding to a spur, leaped forward, down Myrtle Avenue: "To the stone crypt! To the Stutchkoff tomb!"

3

The moon was out. The ground glowed in its beams as if covered with grains of sugar. The gravestones leaned left and right, like uneven teeth in a jaw. Across this landscape stumbled our band of Jews, toward where the pyramid of the mausoleum stood, blotting a portion of the star-filled sky. How much higher, taller, more mysterious the structure loomed now than when, in the light of day, I had attended the funeral of the late Pepi Pechler. Twice we circled the massive base before we found the stone slab of the door. Dick, Ph.D., the most powerful among us, pushed against the smooth surface. It did not yield. Then we all put our shoulders to the rock, sweating, grunting with effort, much as our ancestors had done when laboring upon the tomb of Pharaoh. The portal stood firm. Wearily we sank down, our heads against the solid stone. I drew my Gladstone onto my lap and forced the double hinges. "Friends," I began. "Would anyone care for a Mint Cream?"

The Stutchkoff tomb was located near the highest point of Hachilah Hill Cemetery, by whose outer walls we had maneuvered our hearse-colored Buick only a short time before.

Out we had tumbled, Tartakower propped in our midst, and
began to walk up the curving roadway, toward the wrought-
iron gate. Here was the first obstacle. Locked. We shook the
bars. We rattled the padlock chain. Then H. H. Levine took
from the hair bun of Miss Bibelnieks a bobby-type pin, which
he thrust into the keyhole. "I know how to do this," he said.
Before he could finish the task, however, a new problem arose.
A group of Sabbath-keepers, homeward bound from temple, came strolling down the sidewalk, beneath their beaver
fur hats.

What a predicament! Tartakower's face was green as a
grape, his lips set in a snarl, while between my thongs and
fedora nothing existed save my boxer-length shorts. The
gentlemen stopped to stare. One of them pointed. Another
said, "Is anything wrong? That man looks like a corpse!"

"Stall!" muttered Levine, still crouching behind us. "Make
a delay."

"Ha! Ha! Not a corpse. *Ein Trunkenbold!* Too much
schnapps to drink."

Old Pipe had wits nearly as quick as my own. "We are
Irishmen! Gay revelers! Now we shall sing all together the
'Glocca Morra.' "

Silence. The musicians looked to the waiters, who turned
with shrugs to the cook. " 'La Cucaracha'?" he queried.

Sheftelowitz: "What about 'Danny Boy'?"

The stout believers stroked their beards. The man who
had already spoken stepped nearer, peering at the ex-smoker.
"Why is he grinning that way? Why doesn't he talk?"

Time, it seemed, for another tack. "Ha! Ha! Fraternal
initiation. I must in this haze go pantsless. Our colleague may
not speak a word. Attend the woolen muffler. This is a
Princeton man!"

"Yeah," said Mosk. "Joe College."

Now a second member of the congregation stepped forward. "A Delta Phi? From Nassau? Here is the handshake!"
The next thing we knew this graduate thrust his way among

us and gripped, with his warm hand, Tartakower's cold one. Second by second the light dimmed in the frat member's eyes. The scream that he uttered, as he and the Orthodox dashed away, entirely masked the click of the tumblers and the clank of the door, which swung inward upon its rusted hinges.

A different sound, a rumbling, accompanied the door to the tomb when, of its own volition, with no person pressing even a finger upon it, it slid to the side on its hidden springs. Trembling, we jumped to our feet. A dark cavern, a black tunnel, stretched before us, leading inward, downward, to the secret crypt. "Forget it," said Mosk. "It gives me the willies."

Said Printzmettle, "Unfortunately, I am afraid of the dark."

"Let's wait awhile. Until sunup."

Salpeter: "We cannot wait. The men on the outside saw us come in. We have to hurry. There will be enough light from the moon to light our way." So saying, the leader of the Quintet stepped across the threshold, into the gloom of the vault. Without another word, Murmelstein and Martinez, with Tartakower propped between them, followed after. Printzmettle, Margolies—through all our adventures, he had maintained the white waiter's cloth over his arm—and Ellenbogen went next. One by one the rest of the funeral procession disappeared into the four-sided tomb.

As Salpeter had predicted, faint beams of moonlight, of starlight, fell over the damp, sloping walls. What he had not anticipated, however, was that this dim illumination would begin to fade after less than a half-dozen yards. Crouching, bending, we pushed for a moment through the gloom and murk, only to come to a halt in the uttermost dark.

"Now what?" some person said.

"Back! Go back!"

"Everything is black in front of my eyes!"

For a moment everyone was milling around. More people started to shout.

"Someone has stepped on my corns!"

"A match! Light a match!"

"Heavens! We dropped Tartakower!"

"I got to do something. You know. Pee-pee."

"We'll be buried alive!"

Those in the front of the line turned back, trampling the people behind them. The ones in the rear fell down, or slipped to their knees. It was a panic. Above the tumult, one voice rose above the others: "Quiet, Jews! Listen! Do you hear?"

At Salpeter's words the cries, the exclamations, dropped to a mere whimper, to quiet weeping. Then, echoing from the walls, the stone ceiling, the way the voice of a bather reverberates from the tiles of his douche stall, came W. A. Mozart tones:

> *Nun komm und spiel die Flöte an,*
> *Sie leite uns auf grauser Bahn.*

Here were the notes, the magic melody, that led the young lovers, Tamino, Pamina, through the cave and the night. In this case the instrument that played it was—no need, friends, to tell you—a London-made Rudall & Rose.

"What's that racket?" someone said.

"What a squeaking!" exclaimed another.

A third: "It must be a bat!"

With the flute pressed to my lips I made my way to the head of the procession and, still playing, hardly pausing for inhalations, plunged onward, toward the depths of the vault. The others grew calm. They dried their tears. As Eurydice followed Orpheus, or the children of Hamelin the friendly Pied Piper, the Steinway employees and patrons followed me.

Our human chain—the hand of one man upon the shoulder or shirttail of another—wound ever deeper, until it seemed we must reach the bowels of the earth. Still the long moments went by. The weight of the pyramid pressed upon us. The ceiling dropped lower, the walls steadily narrowed: Soon we would crawl on hands and knees! It was I, at the caravan's head, who saw first the gleam of light. My thought was that my eyes had betrayed me; but with each step what had been a dim glow, a bare flicker, grew steadier, brighter. Soon the others saw it as well. There was a gasp, a cry: Then, like thirsty men, desert travelers, who see distant oasis palms, everyone rushed with eager steps to the lit-up burial chamber.

There we halted, amazed. The room, the color of alabaster, was square, its high ceiling resting upon four stout columns. The light came from the bowl of an oil lamp, which hung on a chain, and from candles, in candlesticks, spread through the chamber. But how could such a thing be? Tapers that burned and were not consumed? Lamps that never ran dry of oil? Was this not a mystery, a miracle to rival that of Chanukah, the festival of lights?

Mosk, beneath his stiff-billed cap, scratched his head. "It smells fishy to me."

"Look! Look over here!" Ellenbogen was pointing with a shaking finger to where a series of marble slabs lay on the floor. The tombs of the Stutchkoffs! M.P., the founder; Shinagel, his devoted bride; the tragic V.V., their only child: These names had been expertly etched into the solid stone. Here was a newer, shinier marker: Pepi Pechler! Cherished schoolmate! Spouse of H. Stutchkoff! The words of the great Longfellow leaped to my mind:

> *How strange it seems! These Hebrews in their*
> *graves.*

It was at that precise moment, while we mourners were still struck with wonder, that the ground beneath us began to shiver, to shake. Salpeter, through the thin leather of his tasseled loafers, sensed it first. "Earthquake!" he cried. By then, all felt the churning vibrations. Not only that, we heard, above us, behind us, a low rumble, like far-off thunder, followed by a definite thud.

"It's the door!" Murmelstein shouted. "We've been locked in!"

Everyone wishes to live. Even aged men. No youthful athlete, no Olympian, could have dashed with more speed than our team of elders back toward the underground passage. None entered, however. The way was blocked by the outstretched arms of a man in a herringbone coat.

"The Assistant D.A.!" cried Levine, clawing at the spot under his armpit where the Roscoe was usually stored. The reason he could not find the weapon was because it was clutched in his antagonist's hand.

"Stop!" our employer commanded. "Turn around. All of you. Go there!"

We followed his gaze, his outstretched arm, to the newest of the sarcophagus stones. Blank. No words etched on its shining surface. "Move! Bend down! Lift it up!"

No one knew what to do. Obey? Attempt to run? And where run to? A terrible thought: Were we to be forced into the pit ourselves? Then, from behind one of the columns, wearing her fox fur, stepped the golden-haired Hildegard Stutchkoff, with whom I had been keeping company only a short time before.

"Please, misters; is in such emergency not to delay. Lift, please, the tomb top."

The waiters bent on one side, the musicians on the other. The patrons, too, lent a hand. Groaning under the immense weight, we inched the tablet upward, until it fell to the side of—yes, there it was: the pit, the hole, the grave.

Mister Schwartz: "Now, take Tartakower. Put him inside."

"You mean," Margolies began, "it's a funeral?"

"Of course is a funeral. What else but a funeral? Having a rabbi and also nice candles, lit by dear Harry Schwartz."

That man stepped from the tunnel entrance. With satisfaction I noted he wore his wingtips, much as the widow wore her stole, about the neck. "We knew you would come here. Where else would you go? We are the ones who opened—and closed—the door to the tomb. We have no choice but to let you use it. If the body were found, if the news came out, the Steinway Restaurant, together with the name of Stutchkoff, would be ruined. But you, too, the murderers, standing here red-handed with the corpse, have no choice: You must do whatever we say."

Here Sheftelowitz, the cod-monger, sank down against the wall, softly saying, "I'm a little dizzy in my head."

Pipe, in feather bedding, sat beside him. "Me too."

Madam Stutchkoff-Pechler: "Is soon to be extinguished the lights. Good friends, is remaining no time! With every breath is using fresh air."

This was so. The oil lamp was almost out. The candle flames were sinking, flaring, sinking again, as if they too were laboring for breath.

"Hurry!" said Printzmettle. "Somebody help me!" He had Tartakower under the shoulders; Murmelstein hastened to take him by the feet. Together they dragged him to the side of the open pit and—he might have been a sack containing potatoes, or citrus, and not a human form filled at one time with the spark of life—threw him within.

"Let's get out of here," said Ellenbogen.

"Wait. Wait one moment." The speaker was Julius Dick. "Rabbi—" He motioned to Jack Rymer, who was already halfway inside the tunnel. Quickly the clergyman turned about. His face, all around his moustache, had a greenish hue.

"*Baruch Attoh Adonoi*, and so on and so forth," he said.

Salpeter, alone of the musicians and waiters, stood gazing down at his former colleague. "Here was a Bialystok man, a widower, no children, who lived for music alone. A Quintet member twenty years, excepting a single season with the Gumbiner Brothers Bar Mitzvah Band. A lilting tone. Intonation perfect. For our cause, the Jewish element in music, he sacrificed first his flute, and then his life. Farewell, good, trusted friend! We shall never find one to replace you."

"No? Ha! Ha! No?" It was I who, coyly laughing, asked the rhetorical question. For all to see I held up my silver Rudall & Rose. "Can you be so certain?"

Salpeter: "Ah, yes; of course, you have a flute. That will be most welcome."

Eagerly I looked about me. Murmelstein, my former colleague, was nodding, smiling. Dr. Dick, my co-worker to be, was, with tearful eyes, smiling, too. "Excellent," said the former; and, from the latter, "Perfect. Wonderful. Very good."

Was it the thinness of the air? The conflicting emotions within my breast? My heart felt as if it must burst like a ripe honeydew from the joy. A member of the Quintet again!

Now Salpeter extended his hand, so as to examine the newest instrument in our ensemble. Gladly I passed it to him. What he did was turn, bend, and place it in the stiffening grip of Monroe Tartakower's hands.

A foam of sorts rose behind my eyes. A roaring, as in certain seashells, filled my hearing canal. Drowning! That was my sensation. "Gentlemen," I called to those about me. "Help!"

Now Schwartz—or was it Maltz? Or perhaps, in herringbone, the devil himself?—came forward and added the fatal revolver to the contents of the tomb. Then he addressed his staff.

"In one moment you will be leaving. You must go directly to your homes. Take care that no one sees you. But remember this: You are to return to work tomorrow, at ten A.M. sharp."

"Ten? In the morning? But we're a night spot. And tomorrow is the Sabbath."

"From now on the Steinway Restaurant will be open three hundred and sixty-five days a year! That's the least of the changes. I've got big plans. In a month no one will recognize what existed before. The jukebox is just the start! We'll have arcade games. Skeet ball. MTV!"

"Is for better or worse the end of an era this new sensation club." With these words Hildegard Stutchkoff manipulated a hidden switch at the side of the column. From above, at ground level, came the rumble of the stone slab sliding away.

Ellenbogen said, "Do you think we'll have to serve lunch?" No one responded. The entire band of Steinway Restaurant employees and patrons gathered at the tunnel entrance, hoping to make their exit.

I lingered. There lay Tartakower, with sunken cheeks, with jutting chin, his dry eyes half open. His hands, with their nicotine-colored fingers, clasped the Rudall & Rose. Poor fellow. Agreed: a lilting tone. But a small sound, owing to lack of breath volume. Such poor technique would not hamper him now. In truth, what further need had he of this instrument? For what purpose? To play, in heaven, duets with purported harps? What if I should retrieve it? Would he, himself, not wish me to do so? Oh, horrible sin: to steal from the dead! Steal? Can one in such circumstances use this term? What harm would be done? Who would suffer? But the others, my fellow workers, would know. They might express disapproval. Ah! surely I might explain that this was my own instrument, a gift from Franz Josef the First. Well: not the precise instrument. I could not but notice a slight difference in tone. But the identical brand, of London manufacture. There is no telling how long this debate might have raged, nor is it possible to predict its outcome, had not the dictator of the Steinway ordered his employees to return to the tomb, where they heaved the stone tablet, as weighty as a Bösendorfer grand, over the poor player and his priceless instrument.

Some hours later I woke to find myself by the far simpler headstone of Mistress M. Goldkorn, lying flat upon the little mound of her frozen grave. Through the crushed crown of the fedora I felt a throbbing, and several bumps; dimly I recalled my flight through the tunnel, blinded, breathless, stumbling, with repeated knocks to the head. But anything further—how long I had lain here, and in what manner I had arrived—was a mystery I could not solve. It was, I saw, still night. My empty Gladstone was by my side. No sign of the Steinwayites. Alone.

Martha! Dear daughter! Where were you now? If only the words on the stone were true! Only sleeping! One day to wake! In heaven! Imagine her there: a pretty pink dress, black buckled shoes. Fortunate Tartakower! He could play a pavane, a ballet selection, the "Sleeping Beauty." How she would dance, the darling, with her little plump arms over her head and her girlish thighs whirling beneath her tutu. I could definitely see her. Look! A ribbon in her hair! The bile of envy mounted from my liver ducts to my tongue. What if she mistook that flautist for her natural dad? Ha! No reason to worry. I had only to remain at this frozen spot a short while longer in order to join the dance. And was there not room enough, in this family plot, for Clara? Reunited! We three! At the tomb of the Goldkorns!

But the vision before my eyes—her black hair, her creamy brow, the pink ribbon: All that was fading. I pressed my body to the cold clods. Tears in the form of crystals froze upon my cheeks. "Martha! Miss Martha!" I called aloud. "Leib Goldkorn speaking! Papa! Do not go away. Say something, sweetheart! Speak!"

As if in response, I heard a gentle sound, a kind of sigh; and a warm breeze, like a breath, passed over my shoulders and neck. I rolled onto my side. There, hanging above me, I confronted a pair of dark eyes, a nose, and teeth in a mouth. Could this be? Were the Hindoos correct? The doctrine of Pythagoras confirmed? I stretched upward, so that my own face was only inches away from the rubbery, bewhiskered lips. I could hardly believe my eyes. Had my daughter, like K. D. von Dittersdorf, turned into a horse? I sat fully upright. Four legs. Bushy tail. A mane and a forelock. No room for doubt:

a horse indeed. And seated on top, with a gun on his hip, a cap on his head, was a New York City policeman.

"I confess!" I shouted, jumping to my feet. "It was my deed! Guilty of murder!"

"All right, buster," said the officer of the law, while his steed snorted and impatiently struck a hoof against the earth. "You're under arrest."

4

Skoal! to the Northland! skoal!
There the tale ended.

Thus, with the verse of the poet—a toast! a salute!—my tale ends, too. The sun has replaced the moon. The last of the downtrodden, the darkies, have been summoned: And still the callous carpenters go about their task, hammering, hammering, even as their victims hang in the wind. May I go as bravely as they! With laughter, gestures of courage, and the jaunty chewing of gum. What little I possess—the paper pledge for the Bulova watch, the Toscanini medallion, and, within the cube tray of the Frigidaire, a United States Savings Bond for the sum of fifty dollars: These valuables are of course to be given to Madam Goldkorn. Goloshes, M.D., is to be the executor of the estate. Doctor, the medicament syringe is also in the fireproof icebox, within the garden crisper. Should at any time the Widow Goldkorn become the wife of landlord Fingerhut, these provisions are to become null and void, and the valuables in that case are to be transferred to the Widow Stutchkoff-Pechler. Unless, of course, she has in the meantime wed Mister H. Schwartz.

What is that sound? Fatal footfalls! The jangle of the jailhouse keys! There: the face, long grown familiar, of the death's-row guard.

"Korngold!"

"You have mistaken me for a different Viennese. Also a musical figure."

"Goldkorn, then. Goldkorn, L."

"*Ja!* Here am I."

I stood. But what the keeper said next made me sink down again, with a heart beating faster, far, than it had at the approach of death. Here, in a scrawl, with the last nub of pencil, I repeat his message, word for word:

"Let's go. You're free. Your daughter made the bail."

Here I sit on the banks of the Hudson. Overhead sail the white, puffy clouds. Feel the warm breezes! See the circling gulls. It is, in the middle of January, a springlike morning. Why not dangle one's feet from the piling? Like a lad who fishes, drowsy and dreaming: without willow pole, however; without worm can, without hat of straw. All about me the New Yorkers are slowly strolling, their hands clasped behind them, taking enjoyment in the balmy day.

Let us go back a mere quarter hour, to the moment when, with a cold sweat upon every inch of my body, I followed the warder to the prison's front room. "Where is she? May I make her acquaintance? What does she look like? Is she, by chance, a dancer in the ballet?" These were only a few of the ceaseless questions with which I assailed the fine fellow. Here follows the brief reply:

"She came and went right away. She paid the bail. And she brought you these clothes." As he spoke, the guard handed me, along with my Gladstone, the trousers, the lumberman's jacket, the shoes I had left in the Beaux Arts Baths! He looked closely as I stepped into the generous gabardines. "You're lucky you only got hit with a drunk and disorderly. It could have been indecent exposure."

But my questions were far from concluded. "Did she leave

an address? A Bell telephone number? Did she say she would return? Can you make, sir, a physical description? Black hair? Full lips, perhaps reminiscent of my own?"

"No address. Nothing. Not black hair. Reddish. Reddish brown. A raccoon coat. Big teeth. That's what I noticed. A big, toothy smile."

Friends: It has doubtless struck you, as at once it did me, that this was a portrait that somewhat resembled Miss Bibelnieks. But did this necessarily mean we must give up the possibility that Martha, my daughter, had returned? Consider: The cocktail waitress was the proper age. She had made it a point to seek work at the same establishment in which I was employed. And it was she who brought me cutlets, paste of liver, and odd broilings. True, my own teeth are small, almost like the milk teeth of a child; but those of Madam Goldkorn, in the days when she possessed them, were large, vigorous, gleaming. Madam Goldkorn! It was she who had made this plot! With the assistance of Goloshes, M.D.! Pretending the newborn child was dead! They had put her out for adoption. Certainly not for profit. That could not be. No: They could not know I would soon become an NBC Orchestra member. What they wished for her was a better life. Ladies and gentlemen! L. Goldkorn: a father!

A morning of miracles: with further wonders to come. I opened my Gladstone, with the hope that a Cream of Mint drop yet remained in the half-pint bottle. What I found was my Rudall & Rose! The original model! A gift from the Austrian Emperor, the Hungarian King! This was the one stolen upon the Avenue Amsterdam. Wrapped around it, held by a rubber, a message from the Moor:

This don't work. Not one damned note in 20 years. Maybe it will play for you.

I held the instrument in my hands. It jumped, it leaped, it quivered. Even before it reached my lips, I heard sweet melodies. Now came the strangest of all these marvels: not the music, for a flute will sound whether a musician breathes upon it, or only the wind. But at these notes, the ice on the river broke, heaved, and parted before me. It was this, I realized, that had made the sound of the *crack-crack*ing gallows. A thaw! The gulls above dipped lower, soared, and dropped again. The city people, a sweet folk in my opinion, stopped to listen as well. The Hudson, set free, tumbled, dashed, and sent up a lively foam. We know, do we not, where these shining waters, sparkling, winking in the sunlight, come from? Past the Palisades, beyond the fine capital of Albany, high in the mountains, lies Lake Tear of the Clouds. That is the distant source, where all things lost are restored, and all aged things renewed.